Recipe for Disaster

'I don't want to lose my job,' Zoe said, stumbling over a tree root that rose up over the trail.

Suddenly, he stopped. Frowning, he studied her. 'This isn't a condition of your working for me.'

'It's not?' She had no idea why she had said it. Jackson wasn't forcing her to follow him.

He sighed heavily. 'Is this what you normally do for your bosses?'

'What?' She gasped. 'No. No, I don't do this ... I haven't ... Why? What did Contiello tell you about me? Did he say I slept with him? Because that's not what happened. I never touched him. Well, of course, I touched him, but I never ...' Zoe took a calming breath, realizing she was babbling. 'I don't normally sleep with my bosses.'

Jackson quirked an amused brow. 'You're adorable when you're flustered.'

'I'm not flustered,' she lied.

'Good. Because I like women who know what they want.' He took her hand and held it firmly against the bulge in the front of his pants. 'And who can finish what they start.'

Recipe for Disaster

Michelle M Pillow

This edition published in 2008 by
Cheek
Thames Wharf Studios
Rainville Rd
London W6 9HA

A catalogue record for this book is available from the British Library.

www.cheek-books.com

Typeset by Palimpsest Book Production Limited, Grangemouth, Stirlingshire

Printed and bound by CPI Bookmarque, Croydon CR0 4TD

Distributed in the USA by Macmillan, 175 Fifth Avenue,
New York, NY 10010, USA

The Random House Group Limited supports The Forest Stewardship Council (FSC), the leading international forest certification organisation. All our titles that are printed on Greenpeace approved FSC certified paper carry the FSC logo. Our paper procurement policy can be found at www.rbooks.co.uk/environment

ISBN 978 0 352 34177 8

Chapter One

'You are an arrogant, no-talent jerk-off who wouldn't know the difference between tagliatelline and conchiglioni pastas if they bit you in the ass!' Zoe Matthews yelled, hands on hips as she glared up at the head chef who happened also to be her boss. Chef Antonio Contiello's deceitfully charming smile faltered and his dark-green eyes narrowed in warning. She didn't care if he was angry with her. 'And by ass I mean that over-bloated thing you call a head!'

Dark-brown hair would have touched Contiello's chin, had it not been smoothed back into a short oily ponytail. Unlike the others in their white traditional hats, her boss didn't wear anything over his head – unless it was for a publicity photo shoot. Zoe often mused that he was so arrogant he probably thought a piece of his hair in someone's meal would only enhance the flavor.

Zoe sucked in a deep breath, barely aware of the audience their argument created in the back kitchen of the upscale Italian restaurant, *Sedurre*. The room gleamed, from the silver countertops to the brand new appliances and the stainless steel pots and pans. They were cluttered together to make the most of the tight space. The metal shone because it had been freshly polished. She'd spent an hour and a half cleaning before starting her prep duties. Janitorial services were not exactly what she'd been hired to do, but ever since the original owner, Mr Gregor, had died of a heart attack, Chef Contiello had become even more of a tyrant – at least towards her.

Apparently, Widow Gregor had a thing for cute, rumoured-to-be-gay men who got television air time. She let him have complete run of the restaurant, making the entire staff's lives hell. At least when Mr Gregor was alive, he had been able to keep Chef Contiello's totalitarian urges reined in. Life inside the kitchen wasn't like anywhere else in the world. There was a hierarchy, a code, and in this world Chef Contiello ruled supreme. What the chef wanted, he got. Until now. Until Zoe.

The evening workers were there in full force, preparing for one of their busiest nights. Each of them had matching eight-button conventional chef jackets with stand-up collars and vented cuffs for easy rolling – not that Contiello ever allowed rolled cuffs in his presence. Cooking was dirty work, but you'd never know it by looking at their boss.

Tonight was special and only one dish would be prepared for the exclusive crowd. The renowned Chef Contiello planned to debut a new culinary masterpiece. Tables had been booked for weeks and the waiting list could fill the restaurant to capacity three times over. Tension ran high behind the scenes, but it wasn't the extra workload that had caused Zoe to yell.

'Watch your tongue, Matthews,' Contiello warned, his Italian accent a little too thick, especially for a first-generation American who'd been raised in English boarding schools. His parents had been born in Tuscany.

'I can't! I'm too busy watching my back, you son of a –'
Zoe couldn't finish. Contiello slashed his hand up in the

air, as if threatening to strike her. The moment was brief before he pointed to the back-alley door.

'Get out of my kitchen, Matthews,' he yelled. 'You're fired! I never want to see you back in here, not even to pick up your last check. Send one of your sisters because if I ever see you in my restaurant again, I will have you arrested.'

It became hard to breathe. Suddenly, the kitchen stoves seemed to surge with heat, stifling her until she wanted to scream. She fought the urge to claw at her chef jacket. The need to get out of the kitchen, out of the restaurant, Contiello's presence, the very city, overwhelmed her.

'You're the one who should be arrested,' Zoe swore under her breath. Her oldest sister, Megan, was a police detective. Surely Megs could find something to throw this guy into prison over. Or perhaps her photographer sister, Kat, could take some pictures of him with a male lover and ruin his reputation. Contiello might act like the sophisticated lady's man who flirted with rich old ladies, but everyone on his staff suspected the truth he tried so hard to hide. And the sad fact was that no one cared, no one but perhaps the rich, old sugar-mamas that toted him around like a big, male doll.

'You are just jealous that you will never possess one ounce of the cooking talent I have in my pinkie finger!' Contiello held up the small digit, pointing toward the ceiling in vindication. 'It is my pleasure to be rid of you. Gregor should never have promoted you to sous chef. The only reason he gave you the job was because your brother-in-law, Dr Richmond, bribed him with museum function patronage. Now go, you no-talent dishwasher.'

She wanted to insult him, but nothing would come from her closing throat. As she stepped toward the back door, a violent shiver worked its way along her spine. What had she done? Chef Contiello would never give her a recommendation for a new position. Without his word, no one would hire her.

Zoe kept her head up, faking a confidence she no longer felt as the last threads of her temper slipped, only to be replaced by fear. Everything she had worked so hard for lay behind her. A low murmur started amongst the staff and a heavy pot clanged, causing her to jolt in surprise. Soon, other sounds of cooking stirred behind her. Life in the *Sedurre* kitchen was going on without her.

Turning, she glanced at Contiello who still watched her intently. For the briefest of moments, she thought to beg his forgiveness and try to salvage what career she had left. The head chef gave a smarmy, knowing look. He wanted her to beg him, but he would never forgive. Her chance to be a great chef with her own kitchen someday had never seemed so far away. At the age of 27, her life was over.

She had two options. Cry and run, or scream and run.

Ah, what the hell, she thought. Zoe chose neither.

Arching a brow, she stated so everyone could hear, 'And your new walnut sauce tastes like boiled sewer rats!'

Contiello's expression hardened. Those in the kitchen gasped in shock. Zoe gave him a vindictive look and stormed her way out of the restaurant, slamming the metal door shut behind her. Anger kept the ominous, anxiety-causing walkway between buildings from penetrating her senses as she marched along the uneven concrete toward the lamplit street. Pale evening sky darkened the sidewalks with heavy shadows and the cool early-spring air gave a chill she didn't feel in her frustration.

Already cars were pulling up along the curb, ushered away just as quickly by red-uniformed valets. Pulling the hat from her head, she found herself walking toward the front of the building, staring into the windows. The long, skinny building could only fit two rows of tables down each wall, leaving a single walkway for the waitresses to go down the middle. Brown vinyl booths were along the sides in the far back, surrounded by more crowded tables. White walls, matching tablecloths and linen napkins gave testament to the minimalist decor. There were a few paintings of Venice and Rome but, aside from the vases of fake flowers, that was it.

'I should have just kept my mouth shut and let him have the damned recipes,' Zoe whispered to no one in particular. A valet brushed past her. Normally, they didn't have workers parking cars, but this was a special night after all. If people liked Contiello's new dish, he'd be offered his own cooking show and endorsements, and with them a lot of fame and money. Every part of her wished she could say he didn't deserve it but, though an asshole, Contiello was a well-trained, talented chef.

A slight vibration along her thigh caused Zoe to look away from the window. She reached for her phone and pulled it from her pocket. Flipping it open, she said, 'Hello?'

'Hey, sweetie, I thought I'd get your voice mail,' Kat said, her voice bright. 'You have a second to talk?'

Zoe glanced around. 'Yeah, I think I have a second or three.'

Kat couldn't have called at a better time. Even though it was through a phone line, just hearing one of her sisters' voices made her feel as if she wasn't so alone. She sniffed. Though her nose burned with the threat of tears, her watery eyes began to dry. In total there were five sisters – Megan, the oldest at 30, then Kat, Zoe, Sasha, and the baby, Ella. Zoe didn't get to see Ella as much as she'd like, because the youngest had joined the navy. The other three often came to *Sedurre* for lunch when Zoe was alone cooking in the kitchen.

Their parents hadn't been blessed with sons, so instead they'd pushed for son-in-laws. Megan was married to a forensic photographer. Kat had married an entomologist, Dr Vincent Richmond, who ran his own laboratories in the DJP Department of Entomology at one of the museums on the Upper East Side. He was filthy rich, adorably absent-minded, and lacked the arrogance that ran prevalent in the rest of his family. Kat had just given birth to their daughter, Mariah. The chubby babe had the same fair complexion as all Matthews women and the blonde hair inherited from Zoe's mother, Beatrice, just like Zoe, Kat, and Ella. Megan and Sasha took after their father's dark brown.

'I just wanted to wish you luck tonight on the big event. May Chef Tyrant meet with success that takes him far from *Sedurre* so you can have his kitchen!' Kat laughed.

Zoe sighed. 'You should've called ten minutes ago and wished me a quiet tongue. I just yelled at my boss and got fired.'

'What?' Kat demanded, her tone instantly changing. 'Where are you? At the restaurant?'

Zoe started walking down the long street. She hadn't taken anything to work with her besides twenty dollars in her shoe and her phone. 'I'm walking home.'

'Are there no taxis?'

'Can't afford it, especially now,' Zoe said. 'But stay on the line and keep me company?'

'Hail a cab and get over here. What's the point of a rich husband if I can't at least buy you a ride? Vincent's still at the lab working, but one call to his mother and I'll have

Chef Tyrant out on his ass by morning. And one call to an old friend who shall remain nameless and that restaurant will be filled with rats and cockroaches.'

'I'll be right over.' Zoe gave a small laugh. Even as everything around her crumbled her sister still managed to cheer her. 'Don't call Mimi and don't sabotage the restaurant. Too many people work there. I just want to get out of this uniform and maybe drink up a good portion of your husband's wine collection.'

'I still have a bottle of Cabernet Sauvignon, the vampire wine Ryan brought me from Transylvania.' Kat lowered her tone. 'Hey, Zoe?'

'Yeah?'

'You're a great cook and you didn't deserve to be fired. Contiello is an ass.' Kat sighed. 'You know that, right?'

The fact that her sister could support her unwaveringly without knowing what had happened made her feel better. 'I know, Kat.'

'Great! Now get your butt over here. I'm in the kitchen and I'm trying to turn on the oven. Stupid thing won't work and I'm not sure where to throw this match.'

'What? Why?' Zoe waved her arm at a passing taxi. 'You don't need the stove to chill wine. Kat, stop, you'll burn your penthouse down. You don't use matches in electric ovens.'

Kat merely laughed. 'Then you'd better hurry.'

Two months later

'Two sisters happily settled and all I have is you, Prince Falke.' Zoe Matthews sighed, staring at the indecently clad man refusing to look at her. Too bad he was made of paper, about five inches tall and didn't have anything under the

7

waist where the edge of the book cover cut him off. 'Megan was right. Romance novels rot the brain.'

Even as she said it, she flipped open to the page marked by her finger and continued to read. She'd just have to avoid telling her police-detective sister about this story, like she did all the others. But, really? What else was she to do? She worked all the time – either at her new part-time job or hunting for a better one. Real-life romance never really fitted into the equation. She was too busy for love and too timid for one-night stands. That left novels.

Zoe frowned, again lowering the book. Did slinging drinks at the Phoenix Arms count as work? It hardly seemed like a credible job. Bartending gave more the impression of a 'working your way through college' kind of a gig. Unfortunately, it was the closest anyone in town would let her get to a kitchen.

Chef Contiello wouldn't give her a recommendation for another cooking position and her options had dwindled down to the pathetic. It didn't matter if she could cook. No one wanted to give her a shot without a culinary degree, loyal cult following or a glowing recommendation from the last employer.

'I can't believe I called my boss an arrogant, no-talent jerk-off.' Moaning softly, she leant her head back, hitting it lightly against the worn headboard in repeating thumps.

In the long hours alone in her bedroom, in an apartment she called home but really had no firm attachment to, Zoe had developed the habit of talking to herself to fill the silence. She had no television, and couldn't afford cable if she did. Since being fired from *Sedurre*, her meager savings had depleted to the point that another month's bills would have been the end of her crappy, so-not-dream apartment.

She'd been forced to find work at a small, old brewery in Greenwich Village.

Since not even her favorite author could take her mind off her troubles, she set the book aside and stared at the sparse bedroom. The furniture, covers, even the sheets, had been with her since high school, taken from her childhood home until she could afford her own adult things. That had been almost ten years ago.

Zoe traced a worn flower pattern on the sheet. The brewery was only part time. If she didn't figure out something better soon, she'd be mooching off her sisters and parents. Her neighbor, Cindy, had offered to put in a good word at a cousin's diner. But bussing tables didn't sound much better than bartending.

Sighing, Zoe crawled off the bed. She'd have to get going if she was going to be in work on time for her seven o'clock shift, at the tail end of happy hour. As it was the beginning of the weekend, she'd be there all night. Legally, the bar could only stay open until four in the morning, otherwise the owners would probably keep the party going. With an hour of clean-up, she'd hopefully be back in bed in time to skip breakfast.

Slipping the pair of red polka-dotted pyjama shorts from her hips, she walked across the small room barefoot, kicking them off as she moved. Inside the closet, a strange combination of chef uniforms and formal gowns hung on the rod. Zoe kept the gowns because of the occasionally elitist nature of her old job. Whenever there was a fundraiser or cocktail party with some of the more well-known chefs, Zoe needed to look her best while hobnobbing.

'Not that it matters now,' she mumbled, running her fingers along the crinkled gold sateen skirt of her favourite Vera Wang gown. On impulse, she gently grabbed the hanger and unhooked it from the rod. Turning to the tarnished full-length mirror on the door leading to her bathroom, she held the gown over her white tank top and lacy pink panties. Her blonde hair, cut straight just below her chin, spiked around her face in a messy, unkempt disarray of waves.

The last time she dressed up, she'd been at a museum fundraiser that Kat and Vincent put together for his entomology department. One of the historians, a stately gentleman with a dry sense of humor, had tried to pick her up with lines from the sixteenth century. Though not exceedingly handsome, he'd been charming and sweet, smelled of cologne and wore a nice black suit. And there had been something about his crooked smile. Zoe had been completely uninterested. All she could think about was how she would have made the shrimp puff hors d'oeuvre differently.

'I should have gone on one date with him. At least he had a job and a car and was sober.' Zoe turned, hung up the dress and opted for a T-shirt more suited to her new career. Her current dating pool consisted of men who reeked of alcohol and cigarettes. Even though cigarettes were banned from the bar itself, the specially ventilated room designated for their use tended to trap more smoke in than it let out. Not that she cared if someone was a smoker. Zoe could care less what someone else did to their lungs. What she didn't like was the watery eyes and stuffy nose she got when exposed to it for hours a night.

Throwing her T-shirt onto the bed, she walked to the folded pile of laundry stacked in the white basket on the floor. Her favorite pair of faded denim jeans was clean. As she picked them up, she again caught her reflection in the mirror. Maybe Kat's constant teasing about her weight was right. Maybe Zoe was too skinny to be a chef. She'd gladly gain fifty pounds in order to live her dream. It wasn't her fault that her metabolism paralleled that of a humming-bird, or that she had a natural abundance of energy flowing through her veins. Her normally thin frame was skinnier than usual. At least as a chef, she'd always had food to eat.

The dusky hue of her nipples through the white tank top drew her notice. She dropped the jeans on the bed next to the T-shirt. Studying her frame, she lifted the tank over her head. Her small breasts were flushed with heat, the nipples peaked from the caress of the material running across them. Thin ridges pressed along the right side, indenting the soft flesh with the pattern of her ribbed tank top from where she'd lain against the bed.

Taking a slow, deep breath, she ran her fingers along her stomach. It had been a long time since she'd had a lover. Sometimes she wished she was confident like her sister, Megan, or free-spirited like Kat, adventurous like Ella, even self-assured like Sasha who seemed to have both her love life and future under her own control.

Zoe glanced at the bed, where the prince stared out from the book cover. Sadness overwhelmed her and she longed for his world, a magical world where there were always happy endings and true love existed. She closed her eyes, vividly imagining a palace bedchamber. He was there, a prince – perfect, built, seductively handsome and confident with a surprisingly tender side he would show to no one but her.

Licking her lips, she lightly ran the pads of her fingers along them, imagining a kiss. It had been so long since she'd been touched in passion. She needed a man, someone to hold her and watch movies with, someone who smelled nice and knew how to kiss, who would laugh and look at her like she was the only one in the world.

Moaning softly, she drew her fingers down her neck, rolling her head back slightly. Her pulse quickened and she clung to the image of a magical prince in her head. She wished it was his hands in place of hers, warm and strong. As she cupped her breasts, rolling the nipples delicately between her fingers, she moved to sit on the bed.

She imagined green eyes, deep and penetrating, staring into hers. Naked muscles, glistening with exotic oils, would move in streamlined grace, crawling over her, forcing her back onto the bed so her limbs sprawled over the expensive silk comforter. Zoe rolled back, keeping her eyes closed, ignoring the stiff brush of her blue jeans against her bare leg.

Her heart longed for this daydream to be real. She refused to open her eyes and return to reality. Running her hands down her flat stomach, she wiggled her hips. How would the prince smell? Sound? Spreading her thighs, she ran one hand down between them to stroke her sex through the lace of her panties. She brushed lightly at first, a gentle caress. A little jolt of pleasure traveled up her stomach. With her free hand, she massaged her breast.

She kept the magical prince in her head, imagining his mouth kissing her hard nipple. If she stopped to think about how this fantasy was all she had, she'd start to cry, so she pushed it from her mind and ignored the ache of loneliness in her heart. Instead, she concentrated on her fingers, dipping them beneath the lace of her panties. The slick folds of her sex parted easily and she rubbed along her clit, massaging the sensitive bud as arousal continued to build.

Though Zoe knew how to touch herself, there was still

a terrible emptiness deep inside. For some reason, she'd always been too shy to buy a vibrator, and perhaps too cheap, though there were times she wished she owned one. The image of the prince had slipped from her mind as real life tried to invade. She pulled him back, focusing on his long brown hair, his illusory kiss.

Zoe gasped as she stroked herself harder, moving her hips against her hand. He had firm lips, a war-hardened physique and a thick cock ready for action. Knowing no one would hear her, she let a soft cry escape her lips. The first hint of an orgasm caused her to stiffen in anticipation. Almost desperately, she cupped a second hand over the panties to cover the first. She pressed down, jerking slightly as she reached climax. After, she let her legs drop to the side, and weakly drew her fingers from her sex. Her heart beat fast, but her breathing only rasped a little.

Turning her head to glance at the clock, she exhaled noisily, 'I'm going to be so late.'

Chapter Two

'If one more guy asks me to dance on the bar, tries to put a cheap-ass one-dollar tip down my shirt, recites me a poem or even so much as looks at me with interest, I swear I'm going to rip off his manhood.' Zoe forced a smile so none of the bar patrons would see her anger – not that a bad attitude mattered in this place. In fact, rudeness was almost encouraged by the owner. It gave the bar atmosphere. Turning her attention back to her sisters, Kat and Sasha, and her brother-in-law, Ryan, she frowned. They had come to visit and all three sat at the bar as Zoe provided them with generous mugs of draft beer.

'Only you would threaten someone's manhood.' Kat giggled. 'You and those damned novels. Why don't you try a threat that isn't so "nice"-sounding?'

'Drink your beer,' Zoe ordered, making a face at Kat as she swiped Sasha's mug to refill it without being asked.

Loud music pumped from the speakers, forcing everyone to speak even louder to be heard. The songs in the jukebox were a mix of classic and modern rock. The Phoenix Arms dated back to the late 1800s and looked as if the decor hadn't been updated too much since then. Old photographs had been added to the plaster-covered walls. The red bricks underneath showed through in some places. Wooden booths with worn tabletops lined one wall, with smaller tables and chairs along the other, reaching all the way to the far back wall. There was no room for bar games or pool tables, except for an old dartboard that hung on the wall and was only played on weekdays when the bar wasn't crowded.

Surviving more on its landmark status than anything, the bar filled to capacity almost every weekend when partiers came out to play – mostly yuppies blowing off steam. Muscled hard bodies in tight shirts and even tighter pants hit on young things in short skirts and the latest trend. Women air-kissed their girlfriends, making sure to hit each cheek, and men shook hands and postured like they were all rock stars.

The atmosphere seemed to both reflect and reject the bohemianism of the surrounding Greenwich Village. Business stayed steady throughout the week with the usual gathering of troubled writers and poets who claimed to be more creative when drunk. Zoe didn't know anything about that, as she thought their drunken limericks quite horrendous.

'Can you believe that guy actually licked his finger, pressed it to my shirt and asked me if I would like to get out of my wet clothing?' Zoe grimaced, nodding her head toward the young man at the end of the bar. His boyish smile made him look seventeen, but his ID said he was of age to drink. The sad thing was she'd, for a brief second, considered taking him up on his cheap come-on. Pleasuring herself earlier had left her feeling a little ... empty.

'Oh, hey, look at that, my pager,' Ryan said, pretending to glance at his waist. He wore his customary jeans and T-shirt, the easy style perfect for his relaxed nature. When he looked up, chin-length brown hair framed his face and he gave Zoe a lopsided grin. 'Hand me my camera?'

She arched a brow.

'Sorry, sis, but this looks like it's turning into a girls' night and the last time that happened I woke up in a dress and my oestrogen levels skyrocketed.' Ryan held out his hand. Zoe handed him the camera bag from behind the bar, unable to help laughing.

'Don't even go there,' Kat said, looking very chic with her navy-blue-streaked bangs and matching silk voile shirt with contrasted piping along the seams. A thick band around the waist showed her trim stomach. Kat had been one of those women who looked gorgeous pregnant and who other pregnant women tended to hate because of it. 'It was a kilt, not a dress, and it was for a Halloween party.'

'The five of us bar-hopping in the middle of December does not count as a Halloween party,' Ryan protested, slipping the strap over his shoulder.

Zoe chuckled. 'That's probably why your oestrogen levels were up. It had nothing to do with us women and everything to do with being bare-assed in winter.'

Ryan gave a dramatic shiver. 'I wasn't completely naked and still my balls nearly froze. I had never been so glad in my life that I didn't listen to Megan. She told me real Scotsmen don't wear anything under their kilts and I should do the same.' Winking, he lifted his hand in farewell.

'Tell Megs hi for us,' Sasha said.

'Tell her to call me,' Kat added.

'Will do.' Ryan nodded once as he headed toward the door, weaving his way through the thick crowd.

'Why can't I find a guy like that?' Sasha sighed heavily. 'Only one that doesn't feel like a brother.'

Sasha wore her bobbed brown hair in two small pigtails right behind her ears. The lightweight, classic black button-down shirt had pleats along the sides, causing it to fit snugly along her waist. After gaining twenty pounds her first two years in college, Sasha had become an exercise fanatic. It showed. She looked fantastic. Split cuffs on the three-quarter-length sleeves showed off a new, small tattoo on the inside of her forearm. Whenever her sisters asked her about it, though, she'd just laugh nervously and say it was some stupid college night.

'Mom would be thrilled if you did,' Zoe teased. 'Why don't you bring home that college boy of yours and let us meet him and get mom off my back for once. She seems to think that I'm next in line. Though, it does occur to me that this might be why you keep switching majors. Tell the truth, do you do it so mom doesn't pressure you to get married?'

Sasha grinned mischievously, only to take a long drink of her beer by way of an answer.

'I think dad would be happy if you just found a major and stuck with it,' Kat said. Sasha had turned into a career college student, or at least that's what it seemed like to her family.

'Have you noticed that she's gotten much sassier since becoming a wife and mother?' Sasha asked Zoe. 'A little too know-it-all?'

'Don't bring me into that one.' Zoe lifted her hands, seeing a couple of expectant eyes looking at her from the other side of the bar. One of the men waved his hand impatiently and the bleached-blonde woman with too much make-up next to him frowned before turning up her nose. One of the waitresses hadn't showed and Pete, the second bartender on staff, was out in the crowd helping out with orders.

'Hey, Zoe, feed us when you're done!' Kat hollered as she

walked to the waiting couple near the front door.

Zoe lifted her hand, not turning to look at her sisters as she made her way down to the end of the bar. Kat must have been getting tipsy. There wasn't really anything worth eating in the place, beyond nachos with an unpalatable processed-cheese sauce, oversized pickles and shelled peanuts. 'What'll it be?'

'Cosmopolitan,' the blonde said, her voice as nasal as could be expected. Zoe leant forward, having a hard time hearing her. 'And he'll have a dry Martini.'

'We have beer,' Zoe answered evenly, placing her hands on the bar top.

'I want,' the woman said louder, 'a Cosmopolitan and a dry Martini.'

'We have beer,' Zoe repeated, jerking her thumb to point at the wall of beer bottles behind her. 'Over three hundred flavours. Which can I get you?'

Behind the couple, the door opened and Zoe glanced to see who came in. She smiled out of habit, only to stop in mild shock at the dark eyes that met hers. Silky lashes swept down, leading her gaze to a crooked grin. Sexy men weren't lacking in New York, but there was something about the way his eyes glanced around only to land back on hers that held her notice. Most men either looked with a piercing intensity that revealed their true primal designs or didn't look at all, using the city dwellers' innate habit of minding one's own business.

A fine, dark stubble shadowed his chin. Zoe shivered to see the small detail in the glow from the streetlights outside as the door slowly closed behind him. She wondered what it would feel like scratching against her skin. The thought was fleeting, an instant sensation so real it left her body tingling and her pussy wet.

The blonde's whiny voice instantly drew Zoe back to her job and she didn't dwell on the new customer. '... get you fired. I want a Cosmopolitan.'

'It's the owner that picks the beers from around the world. It's the owner who makes the menus and it's the owner who says Cosmopolitans are for whining sissy girls trying to act more sophisticated than they really are.' Zoe forced a fake smile to her lips, only to add sarcastically, 'Should I get you his number? He likes nothing more than to be woken up late at night by drunks.'

'Ah! I heard the help at this bar was rude.' The woman made an awful, high-pitched noise of displeasure. 'I'm going to tell everyone I know *not* to come here.' Her nose scrunched as she grabbed her boyfriend by the arm and forcibly dragged him with her toward the door. The man glanced back before leaving, winking at her. Zoe rolled her eyes heavenward, really not in the mood.

'Don't worry, ma'am, I just came for a beer.' A loud voice drew her attention, mostly because the Southern inflection seemed out of place. It wasn't so heavy as to be Deep South, but enough to be far away from New York.

When she turned, she saw it was the man with dark eyes. Her heart skittered a little in her chest. His medium-blue dress shirt lay open at the collar and was rolled up at the cuffs. Tan arms rested on the bar top, but when she looked at his face, she didn't see the telltale white around his eyes that people got from wearing protective glasses in a tanning bed. As she studied him, something in the curve of his mouth reminded her of a romance-novel hero. It was a small thing, a fleeting passage in some book she couldn't quote, recalling a flutter she got in her stomach when reading.

'What flavour?' Her strained voice came out breathy. Zoe

didn't move, couldn't force a smile, so instead she just stared rudely at him. Inside, she trembled with a desire she'd not felt outside of a fantasy. Part of her wanted to flirt, to bat her eyelashes and secure a date for after the bar closed. She'd never picked up a man at work, but the idea of being with this one after hours caused her stomach to tighten. The more she wanted him, the more her face tightened in what would appear like irritation. It was a reaction she couldn't seem to control.

The sudden surge of rock music made it hard to hear the exact tone of his voice beyond the drawl, so she watched his full mouth. 'You pick.'

Zoe nodded once, turned, pulled open a standing cooler and grabbed the first beer her hand touched. She thought about pressing it to her flushed skin to cool the sudden flame of heat that rushed over her neck and face. She refrained. Opening it without thought, she slid it toward him. 'That'll be eight dollars.'

'Keep the change.' The man tossed down a folded ten-dollar bill. She picked it up and moved on to the next customer, refusing to look at him even as her knees tried to wobble. After a few more orders, she was back beside her two sisters.

'You know him?' Sasha asked instantly, as if the question had been burning on her tongue for quite a while.

'Who?' Zoe didn't bother to follow her sister's gaze. She'd been pointedly ignoring the handsome stranger. Talking to him would only bring disappointment and she really couldn't use any more disappointment right now. Surely that was all that would come from a relationship.

'Mr Tall, Dark and Delicious,' Sasha said. 'If you don't know him, then I think it's obvious that he wants to know you. He's been staring at your ass like a man ready to jump onboard for a ride.'

'I don't want to know him.' Zoe ignored Sasha's crudeness. The woman always got a little crass when she drank. And her answer wasn't a complete lie. Some animalistic part of her did want to know him, but the logical part knew better. She had to get her life on track first. Didn't all the experts say that a person couldn't be happy in a relationship until they were happy with themselves? Still, it didn't stop the fantasy of straddling his lap as he sat on the barstool from entering her thoughts. In her mind, everyone disappeared from the bar, leaving them to their sexual devices. Her lips tingled. How would he kiss? Gentle and soft? Hard and desperate? Warm and probing? She knew the beer she'd given him would flavour his tongue if she were to suck it. Hearing one of her sisters clearing their throat, Zoe shook the images from her mind.

'At least Contiello isn't here again,' Zoe continued. Other lurid thoughts about the handsome man tried to surface, but she pushed them away. 'I swear I could kill the person who told him I work here. He's been here twice this week for drinks, once with a big-name chef and another time with a publicist that has a lot of connections.' At her sisters' looks, Zoe nodded. 'Oh yeah, he made sure to point that out. He also made sure to introduce me as "that one who did that thing I was telling you about."'

'What do you think he told them?' Sasha asked.

'Who the hell knows? Whatever it is, it's not the truth. If I didn't need this job so badly, I'd have told him off ... again.' Zoe sighed, rushing off to take more drink orders as a new group came to the bar. Pete had come back from working the floor and was filling the waitresses' drink orders along with his own. An unkempt college dropout, Pete had a habit of quoting old writers while he worked, often answering questions with some line only the literarily inclined patrons could understand.

'"Lord, what fools these mortals be,"' Pete said to Kendra, the waitress.

'Lord Byron?' Kendra asked, tilting her head to the side. Her soft curls bounced, as if an extension of her energetic frame.

'That's right, love.' Pete nodded, grinning. The woman giggled and walked off.

'Byron?' Zoe arched a brow. 'Don't you mean Shakespeare?'

'Zoe, baby, I've learnt never to contradict a woman you're trying to get into the sack. It hurts the odds.'

Zoe gave a small laugh, before drawling sarcastically, 'You truly are a poetic soul.'

He wiggled his eyebrows, picked up a tray full of beers and disappeared into the crowd.

'Guys like you, Pete, are the reason I don't date,' she muttered under her breath.

Obviously hearing her, Sasha laughed. 'Zoe, you don't date because you don't take chances. I say you give Mr Fine over there a shot and don't give him one of those snobby looks you get around cute guys. What is the worst that could happen? You get a little action? Maybe have a little fun? A free meal at the very least?'

Zoe glanced down the bar to where the handsome stranger still sat. His eyes were on her and he smiled. Could she take a chance like him? She thought about apologizing, of seeing where things led, of a one-night stand. The thoughts only made her tense. She quickly diverted her attention, ignoring whatever attraction tried to form inside her. 'You go for it. I'm not interested. By the sound of his fake accent, he's an actor. You wouldn't believe how many men come in here with fake accents trying to pick up women. I hate people who aren't real.'

'How's it not real? They're just doing a job,' Kat pointed out. 'Besides, actors can be fun.'

'Ah, forget it.' Zoe swiped her hands through the air. 'Let's talk about something besides men.'

Jackson Levy tapped his foot in time with the music. 'Take It Easy' by the Eagles played. The song was much better than some of the other music that had been blaring over the bar. Back home in South Carolina, in the small town where his family still lived, they played nothing but country music and a few rock classics. This song reminded him of home and how terribly he missed it.

As a young boy, he could dream of nothing more than getting out. It was a generic dream, a dream had by all young boys who grew up in small towns. Places like New York seemed so exotic. But what reality made clear, and dreams never touched upon, was how rude and busy everyone was in big cities. Everything was impersonal, everything had a time and a schedule. That's why he hated coming here, hated coming to all big cities. But with work he had little choice. When it came to his job, whatever he did, he succeeded. Too bad his love life wasn't so golden.

Jackson glanced down the bar to where the bartender spoke with a couple of women. When he had first walked in and seen her brief smile, he had hoped that maybe she would be different from the others he'd met each time he came to New York. Her wide, dark-blue eyes captivated him. Straight blonde hair framed her face, the bangs long but tapered. Normally, he liked a woman with flowing long hair, but the cut suited her slender face and small, energetic frame.

His initial hopes for a pleasant conversation were crushed when she merely stared at him, like he was another drone in her long line of customers. Well, his momma hadn't raised a quitter. Maybe he needed to try a different approach. Wasn't his family always on him to try harder in the female department?

With that in mind, he hurried and finished his beer. The deep ale had an orange and ginger aftertaste he didn't care for. Where he came from beer tasted like beer. It was just one more thing separating this world from his. After a dinner meeting filled with scotch and sodas, he felt himself entering a pleasant alcohol haze – not so much to impair judgment but enough to loosen his tongue so he could make small talk with a pretty woman.

Jackson lifted his empty bottle as soon as the male bartender disappeared into the crowd. For all the people in the place, the woman didn't look too busy. It took her a moment to see him. She said something to her friends, causing them to laugh before she walked toward him.

'Another of the same?' Even before he answered, she started reaching for the bottle.

'No, actually, I didn't like this one.' He gave her a small smile, one he hoped appeared charming. For some reason, he really wanted this woman to notice him. It was more than the stirring of carnal interest between his legs, but a desire to connect, to know who she was.

What the hell was wrong with him? Jackson suppressed the urge to frown at himself. He wanted to get to know a bartender? What he should be concentrating on was getting her into the sack. He needed release, wanted to find it buried inside her.

'How about something that actually tastes like a beer?' His smile widened.

'How about you actually order and stop wasting my time? I'm not a mind reader.' She arched a brow impatiently. She reached behind the bar to grab a menu then slid it in front of him.

'Important conversation to go back to?' He told himself to keep the Southern charm in his voice. Slowly, he glanced toward her friends. 'Or are you like all Northerners? In too big of a hurry?'

'Wow,' the woman drawled wryly. 'Listen, confederate, the war is over. Y'all lost.' The last was said mimicking his accent, and not in a flattering way.

'I didn't mean to offend you.' Jackson gave her another small smile. 'Just trying to make conversation.'

'Do I look like I'm lacking in conversation? I've got two sisters right over there.' She glanced down the bar. 'And do I look like I'm searching for a good time tonight?'

'Sisters? So you're a . . . ?' He glanced at the pretty women at the end of the bar.

'Uh, my sisters – my mother gave birth to all of us.' The small crease between her furrowed brows deepened.

'Oh.' He gave a nervous laugh. 'I thought you were saying you were . . .'

'Into ladies?' The brow arched. 'Not that it matters, but no.'

Fucking smooth, Jackson. The sarcastic thought filtered through his mind. If it were physically possible, he'd beat the crap out of himself right now for being such an idiot. *Nice and subtle, moron. Why not just pass her a note? Will you go out with me? Yes. No. Maybe?*

'I apologize if it was rude of me,' Jackson said. 'You must have a boyfriend.'

What else could all this hostility be? It wasn't like he had tried to paw her or drag her onto his lap.

'No, I just don't like being hit on by drunks.'

'I'm not drunk. Not on this fruit water you served me.' Jackson let loose an aggravated sigh. A beautiful woman such as her, working in a bar, should expect men to come on to her.

'Listen, pal, how about you leave acting school back at whatever second-rate studio you've crawled here from?' She placed her hands on the bar, leaning forward. The movement accentuated her rounded breasts beneath her T-shirt. He found himself glancing down, even as he told himself not to look.

'Do you ... ?' Jackson forced his eyes away, glancing around the bar. 'Do you have me confused with someone else?'

'Your crowd is usually here on Tuesdays. Last week you were pirates and some oily-faced jerk-off called me his matey. The week before I was a serving wench. Before that a ho talk'n back to her pimp daddy. Before that Mrs Claus, my lady, doll, dame, lassie, bella, Goody Prudence-something-or-other and apparently now it's to be ma'am.' She took a deep, annoyed breath. 'I appreciate that your teacher makes you go out into the "real world" and practice your five-dollar acting skills with promises of Broadway. But I'm not the girl to run your accent by. I'm tired. All I ever wanted to do is be a chef but instead I have a crappy job slinging beer and the last thing I want is to deal with some guy coming on to me.'

So much for charm.

What did he want with some hard-nosed city woman anyway? He could easily pick up a woman for the night, if that's what he wanted. If he wanted one guaranteed, all he'd have to do was call a number he had for a discreet escort service. With a few words he could pick a sure thing from a catalogue for the evening and have his every sexual desire met without questions. However, he didn't like hookers, didn't like the seedy feeling of paying someone to be with him. He wanted a woman to be with him because they wanted to be there, not because he could pay well for the service.

'Wheat beer, dark is fine, no fruit flavours, can you do that?' Jackson just wanted to get his late meeting over with and go back to his hotel to sleep.

'Coming right up,' she said, turning around to grab a chilled glass mug. Pulling the tap lever, she filled it before sliding the beer in front of him. 'That'll be —'

'Run a tab.' Jackson lifted his credit card between his middle and forefinger. He noticed that he had automatically lessened his accent and it annoyed him greatly.

She snatched the card, turned and slid it next to the cash register, quickly scribbling a note on a pad next to it. A shout from a group of young men drew her attention down to the other side of the bar. Jackson watched her, strangely drawn to take in each and every movement. She focused on her task, slipping a paring knife from behind the bar to cut a lime. He watched how she handled the blade, barely looking down as if she'd cut such things a billion times before. After shoving the lime slices into the tops of beer bottles, she slid the bottles over and picked up a new piece of fruit. Walking back to her friends, she slowly cut the peel from the lime, spiralling horizontally around the entire thing so it came off in one continuous piece. Then, dropping the fruit, she formed a rose out of the peel and stuck two toothpicks in the base before placing it on the napkin. The woman had said she wanted to be a chef in her little tirade, but seeing her make a rose peel hardly gave credit to her talent.

Jackson turned his attention briefly to the door before again looking at his beer. Behind him, someone bumped into his back, giggling softly. He ignored them. The barely rock stylings of some underage girl blared over him, adding to his bad mood. He knew what he was doing here. He'd heard of the bar, wanted to see it someday just to say he'd been there, and when Chef Contiello had mentioned meeting up for drinks he hadn't thought twice about saying yes. It had been his hope that loud music and alcohol would drown out the insufferable man's yapping. Jackson knew he didn't have to like a chef to hire him and the client wanted someone semi-famous – not so big as to be un-gettable, but poised for greatness so that whatever restaurant possessed him would benefit.

'Where the hell are you, Contiello?' Jackson swore under his breath, glancing at his watch. The man was beyond late. Even after having his efforts shot down, the semi-erection between his thighs remained to remind him how long he'd been without sex. The last time had been a wait-ress in Paris nearly four months earlier. He again looked at the bartender, his gaze roaming the back of her ass. 'Fuck.' Swallowing deep, he chugged half the mug.

'What were you and brown-eyes over there talking about?' Sasha asked when Zoe again came over. 'Seemed like quite a conversation.'

'You can't see that his eyes are brown from over here,' Zoe said, pointedly refusing to look.

'She wandered by when you were busy with the frat pack.' Kat laughed.

'He smells nice.' Sasha giggled. 'Why don't you go ask him to see his, ah, "cologne bottle"?'

'I hardly think he'll want to show me anything after the way I just shot him down.' Zoe glanced up and down the bar, making sure no one wanted a drink. More to herself, she said, 'I should send Pete out to work the floor more often. He's worth about five waitresses.'

'Forget Pete, what did you say to brown-eyes?' Kat asked.

'I took my frustrations out on him,' Zoe admitted. 'I don't know what came over me. I'm just sick of this place and that damn fake accent of his made me crazy, probably because it was a little too sexy and that just annoyed me more.' Groaning softly, she lowered her head. 'I'm such a bitch. I need to get out of this place.'

'I agree. Quit.' Kat rustled her hair. 'And I'll hire you to be my personal chef. In fact, I'll get Vincent's parents to buy you your own restaurant.'

'I don't want charity,' Zoe said, grabbing a nearby empty bottle and tossing it toward a trashcan.

'Since when is helping out a sister charity?' Kat demanded.

'Kat, you'd be indebted to his parents forever after a favor like that and I would be stuck cooking for their cocktail parties until the end of time.' Zoe pushed away from the bar and grabbed the little lime-peel rose with the napkin it sat on and wadded it into a ball. 'I got to get back to work.'

'I see you started without me, friend! I'm not too late, eh?'

Jackson glanced up from his row of empty beer bottles to

see Chef Contiello. The man smiled, his eyes glassy as if he were already drunk. Jackson found no fault in that; he was well on his way to the exact same condition. 'Not at all.'

'Yes, I am.' Contiello laughed, his thick Italian accent slightly slurred. 'But that is OK for me, because I am the talent and you need me to say yes to this project.'

'Let me buy you a drink.' Jackson lifted his arm. The chef was right. He did need him to say yes. It would make his life a helluva lot easier.

'What do you think of this bartender?' Contiello motioned toward the woman who'd shot him down earlier.

'A real piece of work,' Jackson drawled.

'You know, she used to work for me and now look at her. She tried to steal my recipes and this is what she's become. That is the kind of power I have, but you know this, don't you?'

Jackson frowned. He knew no such thing, but had a feeling people in Chef Contiello's life had been telling him exactly what he wanted to hear for a long time now. The man truly believed the celebrity hype surrounding him.

'My usual!' Contiello yelled.

The bartender stiffened and turned at the sound. She stood so long, staring at Contiello, that Jackson wasn't sure she'd come to take the order. Slowly she stepped forward. 'Sorry, we're fresh out of goat piss.'

Contiello gave a wry laugh. 'Zoe, why so bitter? Don't you like mopping vomit for a living?'

'Better than working for vomit,' she answered, her tone sickeningly sweet.

'What did I tell you?' Contiello slugged Jackson on the arm a little too hard.

Zoe's eyes turned to him. Her gaze hardened. 'You're with him?'

'Zoe, you didn't introduce yourself to Mr Levy?' Contiello laughed. 'Oh, I forgot, you aren't important enough to know who he is.'

Jackson didn't care for Contiello's tone, but he didn't take his eyes off Zoe. The changes on her beautiful face were slow and unmistakable. First, the hardness turned to surprise, then disbelief as she slowly glanced from Contiello to Jackson. She shook her head, mumbling, 'No, you're joking. It can't be Jackson Levy because he ...' She reached behind her back, fumbling for the credit card she'd placed by the cash register to run his tab. Knocking several papers onto the floor, she finally grabbed it and held it up in a narrow stream of light from a neon sign. 'You're Jackson Levy.' Her eyes round, she looked back at him. 'You're –'

'Jackson Levy,' Jackson finished for her. 'The confederate who doesn't know the war is over.'

Her face paled. 'Mr Le – sir, I'm sorry about that. I had no idea who you were.' She quickly turned and grabbed a ticket from the bar. Without even looking at it to make sure it was his, she tore it up. Zoe put his credit card down on the bar. 'Your drinks are on me. There is no excuse –'

'For grovelling,' Contiello put forth, laughing noisily. 'Zoe, have some pride. First you beg me for a job and now this?'

Her mouth opened as if she wanted to say more, and Jackson almost felt sorry for her. Almost. Until he remembered how she'd treated him and how her tone only changed when she discovered who he was. He might not be a movie star, but in culinary circles people knew who he was. If Zoe had worked for Contiello, she'd been in those circles.

The bartender nodded once, not deigning to answer the boisterous chef, and turned without saying another word.

She grabbed a beer from the cooler and slid it in front of Contiello before turning to walk away.

'What did I tell you?' Contiello slapped him on the arm again. 'Come on, let's go get a seat and hear your proposal.'

'Jackson Levy,' Zoe whispered, coming to her sisters. 'That cowboy is Jackson Levy and he's really a cowboy.'

'Are you getting this?' Kat laughed, taking a drink. She swayed slightly on her seat, more than a little tipsy.

'Something about cowboy levies?' Sasha answered.

'They tax cowboys?' Kat giggled.

'That man I yelled at. That's Jackson Levy. Kat, do you remember that magazine article I showed you a year ago about the mysterious restaurateur? You know the one, everything he touched turned to crème brûlée? That's him! He's the guy investors pay thousands of dollars to so he can design them restaurants and every one of them is in the black within a year. He picks the location, the theme, the staff, the cooks, the ...'

'Whoa, take a deep breath.' Kat reached across the bar. 'You look like you're about to pass out.'

'He could get me a job,' Zoe said, feeling the first real ray of hope since she'd gotten fired. 'If he backed me, it wouldn't matter what rumours Contiello spread because that man –' she paused, waving her hand toward the end of the bar where Jackson had been sitting '– is a restaurant genius. And I was such a bitch to him.'

'You didn't know,' Kat said.

'You've done it now,' Sasha teased.

'Sash, now's not the time to rub it in,' Kat scolded, giving their sister a disapproving look. Turning her attention once more to Zoe, she continued, 'Apologize to him and if he seems reasonable, explain what happened between you and Contiello.'

'What did happen between you and Contiello?' Sasha interrupted.

'He wanted her recipes.' Kat continued to stare at Zoe. 'And she didn't want to give them to him to use. He tried to say they were his anyway since she worked in his kitchen when she invented them.'

'Pfft!' Sasha snorted. 'She'd been inventing those long before his kitchen.'

Zoe looked to where Jackson sat, well away from both her and the bar. 'Who knows what lies Contiello's telling him now?'

'Want me to have him eliminated?' Sasha narrowed her gaze, taking a swig out of her bottle as she glared across the room.

'Thanks, gangsta, but I think we'll follow mom's advice on this one.' Kat gave Zoe a pointed look. 'Go defeat him with kindness and honesty. Don't let Contiello win. You're too good for that.'

'Since when do we listen to mom?' Zoe asked, too nervous to take a step.

'Since the tea leaves told her we should.' Kat laughed, poking fun at their divining mother. 'You want me to call her and tell her to put on a kettle?'

'Uh, no,' Zoe said, knowing her mother's assistance at this moment was the last thing she needed. 'I'll talk to him just as soon as there is an opening.'

'Smart choice.' Sasha winked. 'Now, how about beer number 159 on the list? I haven't tried that one yet.'

Zoe waited nervously for over an hour, watching for her chance to bring Jackson another drink. Once, Kendra beat her to it as she was tied up with the rowdy college boys. A part of her cringed since she had said she'd pay for them, as she mentally tallied how many beers the two men drank. She could little afford to fund their meeting.

But covering the tab was the least of her problems. She wasn't sure what she would say to Jackson when she finally got the chance, how she could possibly say she was sorry. In truth, she would never have imagined Jackson Levy to be so young, or so cute. Whenever culinary magazines talked about him, they showed pictures of his restaurants, never of the man. By his accomplishments, she just assumed he'd be much older.

Zoe paced the bar. What could she say to him? The truth?

Please hire me, I'm desperate. I'll do anything for a job and I do mean anything. You're my last hope, if you don't give me a job I'll die in bartender hell.

When the moment came, she still hadn't come up with the right words. Her sisters left, Kat to go home to her husband and daughter and Sasha to bum a cab ride from the richer sister. Zoe missed their silent support.

Contiello stood, shrugging and laughing as he backed away from the table. Then, pointing, he yelled something along the lines of, 'You know what I want, let me know when you decide.' Zoe couldn't be sure of the exact words, as the bar was too loud, but she saw his lips move in the dim light. As he sauntered toward the door, he winked at Zoe. She glared at him and he laughed, tossing his head back in a way that made her want to jump over the bar and pull out all his shiny hair by the roots.

Her eyes turned to Jackson, meeting his gaze. Slowly he stood and walked toward her. The music coming from the jukebox played low and soft, a love song, as if cued by some demon force to torment her. Her heart beat just a little faster. Somehow knowing who he was, knowing he wasn't just some actor but a man with a real job and a real accent, made him intimidating. And, oddly, it made him more attractive. Power in and of itself was a heady aphrodisiac and this man had it in spades.

Focus, Zoe, you want a job, not a date.

'I'd like to pay my tab.' Jackson tried to hand back the card he'd originally given her.

'I said I'd take care of it, sir,' Zoe answered.

'I insist.' He didn't smile, didn't let on that this was anything more than a business transaction. All the charm he'd tried to bestow upon her earlier was gone. Why hadn't she just been nice to him when she rejected his advances?

Zoe nodded, already knowing their total bill in her mind as she turned to the credit card machine. Putting the receipt on the bar with a pen for him to sign, she said, 'Mr Levy, sir, I'd like to apologize again for earlier. This isn't exactly my dream job, but that was no excuse for being in a bad mood and taking it out on you. In fact, I would love the opportunity to cook for you.' He glanced up from signing his name and she stumbled over her words as she looked deep into his steady brown eyes. 'For, ah, a, um, interview. I promise it won't be a waste of your –'

A loud ring sounded and he reached for his jacket pocket. Pushing the receipt toward her, he grabbed his cell phone and flipped it open. To her, he said, 'I'll need a copy of the receipt,' before saying into the phone, 'Hello? Yeah, give me a sec, my meeting with Contiello just ended and I'm waiting for a receipt.'

'Receipt,' she repeated softly, turning to take the customer copy from the printer. She closed her eyes tight when he couldn't see her and took a calming breath. When she again faced him, his hand extended before she even reached to hand the receipt over.

'What? No, he wants to negotiate salary. I expected it, but his terms are ridiculous. I'll let him think about it and contact him in a week. Let him think we've changed our minds until then. After he starts to sweat, we'll re-approach him if he doesn't come to us first. That restaurant he works for is in the red since the owner died. I talked to the bank president today.' His eyes shifted up, as if realizing Zoe still stood in front of him, listening to every word. Nodding once, he said, 'Ma'am,' and walked out of the bar.

Zoe stared after him, ignoring a loud call for raspberry beer. Streetlights silhouetted Jackson as he stood outside, glancing up and down the street before walking along the sidewalk, out of her eye line.

'Hey, Zoe, you all right?' Pete asked, bumping her lightly as he passed to grab a raspberry beer from the cooler.

'Ah, yeah,' she lied, fumbling around for a towel. 'Just tired. Long night.'

'I hear ya, doll.' Pete walked away, leaving her alone behind the bar.

Grabbing a rag, she began scrubbing her workstation with irritated force. 'Good going, Zoe,' she berated herself, 'way to fuck up your life more.'

Chapter Three

The loud, startling words came from behind her. 'Do you know what the original recipe for Southern pound cake is?'

Zoe gasped, just short of screaming. This time of day the street was usually abandoned. The early-morning hour stretched before her and she could think of little else beyond finding her bed. Her T-shirt stuck to her underarms. Sweat dried on her face and neck combined with the smell of bleach water on her hands. Tired and aching from a full shift that had ended in cleaning the entire bar, she wasn't in the mood to defend herself from an attacker. She reached for her hip, pulling Mace from the clip on her waistband. Turning, her arm raised, she gasped again. 'Mr Levy.'

'Do you or do you not know what the original recipe for Southern pound cake is?' Jackson's arms hung easily at his sides as he studied her intently. A light-grey button-down shirt with darker grey stripes replaced the blue one he'd worn earlier, testifying to the fact that he'd changed and come back. His black suit stood in sharp contrast against the lighter-coloured shirt and succeeded in making her feel all the grungier. The elegant drape of black material and the perfect cut confirmed the suit's custom tailoring. By the alertness of his gaze, he appeared as if he'd slept a full night when she knew for a fact he'd been up late drinking. 'Do I take your silence to mean you don't know?'

Zoe opened her mouth, still trying to process his question through her tired mind. Jackson began to reach for his jacket pocket and she hurried to speak, stopping him. 'I can't be sure. Southern cooking isn't my area of expertise, but I'd say basic cake ingredients – flour, sugar, eggs, butter, maybe salt or vanilla to flavor, baking soda.'

'What is the difference between Cajun and Creole cooking?' His expressionless face gave nothing away.

'What is this about? Is this a job interview?' Zoe took a slow step toward him, only to stop when she remembered how badly she needed a shower. She imagined her eyeliner to be smudged, creating dark circles beneath her eyes. Her eye shadow and blush would have surely long faded and her hair had to be frizzy.

'I haven't decided yet. Do you know the difference?'

'Creole is French-based –' Zoe paused, her mind not wanting to work past the dull headache of fatigue '– ah, Cajun is Louisiana … It's a trick question. They're the same.'

His mouth shifted into a slight frown. 'Can you make grits?'

'I can make anything you want me to if I have a recipe. Give me a day with that recipe and I'll most likely improve upon it.' Zoe proudly lifted her chin, trying to force a challenge to her gaze.

'Southern folk don't really cotton to people changing their tried and true recipes, ma'am.' Jackson's drawl thickened and she wondered if he did it to annoy her.

'Then I can make it exact,' Zoe answered, too weary to debate. This strange interview couldn't be going well anyway. Southern cuisine was more of a regional thing and she'd never really paid attention to it. Italian cooking was her strongest suit, with French and Mediterranean following far behind.

'Hmm.' Jackson stared at her, giving nothing away. His piercing gaze bored into her, as if taking in every nuance of her expression. She made an effort to keep her features blank yet pleasant, but as she imagined what her hair and make-up must look like, she found herself frowning. 'All right.'

Zoe blinked several times, shaking her head slightly. 'All right?'

'I have an urgent position open for a head chef, one I have to fill today, and unfortunately for me I have more pressing matters with a new restaurant proposal in Texas. The job I'm offering is nothing glamorous. Ah, here we go.' He motioned to the side. Zoe turned to see a limo pulling along the quiet street only to stop nearby. Jackson walked toward the driver side of the car, meeting the chauffeur when he opened the door. 'Thanks, Chuck.' When he turned to her, he held two large paper coffee cups. To Zoe, he said, 'Well?'

'I need more information.' Zoe took a slow step off the curb, reaching to take the offered coffee cup. Heat flooded her fingers and she tapped them lightly against the sides. What was she saying? The restaurant could be in the pits of hell cooking for demons and she'd say yes. Fingering the plastic lid, she tried to focus past her racing heart. 'When? Where?'

'You'll start in two days, flight leaves tomorrow morning.'

'I have to give notice to the bar and there's my apartment.'

He sighed, taking a step forward. Zoe glanced up, taken

aback by how close he was. A small shiver worked over her, making her forget how tired she was. When he leant over, her eyes automatically went to his mouth and her lips parted. Tingling sensations erupted as she irrationally waited for him to lean closer. He didn't kiss her, but instead reached for the door handle to the back seat. She quickly stepped out of his way and looked down at the cup, only to take a sip to hide her mortification.

'The offer leaves with me and I have a plane to catch. I have a position to fill and either you want it or you don't – on a probationary basis, of course. I honestly don't care if you prefer to work in a bar. I can track someone down with a few phone calls.'

'But you don't even know my name.' She tilted her head in question. 'Do you?'

'Zoe Matthews. Last time I'm going to ask.' He made a move to get into the car.

'I'll take it,' she blurted.

He reached into his jacket. 'Here is your ticket. Someone will meet you at the airport. I'll have my office arrange for transportation and a temporary residence. Don't disappoint me.'

'I – I won't.'

The car door slammed shut. She stepped back as the limo rolled down the street, wishing he'd offered her a ride home. It would have saved her cab fare. Looking down at the ticket, she saw it indeed had her name on it. He'd known she'd say yes. Why wouldn't she? He was Jackson Levy and he was giving her a last chance at fulfilling her dream.

'I won't fail,' Zoe whispered to the ticket, squeezing it tight in her shaking hands. 'I can't fail.'

Scanning the bold print, she gave a short laugh. 'Of course the flight would leave at six in the morning.' Her eyes went to the destination. He never had said where. He'd mentioned Texas. That wouldn't be so bad, not ideal, but not bad. San Francisco or Chicago would be better. Tension instantly worked up her spine as her gaze fell upon the city. 'Columbia, South Carolina?'

Jackson resisted the urge to turn around and look out the back window. Even covered in sweat and looking like she'd hit the end of a triathlon, the woman was gorgeous. There was something to her dirty appearance, the way her hair lay flat, the way her make-up smudged beneath her eyes, making them dark. A base urge boiled inside him, filling his cock and causing him to tremble. Normally, he didn't fantasize about unclean women and dirty sex, but with her his sudden libido seemed to create whole new fantasies. He imagined her leaning over a barstool, bent across a pool table, on her knees in the Phoenix Arms's restroom. He suddenly cleared his throat, slightly uncomfortable with the turn his mind had taken. Instead, he forced himself to think of her in the shower – bathing the sweat from her body, kissing her wet flesh, running his fingers through soapy trails.

This plan to bring her to his hometown had seemed like a good idea when Jackson put it into motion. What better way to teach the rude woman a lesson than to take her out of her element, luring her away with her dream job? Of course he'd been pissed off and drunk and, by the time he'd sobered some, he'd not thought to stop his plans because that wasn't the type of man he was. Once he decided to do something, he did it full on. Besides, he'd already ordered a background check on Zoe's qualifications and purchased her plane ticket.

The limo turned the corner and Jackson glanced at the

dark window separating him from his driver. He slipped off his jacket and placed it on his lap, eager to take care of the growing erection pressing against his dress slacks. He pulled a handkerchief from his pocket before unbuttoning his slacks and slipping his hand beneath the silk boxers. A low sigh echoed from his mouth and he bit his lip.

Zoe's image danced behind his closed lids. The gentle rocking of the car vibrated along his back and thighs. Jackson fisted his cock, hating the dry rub of his flesh even as he imagined what she would feel like instead. It was difficult, stroking in a way that wouldn't be noticed by anyone passing. Even with tinted windows, there were times when the light hit just right and people could see inside.

He gripped tight, digging his heels into the floor as he moved his hips in shallow thrusts. Jackson wanted to fuck her so badly, wanted to order the driver to turn around so he could grab her and throw her down on the limo seat. Sweat beaded his brow. Release was close, so close. He took his handkerchief, cupping it along the tip of his cock, catching his seed as it jetted warm into his palm.

For a long time, he breathed hard, opening his eyes to watch the passing buildings. Jackson righted his clothing, knowing he had to get himself under control. Masturbating in a limo wasn't his style. He pushed all sexual thoughts from his mind and grabbed his cell phone. Only when he'd regained complete control over his thoughts did he punch in number five on his speed dial. It didn't take long before the call was answered by his assistant's enthusiastic voice. 'Jackson! I didn't expect to hear from you again for a few days. Don't tell me you aren't coming home. You know it will kill Tommy if Uncle Jackson isn't here for his birthday party. We have the whole day planned.'

'No, I said I'd be there and I'll be there. I haven't missed one yet, have I, Callie?' Jackson laughed, thinking of his three little nephews. Callie wasn't only his assistant, but his sister. 'I'm actually coming home today.'

'That's great news. I'll tell the family and we'll have a big dinner tonight.' The soft accent of her words made him feel safe.

'That's not why I called,' Jackson said. 'I need to talk to your husband. Is Bob there?'

'He's out back carrying on with Mr Davis about lawn-mowers or Weed Eaters. The old coot was up before dawn mowing his lawn. Amazingly, I was up at that time searching the internet databases for your Ms Matthews.'

'Sorry about that,' Jackson said.

'That's all right. It is what you pay me for, little brother.' Callie laughed. 'I know a drunken man when I hear one. Why do you need Bob? Is something the matter?'

'Not really. I just have to fire him from the restaurant.' Jackson paused, waiting to see if he would get a rise out of her.

She sighed, clearly unconcerned. 'What did he do now? Is this about the industrial-sized pickles? I asked him to bring them. We'll pay for them and for the ketchup.'

Jackson laughed, watching the tall buildings pass in the early-morning light. Streaks of gold and magenta raced over the glass fronts. 'I don't care about the pickles. I told ya'll to take whatever you need.'

'Then, what is this about? You're not really firing him, are you?'

'Just for a few months. I need the chef position for someone else. Don't worry about your bills, they'll be covered. In fact, if he takes the time off, it'll be doing me a great favour.' Jackson knew he'd have to explain why, not

43

only to Callie, but to the rest of his family. 'I've hired a chef from here in New York. A real uppity piece of work.'

'Ah, so this is why you had me looking up Chef Matthews at two in the morning.' Callie instantly drew the connection, not that it was too hard. 'If she was so bad, then why'd you hire her?'

'To teach her a lesson.'

'Sounds like more work for you than her.'

'She insulted me, my accent, my heritage and I'm pretty sure several other things I can't clearly recall right now. I've just had it with these rude, arrogant people who think they're better than everyone else.'

Callie hummed thoughtfully. 'You're telling me you lost your temper and offered her a job in your favorite restaurant?'

'It's complicated.'

'Sounds like it is twelve beers too many complicated, if you ask me.' Callie hummed softly, as if suppressing a chuckle.

'Perhaps,' he admitted. 'I was interviewing Contiello and he went on and on about how she tried to steal his recipes and ideas only to come on to him and how he had to fire her. The guy's a real jerk. I'm not sure how much I believe of his account of things, but then she wasn't the nicest person either until she found out who I was. As soon as she heard my name, she became all sweet, begging for a job.'

'So, what I'm hearing is, you were drunk.'

'Yeah. But I was also fed up with the nonsense. These people are only nice if it suits their purpose. So, I'm giving her what she asked for – a job in her very own restaurant.'

'That poor child. You are going to put some city girl in

that diner?' Callie clucked her tongue in disapproval. 'By the way, little brother, you'll be happy to know there wasn't much information on her. I saw her name listed in a website for some restaurant named *Sedurre* in New York, but nothing else. She's not in any of the normal publications. Want me to check schools and the obscure media listings?'

'No, that won't be necessary.'

'She cute?'

Jackson didn't answer.

Callie chuckled knowingly. 'When do you need him out by?'

'Couple days.'

'I'll let Bob know he's taking me and the boys on a mini-vacation.' Callie laughed again. 'And don't you dare offer to let him use your fishing cabin. I'm going to stay in a place with sheets and cable.'

'You're not going to give me hell about this?' Jackson asked, surprised.

'Oh, I have plenty of opinions about this, but I figure it's best to mind my own business and leave you to yours.'

'Since when?'

'Since you said she was pretty and I know you need all the dating help you can get. And you are my employer giving me a paid vacation.' A series of sounds came across the phone from his sister's house. He heard his nephews running behind her, shouting something about a turtle in the yard.

'It's not like that,' Jackson said.

'Sure thing, Jacky.'

'Stop calling me Jacky,' he ordered, annoyed by the child-hood nickname.

'Then stop making it so darn easy to aggravate you with

it, Jacky,' Callie said. 'Now, I have to go – something about a giant turtle getting ready to battle a neighbourhood cat.'

'Hug the boys for me.' Jackson sighed with longing, trying to catch his nephews' voices.

'Call me when you get back,' Callie ordered. He heard her talking to the boys in a firm voice before the phone connection clicked off.

'Are you sure I'm not bothering you, Kat?' Zoe held her cell phone to her ear, staring at the old suitcase slowly being filled with her clothes. All the chef uniforms were neatly folded, taking up most of the space. Folded and rolled T-shirts lined the edges, crammed in to utilize what was left. 'I know it's early.'

'No, I've been up for an hour. The baby is fussy,' Kat's tired voice answered before she yawned. 'What's up?'

'I'm going to South Carolina,' Zoe said, still a little awed by it herself.

'Things that bad? Did Contiello do something last night after we left?'

'Nothing out of character.' Zoe took a deep breath, shoving jeans in to make a new layer across the top of her pile. 'I talked to Jackson last night and made a complete ass out of myself.' Zoe quickly told her sister everything from him asking for a receipt to the strange interview, finishing with, 'What do you think?'

'I think you're going to go down to South Carolina and wow the crap out of Mr Levy with your talent.' She could practically hear her sister grinning. 'How can he not be impressed with you? I even bet he offers you a bigger restaurant before everything is said and done. And I don't want you to worry. I'll take care of everything here. I'll deal with your landlord and see about getting you out of your apartment so you don't have to pay rent.'

'But what if I fail?' Zoe swallowed nervously.

'You won't fail,' Kat said. 'You'll be great. Just make sure you call me as soon as you get there. If it looks dangerous, you call me and I'll have the Richmond private jet down there within an hour.'

Zoe laughed. 'Quit trying to find excuses to use the family jet. It's Jackson Levy. I hardly think the job is going to be dangerous.'

'I don't know, sis. Jackson was pretty cute and that can always be dangerous. Feel free to mix business with pleasure, just call me after with the details if you do.'

Thoroughbred County, South Carolina

Zoe blinked rapidly, wondering how long she'd been asleep. Her head hurt from the rude awakening of hitting against the car window. Trees passed by her vision in a long blur of greens and silver. A thin veil of moss draped the limbs like long, tangled strands of gray-green hair drifting in a gentle breeze. Some reached as long as twenty feet and sprouted threadlike leaves. By the light, it was still morning, though how early was hard to tell. Because of her night schedule, she'd not slept well as she'd worried about making her six o'clock flight on time. Only after quitting her job and locking her apartment door for the last time did she realize she'd never really negotiated benefits and pay. She'd been so focused on becoming a chef. This opportunity was all that mattered to her.

'I see you're awake, ma'am. You were sawing logs there for awhile.'

Zoe sniffed loudly, embarrassed to be told she'd been

snoring. At least it wasn't moaning in sexual desire due to the very torrid dream she'd been having about Jackson. Though waking up took some of the dream from her, she remembered there being a lot of whipped cream and peaches involved.

She glanced at the driver, trying to remember the mumbled name he'd given her as she came from baggage claim to find him waiting with a cardboard sign with her name written on it in orange marker. Hands gnarled with arthritis gripped the wheel, as wrinkled as the old man's face. Short, dark hair heavily peppered with gray covered all but the freckled balding spot at the crown of his head. 'Where are we?'

'About five miles outside of Dabery. Jacky boy asked me to drop you at Marta's so you can get cleaned up before going to *Renée*.'

'*Renée*?'

'You're the new cook, right?'

Zoe sighed, hit by just how little she knew about her new job. She told herself it didn't matter. Any restaurant would do so long as she had a chance to run her own kitchen staff, make her own menus and prove herself to Jackson. He had asked her about Cajun food and *Renée* sounded French. It wasn't her specialty, but she could do it. She *would* do it.

'Yes. I am the new head chef.' Zoe lifted her chin, trying not to let her nervousness show. She had to keep a brave front, had to make everyone believe she knew she could do this when in truth she wasn't so sure. What if she failed? What if Jackson hated her cooking? What if no one ate at the restaurant and she was the first Jackson Levy venture to fail miserably? She'd never get into another kitchen again.

'You all right, ma'am?' the driver asked. 'You're whiter than Sunday linen.'

More of the dream surfaced. Her body had been covered in cream and Jackson had decorated her with pieces of fruit before slowly eating his way over her body without his hands. The wave of desire that flooded her made her actually gasp in shock.

'Fine,' she lied. 'It was a long flight. Can you tell me if Mr Levy will be there?'

'Jacky boy? I don't rightly know, ma'am. His sister called me and asked me to pick you up from the airport. She's a good girl, that Callie.'

'His sister lives here?' Zoe asked in surprise. She really knew nothing about the man aside from his work reputation.

'His whole family moved to Dabery when those Levy kids were just young children barely out of diapers.' The man glanced at her through the rear-view mirror, smiling kindly as he gossiped. 'They have lived here ever since, more or less. Jackson's been good to this town and owns a place outside city limits. The baby of the family, Jefferson, left for awhile but is back now. And Callie, the oldest, settled with a local boy right out of high school. They have three boys now – Tommy, Sammy and Peanut – ornery little rascals.'

'And his wife?' Zoe probed, finding herself holding her breath. Peanut? Jackson had a nephew named Peanut?

'No, ma'am, he never did marry. We keep hoping, but no wedding bells yet. Though Jefferson is engaged to a fine lady from Savannah. I met her at the church potluck a couple weeks ago.'

Zoe had a feeling she could get lots of information about Jackson from this man, but refrained from probing further.

Instead, she turned her attention out the window. Trees thinned, opening up to a sloping valley. Nestled along the hillside were houses and farms, as beautiful as a painting. Horses grazed behind stark-white wooden fences, their sleek bodies gleaming in the sunlight. A red barn stood over a shorter brown building with black iron gates. Tall pines swallowed little trails that led off into their shadowed sanctuary, the limbs not as covered with moss as they had been earlier along the road.

'This can't be right. The restaurant is here? But this is ...' Zoe rolled down her car window, sticking her head out to look around. The smell of pine assaulted her, mixed with fresh air and dust. Eerie quiet surrounded them, punctured only by the sound of the car engine. To herself, she finished, 'This place is too small.'

'Is it done?' Jackson asked, leaning against Mac's car. He'd known the old man since he was a boy and Mac looked the same now as he had then, down to the arthritic hands. The only difference was a pronounced limp when he walked, the legacy of having fallen off a horse while drunk. Jackson made sure the man always had work with local stables and odd jobs around town.

'Sure is, boss,' the man said.

'Good.' Jackson discreetly handed the man a couple of hundred dollars before pushing up from his car. The warm spring air scented with wildflowers drifted from the forest behind Marta's Twelfth Street Bed and Breakfast. Trails led from the back of the house into the oak and pecan trees, to a little pond and creek hidden from those not familiar with the area. Bass fishing, camping, hunting and hiking were popular pastimes for the residents of Dabery and they did not share their secret haunts with outsiders. It wasn't unusual for people to see deer grazing along the tree line.

The bed and breakfast was over a hundred years old. Like most of the businesses in town, he'd owned it for a short time until the owners could afford to run it on their own. It was one of the few properties he didn't make a small profit on, though he'd never tell Marta that. He would have been happy just to break even, but it was a matter of town pride that he earned something for his investment and he did not take their pride from them.

Stark-white siding with barn-red trim and green window boxes looked freshly painted. The front porch wrapped alongside the house, sporting wooden chairs with padded floral seats. In truth, the house should never have been a bed and breakfast, as it was too small, but he managed to make it work. Widowed and childless, Marta had no one. So Jackson encouraged her to use her strength, which was taking care of others.

'She asked about you,' Mac said as Jackson began to walk toward the first restaurant he'd ever owned and the only business property still under his name in Dabery. He heard the telltale teasing to the man's tone.

Jackson knew he should keep walking, but he couldn't stop himself from turning back around. Zoe preoccupied his fantasies, stirring the kind of constant lust he thought he finally had under control once he hit his mid-twenties. But one thought of Zoe had him as randy as an eighteen-year-old boy hiding in the girls' locker room during shower time.

'She asked if you were married.' Mac grinned. 'And about your family.'

'Normal questions,' Jackson said, though inside his stomach tightened.

'Did the secret code change? Because when I was

your age and a pretty woman asked if I was married, it meant –'

Jackson laughed. 'Mac, tell the truth. When did a pretty woman ever ask you anything?'

'Boy, you're not too old to bend over my knee,' Mac warned, suppressing a good-natured grin. 'But you are sure as hell old enough to know you won't be young forever and if a pretty girl is interested you ask her out on a date.'

Date his new cook? A woman who he had brought down here in a drunken fit to punish? Jackson gave a small laugh. 'They have laws against dating employees.'

'We're from the South.' Mac winked. 'Since when do we worry about laws?'

'Jackson pumped new life into the town. He bought shares in the old stables, rebuilt them better than ever and created jobs. Now Dabery's stallions are bought all over the world. Once they were operating enough to support themselves, he sold his share to the original ranchers and became a local hero.' Marta smiled, pointing at the pictures along the walls of her bed and breakfast. The old newspaper clippings were from the mid-1900s when horse shows seemed to draw much of the town's attention. 'A run of bad luck struck this town in the 70s and we all struggled. People were moving away and this town almost died, but Jackson brought us back to life.'

Zoe nodded, following Marta's hand to more recent editions of the *Dabery News*. Jackson's face graced the clippings. Some of the earlier ones showed him with hair to his chin, in T-shirts and blue jeans, then later in business suits and a crew cut, to the most recent with short, styled hair expertly mussed with gel, and designer-label clothing.

She paused, captivated by his frozen smile and the happy light in his eyes. Her heartbeat quickened. If she were a teenage girl alone in her room, she would have pressed her mouth to the photograph. She tried to ignore the attraction she felt for her new boss, but it was there – raw and so very real.

Marta's cheery disposition fit the Victorian-decorated farmhouse atmosphere of her business. Her blonde, upswept hair created a curled effect around her smooth face. Tiny lines gave away her advanced age, but it was impossible to tell how old she really was. Dangling crystal earrings and a matching jewel necklace added flair to the rose-embroidered jacket dress she wore.

Wooden floors, fireplaces and antique furniture graced the many rooms. Equestrian-themed paintings and small horse figurines covered the walls and many shelves of the downstairs sitting room. Zoe had already been shown to her room upstairs. According to Marta, it was one of three, though the others were empty. She'd been placed in the largest room, with a king-sized bed, white-painted walls and rose porcelain vases.

'I'm sorry, but I should get going.' Zoe touched Marta's arm lightly as she pried her eyes from the hypnotic smile on Jackson's picture. She hadn't really been listening to what the woman had been saying anyway. 'Can I borrow your phone to call a taxi?'

'Taxi?' Marta laughed, waving her hand in the air. 'Sweetie, the restaurant is only two blocks that way.' She pointed toward the west side of the house. 'And there is no taxi service in Dabery.'

'Of course there isn't.' Zoe looked down at the chef uniform she wore, having a sinking feeling in the pit of her stomach. Though with all the horses it was possible the restaurant had a booming tourist business. A rich, powerful clientele who demanded the best wherever they went – whether it was a Swiss ski resort or Dabery, South Carolina.

She left the house, her head down as she quickly descended the steps. Hearing an engine, she saw the car that had dropped her off an hour before driving away down the street. Her eyes followed it, automatically going down the sidewalk in the direction of the restaurant. Seeing a man in blue jeans and a long-sleeved T-shirt, she stumbled. Without seeing his face, she knew it was Jackson. He might not be in a suit, but the tilt of his head, the stride of his walk, the controlled movements of his arms gave him away.

She made a move to catch up with him, running her fingers through her hair. Suddenly, he turned and she stumbled again. Dark eyes pierced hers and her breath caught at the intensity in his gaze. Nerves fluttered in her stomach, and her heart beat faster. Hating the breathiness in her tone, she said, 'Hi.'

His gaze slowly roamed over her chef uniform and a small smile lifted the corner of his mouth. When she reached him, he began walking next to her, not saying anything.

'I wanted to thank you for this opportunity,' she said, feeling some mysterious need to fill the silence. 'I won't disappoint you.'

'Just try not to be rude to the customers.'

She opened her mouth to speak, but nothing came out. She nodded, not looking to see if he noticed. It wasn't as if she could blame him for the jibe. Businesses clustered the long street, a continuous front that only broke at the end of each block. Wooden signs carved and lined with gold inlay hung along the eaves of each one – a general store, clothing boutique, jewellery, curios, horse supply, shoes. The quaint little shops weren't like any she'd seen in New York. Walking under a sign that said DINER, she looked forward for a restaurant set off from the rest of the town.

Jackson cleared his throat. Zoe stopped, realizing he was no longer beside her. She found him waiting, a door held open to the diner. Unsure, she glanced at the front window. In white and gold window paint, old-fashioned letters like the script from a wanted poster spelt out the single word, 'Renée'.

Her eyes wide, she looked from the window up to the diner sign and back again. 'I . . .'

Jackson motioned inside. 'We're closed today because of the re-staffing. Otherwise, you'll open at nine, close at seven thirty. You're off Saturdays and Sundays when the relief cook comes in. You have no say on the way weekends are handled and the weekend staff will not interfere with what you do. When you arrive is up to you and you leave when your work is done. Come in, get acquainted with your area, figure out if you need to order anything, numbers are on the back wall of the kitchen. Food orders are delivered by the local grocery and they can have whatever you need dropped by with only a day's notice – unless it's something fancy they don't keep in stock. Then you'll want to give them a couple days. The waitress takes care of deposits and you just need to keep your receipts together for the accountant who comes in at the end of each month.' Pulling his key from the lock, he handed it to her. 'Your copy.'

Numbly, she followed him in, hoping the second she entered she'd see it wasn't as bad as she thought. Though clean, the restaurant was definitely a diner, with plastic menus and a long row of booths along a stretch of countertop. It had red and white-chequered wallpaper accented with a large clock and tables whose tops were lacquered newspaper clippings – most with pictures of horses.

'I don't understand,' she whispered, her nose burning with sudden unshed tears. Her hands shook. A diner? She'd left her home, her city, her family for a diner? If she wanted to work in a diner she could have moved somewhere closer to New York City. Unable to stop her feet, she followed him toward the metal swinging door with a small round window leading to the kitchen. Basket fryers were next to a stainless-steel range complete with a griddle and six burners. A high shelf was set right beneath the pick-up window showing out over the main floor. Double ovens lined one wall, next to a worktable with a butcher block and an array of appliances. The red ceramic floors had a darkness to them that would never look completely clean, no matter how hard a person scrubbed. The white walls were constructed of washable panelling, covered with clear plastic splashguards at places.

Jackson stared at her, his face unmoving, his dark eyes searching for her reaction. Was this a test? A joke? Was he waiting to see what she would do?

'I thought you said you needed a head chef.' Zoe tried to choose her words carefully, tried to keep the disappointment from her eyes, tried to look as blank as his expressionless face.

'And I do. You just happen to be the only chef. What do you care? You needed a job, I needed a cook, you begged for this –'

'I didn't beg for this.' She felt as if she were being punished for something.

'You begged for a job. This is a job.' He took a step toward her and she became aware of how very alone they were in the kitchen. The breadth of his shoulders blocked her line of sight until all she saw was his body looming forward. 'I told you the position wasn't glamorous and that I had more pressing matters with a new restaurant proposal in Texas. I don't have time to interview for cooks here. I need someone who can just come in and do it. Did I make a mistake in bringing you here?'

'That's it?' Zoe swallowed, wondering if he knew how close he was standing. The gentle scent of his cologne wafted across her senses. She saw a subtle shift in his expression, a lifting of his brow, a curve of his full mouth. Her breath caught in her throat, even as her heart sped in her chest. She did her best to hide her trembling.

'You want there to be more?' The soft brush of his words fanned her cheek, carrying the accent of his voice. What he implied was not what she'd meant, but as the words left him and he leant his face toward hers, she found herself meeting his kiss. Aggression poured between them, as if they fought with their mouths instead of words. Only, Zoe wasn't sure what they were arguing about. A warm hand gripped the side of her face, holding her tight. His body grazed the length of hers and she touched his firm waist, not pulling or pushing as she made contact.

The forcefulness only increased when his tongue delved into her mouth, conquering the depths with a bruising intent. Zoe didn't back down. She'd never been kissed with such knee-weakening passion. Desire warmed her stomach and thighs, centering its slick burn in her dampening sex. Something grazed her stomach, so lightly she couldn't be sure which part of him it was by feel alone. But when it happened again, she had the distinct impression it was his erect cock. Every ounce of her wanted to grip him tight, force his muscled body to hers, but the mild shock that she was being kissed by *the* Jackson Levy kept her from instigating more.

'Hel-low!'

The loud call punctuated by the bell over the front door caused them to jerk apart at the same instant. Zoe licked her lips, tasting the cool mint of him on her tingling mouth. Jackson's hand stayed on her face, his shocked expression saying more than words ever could. He was as amazed by their kiss as she was. Though their bodies had not pressed together, her hand was still on his waist.

'Jackson? Boy, you in here? Bob said you were coming by today.' The voice that interrupted them continued, the sound tired with the deep gravelly quality of a heavy smoker.

Zoe panted hard. Jackson pulled away, putting distance between them. His hand slid from her face as her fingers left his side. She tried to speak, but had no idea what to say. He visibly swallowed, his gorgeous lips parting in a deep breath. He pointed at her, bouncing his hand lightly in the air. 'We'll, ah . . .'He didn't finish as he turned to the metal kitchen door in time to see it swing open. 'Sheryl, hey there, sweetheart. How's my best waitress?'

Zoe felt jealousy burn through her at his easy tone, until she saw the older woman he talked to. Her dyed-black hair contrasted with the paleness of her wrinkled face. The short locks were cut straight along her chin and the cat-eye style of her glasses was actually pretty trendy in some artsy New York circles. Her white button-down blouse tucked into her black, pleated, knee-length skirt.

'I'm your only waitress,' Sheryl answered with a wink. Her playful expression faded when she acknowledged Zoe.

'You must be the new cook. I'll do the pies and the pound cake. I don't do rolls. I don't cook and if the dishwasher doesn't show, you're in charge of the dishes. I'll need a list of specials at the beginning of the week. I like to tell the regulars what to expect and I highly recommend you make Tuesday meatloaf. If you don't, I won't protect you. Mashed potatoes must be homemade. If it comes from a box the customers will scream louder than a stuck pig. Other favorites include ham and beans with cornbread, zucchini pancakes, potato pancakes, sweet potato pie, meatballs, barbeque chicken, chicken and dumplings, fried chicken gizzards and smothered pork chops. Recipes are in the desk file in case you don't know how to make them right, being as you're from New York and all. Potato salad is homemade, but you don't have to do it. I'll leave it in the fridge every Monday. And it's not on the menu, but when tomatoes are in season, we always offer fried green tomatoes.'

Zoe couldn't answer. Her heart still fluttered in her chest from Jackson's kiss. If his plan had been to throw her completely out of her element, he'd succeeded.

'Good.' Sheryl nodded in approval. 'Quiet ones work harder.'

When the woman left the kitchen, Zoe said, 'I thought I was the head chef.'

'Technically, you are. But Sheryl's been here a long time. I'll leave it up to you if you want to try and cross her.' Jackson nodded once before pulling out a card. He tossed it on the butcher block. 'My number if you need it.'

Zoe watched him leave before growling under her breath. Ranting to herself, she said, 'This is a joke. I finally have control over my own restaurant and it barely qualifies as a restaurant and a waitress thinks she can tell me what to do.'

'Hmm.'

Zoe gasped, spinning toward the door. She hadn't heard it open. Sheryl raised an eyebrow, clearly having heard the rant. Tossing a plastic menu down on the cold stovetop, she said, 'Better have this memorized. I don't want to have to explain my orders.'

Chapter Four

Jackson nodded, listening to Charlie talk about business expansion as he occasionally glanced out the window toward the diner. The general store's front window had a perfect view of the restaurant's entrance. What was Zoe doing in there? Sheryl left soon after she had arrived. He almost felt bad for Zoe, knowing how much of a tyrant the older woman could be. But Sheryl, like most of the town, was like family to him. It was this close-knit feeling that he missed when away in the big city. He knew people here, really knew them. He visited them in the hospital and knew that they'd come and see him if anything happened. He knew their kids, mourned at their funerals, celebrated at their weddings. Then why had he brought Zoe here? Why to a place that was so special to him? To a place he rarely let even the most elite of his clients come to, and then only if they were in the horse market?

'I heard your new cook was young and pretty.' Charlie followed Jackson's gaze through the front window. 'Also heard she wasn't big on the small talk.'

'She's from New York.' Jackson knew that would explain everything. He tried not to think about the searing kiss they'd shared. What had prompted him to kiss her like that? On her first day and so passionately?

Charlie nodded. 'Heard that.'

Jackson chuckled. 'Marta's been by, I see. That woman should write the gossip column.'

'I'll mention it to her.' Charlie laughed.

'Oh, no, please don't.' Jackson tensed as the restaurant door opened. Zoe was on her cell phone and began to walk away before turning to lock the door. Whatever the conversation was, she was deep into it.

'Go,' Charlie said. 'No point in standing around here when she's out there.'

'Nothing is going on. She's just a temporary employee. Bob needed a vacation.' Jackson didn't take his eyes from Zoe's slender figure as she held the phone with one hand and wrapped the other around her waist in a protective gesture.

'He using the cabin?'

'Callie threatened my life. I think they're going to Savannah for a few weeks. Jefferson's fiancée has family there and the ladies are going to do some wedding shopping.'

'I'd prefer the fishing cabin.' Charlie coughed, tapping his chest.

'So would my brothers.' Jackson kept an eye on Zoe as he made a move for the door. 'I'll see you later, Charlie. I need to make sure she's not going to ruin the diner.'

'Now that would be a true tragedy. All of Main Street would starve without it.'

'Kat, it's awful. I mean, the menu is like ... is like ...' Zoe shivered. Out of all her sisters, Kat was closest to Zoe. They just seemed to get each other. 'It's like a diner's. Chicken fried steak, grits, potato salad, ruebens, hamburgers, hotdogs, coleslaw, macaroni with cheese, fried foods –'

'Oh, sweetie, do you want me to send the jet?' Kat interrupted, concern in her voice.

'No, there are a couple of bright spots. I get to choose the soup of the day and I get to do my own specials, except for Tuesday, which apparently must be meatloaf.'

'Ew!'

'Yeah.' Zoe nodded, though her sister couldn't see her. She paced to the end of the block, passing the bed and breakfast. 'But I can do this. I can prove myself.'

'Of course you can.'

'I'm going to go. I'll call you later.' Zoe said goodbye and hung up. She found herself a block from the bed and breakfast in a residential neighborhood. Some of the children playing in the front lawns stared at her, a little girl grinning as she held an enormous rainbow lollipop in her dirty hands.

Giving a brief, uncomfortable smile, she turned and went brusquely back toward Marta's. She watched her feet, not making eye contact out of habit from living in the city. Hearing a car, she glanced up. Her gaze instantly drew forward, magnetically drawn down the sidewalk. Jackson stood before the bed and breakfast's picket fence.

Instantly, her lips tingled, reminding her of what his kiss had felt like against them. She missed her step and tripped on a deep crack in the sidewalk, realizing she seemed to stumble a lot around him. Doing her best to recover gracefully, she cleared her throat and tried to smile. 'Checking on my progress?'

'Do I need to?' The softness of his words was almost as seductive as his dark eyes.

'I can run a kitchen.' Zoe refrained from adding, *especially one as small as the one you gave me.*

'That remains to be seen.' Jackson motioned that she should follow him. Instead of heading inside the bed and breakfast, he made his way around the side of the house toward the woods in back. The combination of foliage, trees and plants created a rich tapestry as it canopied over the worn dirt path leading into the woods.

'Where are we going?' She looked over her shoulder, wondering why he'd bring her to the woods in her chef uniform. Or why he'd bring her there at all.

'The only place in town where we can be guaranteed some privacy.' Jackson's features gave no hint of what he was thinking. Zoe ducked under a branch as he held it aside for her. As it fell back into place, hiding them from the stark white of the bed and breakfast, Jackson grabbed her arm and pulled her against his chest. His lips came down hard, but she jerked back before he made contact.

Zoe fought the tension between them, her mind screaming all the reasons why she should run. He was her boss. He was only doing this as some sort of punishment for the way she had treated him, or simply because he could. He didn't respect her. If he did, she'd be in a better restaurant, not a two-bit diner. Then there was the possibility that this diner was where he brought all young female cooks to toy with them, like some sick rich man's game – not that she wanted to believe he was cruel like that.

But for all the reasons she shouldn't be with him, there was one very strong reason why she should. She wanted him. His eyes pulled her, tugging a cord she kept buried deep inside. Looking at him awakened part of her soul, a longing and desire she often denied. Jackson breathed hard, his eyes narrowed, his mouth open as he looked at her, waiting for her response.

Zoe jerked him forward, kissing him on her own terms. She moaned lightly, pressing her chest to his harder one. Her arms wound around his shoulders and her fingers gripped at the nape of his neck. Spearmint flavoured his lips as if he had sucked on breath mints recently. The taste drew her in and she thrust her tongue past the barrier of his teeth. Jackson sucked on her tongue before letting his dance around hers in small, intoxicating circles.

Warmth curled in her stomach, centering on her sex and causing the slick glide of cream to build between the soft folds of her pussy. She squirmed, suddenly too hot in the thick white material of her chef's uniform. Jackson massaged her lower back, kneading his fingers against her as he slowly drew up her jacket and the tight tank top she wore underneath. Strong hands dipped beneath the elastic band of her uniform pants, taking hold of the cheeks of her ass. The cotton of her panties provided no protection against his heat. Pulling her flush against him, he rocked his erection against her, letting her feel the full, hard length.

Zoe broke her mouth away, gasping. Her heart hammered against the walls of her chest, pounding so loud it echoed in her ears. Jackson spread her cheeks, lifting her so her heels left the ground.

'We should go deeper in the woods,' he whispered, pulling his hands from her pants. His fingers slid along her forearm before gripping her hand. Without waiting for her to answer, he pulled her behind him, walking her deeper into the forest.

Zoe couldn't speak, couldn't breathe. Every inch of her ached to be touched, kissed, loved. She tried not to let her mind romanticize what was happening. As her sister Kat would tell her, this was lust, not love, and there was nothing wrong with it. But Zoe didn't have casual sex and it was harder for her to separate the two.

'I don't want to lose my job,' Zoe said, stumbling over a tree root that rose up over the trail.

Suddenly, he stopped. Frowning, he studied her. 'This isn't a condition of your working for me.'

'It's not?' She had no idea why she had said it. Jackson wasn't forcing her to follow him.

He sighed heavily. 'Is this what you normally do for your bosses?'

'What?' She gasped. 'No. No, I don't do this ... I haven't ... Why? What did Contiello tell you about me? Did he say I slept with him? Because that's not what happened. I never touched him. Well, of course, I touched him, but I never ...' Zoe took a calming breath, realizing she was babbling. 'I don't normally sleep with my bosses.'

Jackson quirked an amused brow. 'You're adorable when you're flustered.'

'I'm not flustered,' she lied.

'Good. Because I like women who know what they want.' He took her hand and held it firmly against the bulge in the front of his pants. 'And who can finish what they start.'

Jackson groaned, tilting his head as he used her fingers to massage his erection. The backyard to the bed and breakfast was no longer in view as the trail had twisted as they walked. All around them were trees and the sound of birds singing. Insects hummed in the background, a gentle yet unfamiliar sound to her city ears. She shivered, glad she wasn't alone. This wasn't her first time in the wilderness, but the isolation did make her uneasy.

'Will anyone come this way?' She glanced around.

'Not likely this time of day. Why? Don't you like the idea of being caught?'

66

Zoe shook her head. 'No. Not in a town of, like, two hundred people.'

'Three thousand,' he corrected. 'Unless we're hosting a horse competition, then it's about double that.'

'Compared to eight million, it might as well be two hundred. I've heard about gossip in places like this. Everyone knows everyone's business.' Still, she didn't pull her hand away.

Jackson didn't seem to hear her words as he again kissed her, sawing his lips against her with insistent passion. Teeth cut the delicate tissue of her lips and she tore her mouth away in pain. 'Ah! Too rough.'

A leisurely smile tugged at the side of his mouth and he leant forward, licking her sore lip lightly. The tip of his tongue darted out, teasing her with its warm caress. With each pass, his kiss deepened, but not like before. This time he was gentle, as if she were a delicate flower. The new tactic caused her to moan. What was it about this man that made her forget herself?

She tugged at his shirt, pulling it up to feel his waist. The hard, hot flesh of his stomach contracted when she touched him. Jackson worked on the black stud buttons along the front of her uniform, expertly unfastening them so the sides fell open. Within seconds, the jacket fell to the ground and a cooling breeze caressed her naked arms. The tank top clung to her skin, but the flimsy white material provided little protection. Jackson pulled it off, and tossed it aside. His shirt followed, landing on top of her discarded one.

Jackson let go, his chin lowered and his eyes narrowed as he looked at her. Zoe wished she had put on a better bra, but she never planned for things like this to happen. The only time she had sex was when in a serious relationship. The sturdy, padded bra was more for comfort than seduction, but at least it was new. Her light-blue cotton underwear cut up to the thigh. The white of her uniform pants was thick enough to hide the colour.

Gradually, he stalked around her, like a beast after prey. Zoe didn't move and every nerve in her body reached for him, followed him. His feet hit the forest floor, crunching softly against the trail. A finger touched the base of her spine and ran up the middle of her back. Arching her body, she held her breath. She wasn't sure how he did it, but as he skimmed over her bra, he unfastened the back clasp and it fell loosely from her breasts, hanging from her shoulders. The finger made its way back down, not stopping as it met her elastic waistband. It drew her pants down, meeting with the top cleft of her ass.

One finger became several and he thrust his hands down her pants. Grabbing her hips, he rocked her butt against his arousal. The stiff denim didn't hide the shape of his erection. Her pants skimmed down her thighs to her feet and with the wide pant legs she managed to get them off without taking off her narrow shoes. Jackson kissed her neck, massaging her stomach and breasts from behind. He slipped his hands beneath her unclasped bra, cupping the soft mounds in his large palms. The achingly sweet rhythm of his hips kept her mind transfixed and she forgot all about the surrounding forest. Closing her eyes tight, she leant her head to the side, giving him better access to her neck.

Jackson reached between her legs, his hand beneath her underwear as he probed her slick folds. His callused fingertip found her clit and he rubbed it in tiny, undulating circles. Throaty growls erupted as he kissed her and his teeth nipped playfully at her neck.

'Jackson, wait,' she whispered.

His growl deepened and he spun her around. Zoe couldn't help the small grin as her instincts took over. Her hands were on his jeans, fumbling to free his cock. Jackson pulled the bra straps from her arms. The heat from his body contrasted with the breeze. Her nipples puckered into erect tips.

Jackson made a weak noise before his mouth took hold of her breast, sucking enthusiastically. She freed his cock from the silk boxers, pushing the tighter material from his perfect hips. Gasping, she wrapped her fingers around the stiff length. His breath caught and she explored the turgid flesh from thick root to smooth tip. Cream flooded her pussy and the cotton underwear stuck to her sex. She shook violently, wanting him deep inside.

'Come on, off the path,' he ordered, leaning over to grab their clothing before leading her into the woods. His bare feet stepped over the forest floor without hesitation.

Zoe glanced around to see if anyone was watching. She wore only her shoes and underwear and this was not how she wanted to be seen by others in the small town. Jackson's naked body moved with streamlined grace as little lights that streamed through the canopy of treetops danced on his tight flesh. He looked like a dream, so powerful and strong, made all the sexier by his success in business. Digging into his jean pocket, he pulled out a condom before dropping all the clothes on the ground.

Jackson pulled her before him, walking her back so she leant against a tree. The rough bark bit into her tender flesh. He kissed her, his hands working to put on the condom without looking. Once more his hands were on her, and he explored every inch of her body with his fingers and mouth. The virile scent of him filled her, carrying on the fresh air. His intense eyes bored into hers, the look saying unmistakably that he wanted her and he was going to have her. She didn't have the willpower to resist.

Jackson watched her face as he tugged the underwear from her hips. Primitive noises escaped him as he frantically worked his hand to feel the wetness of her pussy. She started to shake, her body tightening as she nearly came from the stimulation against her clit. He boldly grabbed her by the hips, pressing his cock tightly against her moist slit. Sliding in her cream, he wet his length. She gasped and arched her back, trembling violently with each pass.

'Mm, you feel like heaven,' he groaned.

The cool brush of the condom bumped against her inner thigh. Zoe ran her fingers into his silky locks. If merely rubbing against his tight body was heaven, what would it be like to have him deep inside her? Every fiber of her being wanted him.

Her skin tingled. They didn't speak, conversing only in a series of light moans and gasps. Jackson gripped her thigh, pulling it up and to the side. She rubbed her body against him, her breasts caressing his chest. He guided his cock to her slit. Jackson lifted her up, holding her against the tree as he thrust. It had been a while and the almost painful glide as he stretched her made her cry out in surprise.

He eased her toward him, keeping his thrusts shallow and easy. His dark eyes locked on hers, forcing her to look at him, to know who it was she was with – not that she could forget. She held on tightly to his neck. Jackson grunted, plunging deep and sure, pushing himself to the brink.

Zoe reached between their bodies, finding the hard pearl

of her clit. Bark scratched her back. He pounded his hips, fucking her hard as he held her legs tight. Each push seemed to build momentum. The heat of his gaze slipped from hers as he leant forward, his face in her hair.

Zoe cried out as she came. Her fingernails bit into his shoulders, trying to hold onto something solid as her world spun out of control. The muscles of her pussy clamped down. Jackson made an animalistic sound as he jerked, joining in her climax.

He held her for a long time, panting for breath. His hot body glistened with sweat. Very slowly, he lowered her to the ground. Her weak knees wobbled before she caught herself. When she stood on her own, she couldn't look at him. A whirling array of emotions assaulted her – pleasure, confusion, fear. What had she done? Sleeping with her boss like some tramp? She never had casual sex. Never. What would Jackson think of her? Could he ever take her seriously as a chef?

Zoe reached for her clothes, somehow managing to get mostly dressed. Her shoe snagged on the pants, but she forced it through the pant legs. She stuffed her bra in the arm of her jacket to hide it before fastening the buttons despite her flushed skin and high temperature.

'Mm,' Jackson moaned lightly. His hand tried to slide over her hip from behind, but she pulled away from him. 'Zoe?'

Wide-eyed, she turned to him. Her thoughts raced as she tried to grab onto the right words to say. She wasn't any good at situations like this. 'I'm not your whore.'

Jackson blinked, his eyes rounding in shock. 'What?'

Instantly, she wished she could suck the words back in and make them disappear. 'I really need this chance and I won't be your whore.' She groaned inwardly. That didn't come out right. She wanted to say she hoped her actions didn't influence her job. She wanted to say she liked him, that she didn't want to like him. Instead, she sounded like a psychotic idiot. Groaning weakly in embarrassment, she shook her head slightly and turned to go.

'Zoe, wait.' Jackson again grabbed her arm, keeping her from going. The softness of the words made her pause and she finally turned to look at him. 'Someone's on the path.'

She could feel the colour draining from her features. Very quietly, she answered, 'I can't hear anything.'

'Shh.' He motioned for quiet, not moving.

Zoe bit her lip, using the silence to compose herself. What on earth had she done?

Jackson took a deep breath, trying to make sense of her reaction after sex. He thought it had gone pretty damn well. When she came, he had felt her pleasure, seen it on her gorgeous face. Now, she barely looked at him as she blurted something about not being a whore. Was that her way of saying she didn't want to do it again? Was this some type of manipulation to drive him crazy? He had never had complaints when it came to sex.

Jackson studied her wide dark-blue eyes, trying to read what she was thinking. He'd lied to get her to stay. No one was in the forest – not this time of day on a Sunday, not when the Thompsons had a new horse out in the north fields. The truth was he didn't know her well enough to read her moods or to understand her responses. It was strange, considering that in business he had an almost surreal sense of the other person. He could read the man across the boardroom table, anticipate the clients' needs before they knew them themselves and could even give the public what they wanted in fine dining. But give him a pretty woman who he seemed inexplicitly drawn to and he was as bad as an untried boy trying to understand the female psyche. All his usual charm failed him.

'I don't hear anything,' she insisted.

'You're not used to the forest,' he continued to lie, not liking the manipulation. Zoe appeared to believe him, holding her body stiff. His mind raced for what to say, how to handle this situation, and came up with nothing. They stood in silence for what had to be ten minutes before Jackson finally gave up. 'They're gone. Come on.'

Jackson held a branch aside and let her walk first onto the path. He'd planned on taking her to the small pond, where soft grasses lined the edge, but when he looked at her mouth as they entered the woods, he couldn't stop from kissing her.

'I did have a question for you.' Zoe ducked under his arm and waited for him to join her on the path. She looked around, searching for anyone nearby.

Jackson wasn't sure why, but it bothered him that she seemed so worried about other people knowing – not that he wanted his hometown finding out about this, but why did she care? She didn't live in Dabery.

'During my interview,' she continued, 'you asked me what the difference was between Cajun and Creole. I could tell by your expression that my answer was wrong. What is the right answer?'

Jackson chuckled, surprised by the unexpected question.

'Please, it's been driving me crazy.' She lightly touched his arm before tossing her hands to the side. 'I'd look it up, but I don't own a computer any more.'

'Don't feel bad, it was a hard question. Many people confuse the two and they are fairly similar.'

'That doesn't answer the question.'

'Cajuns are descendants of French Acadians. They were forced from their homeland by the British in the late 1700s. Creole is harder to define, but commonly refers to people born in the New World, whose parents came from Africa or Europe.' Jackson glanced down at Zoe's hand, thinking he might take it in his. He stretched his fingers, but didn't make a move. Somehow, even after sex, the gesture seemed too intimate. Holding hands was one of those things that said more than a romp in the woods ever could. It was a way to lay claim and show the world that he liked her. But he wasn't any good at that part. He could charm women into his bed, but a real relationship with a real connection eluded him. 'Both are Louisiana, but Acadiana is Cajun country and Creole is more what you'd find in New Orleans.'

Zoe laughed, a pretty, sweet sound that held his attention. 'I meant the cooking, not the cultural background. I mean, I could tell you the difference between almost every pasta known to man. I can tell you the noodle originally came from China before the Italians made it their own, but you threw me for a loop when you asked about Cajun and Creole. What is it? Is Cajun spicier? I know it has a French influence, and I have studied some French cuisine, but it's not the same.'

Jackson liked the way her eyes lit up when she talked about food. There was an innocence to her expression, a wide-eyed curiosity he found endearing. 'Both use a lot of celery, onions, peppers, beans, tomatoes, filé powder and seafoods. They also use reptiles like alligator and turtles, pork, frogs, turkey, pecans, brandy – anyway, you get the general idea.' He again glanced down at her hand, wondering why his mind was suddenly fixated on taking it in his. Zoe nodded thoughtfully, taking in all he was saying. He found he liked having her undivided attention. 'Creole uses more butter and cream whereas Cajun uses more spices, pork or animal fat and a dark roux. Since Creoles historically came from richer plantations, they developed their recipes from those they brought over from Spain and France and modified them to include the local foods, thus giving birth to what we now know as Creole cuisine.'

'Interesting.' She nodded. They came out of the forest and Jackson knew he'd missed any chance of discussing what had happened between them.

Concentrating, he tried to remember what he'd been saying. 'Ah, Cajuns were just the opposite. Their foods came from poorer communities and many of the dishes developed out of practicality. They also used local foods, naturally, but they normally cooked them as a single dish – like jambalaya and gumbo.'

'You know a lot about this.' She gave him a slight smile, looking up at him from beneath her lashes.

'It's my business to know. Several years ago I helped create a restaurant in New Orleans. Unfortunately, it was wiped out by the hurricane, but until then it was doing fairly well. I spent a lot of time with the owners sampling the local foods. Everyone down there has a different recipe for what is essentially gumbo. We had to find one that worked for the new restaurant and then modify it to be original.'

'And what kind of restaurant are you working on now?' She paused. They'd made it to the side of the bed and breakfast and now stood in its shadow.

'A place in Houston for a big hotel that's being built there.

It's not my favourite project because many of the factors are preset, but it's one of those rotating, on-top-of-the-hotel-type places that overlook the city.'

Her eyes fell. 'Is that, um, what you're interviewing Contiello for?'

'No. It was for a different project.' Jackson didn't want to discuss Contiello with her and it wasn't just because he knew they had history. He didn't like the way her expression faded and her eyes dulled at the mention of the man's name.

'Well, I'm tired.' She motioned toward the house. 'It's been a long day and I have to get up early tomorrow for your customers.'

'Zoe, wait.' Jackson grabbed her hand, stopping her from leaving. 'I don't think you're a whore. That's not what ...' Her suddenly mortified look stopped him from finishing his sentence. He felt her closing off to him.

'I don't want to talk about it.' She tugged her hand and he let go. 'Good night, Mr Levy.'

Jackson watched her walk away before shaking his head. With an exasperated sigh, he ran his fingers through his hair. 'But it's still the afternoon.'

What in the world was happening? He'd never met a woman like Zoe. One second she was cold, the next warm. She was passionate, then distant – but always sexy. When they talked about food her eyes lit up, but at a mere hint of something intimate she became strangely reserved, if not a little aloof. Laughing wryly at himself for caring, he rolled his eyes heavenward. 'Jackson Levy, you are a world-class fool. What in the hell do you think you're doing with this woman? You should have left her in New York where she belongs.'

Chapter Five

'What the hell is gaz-pay-cho?' Sheryl frowned, looking at the cold soup Zoe had made for her first official day as *Renée*'s new head chef. Quartz-studded barrettes held the sides of her black hair away from her face and matched the tiny gemstones on her round glasses. The cat-eyed trendy look was gone, replaced with a full black apron over light denim jeans and a floral shirt. Apparently, *Renée* was lax on dress codes. She wished she'd known before packing mainly fancy chef uniforms and hardly anything else. Thankfully she had Kat, who insisted she'd send a care package.

Her late-night phone call to her sister had made her feel a lot better. She'd told Kat everything, knowing that in a small town that seemed to regard Jackson as a local hero, she wouldn't find an unprejudiced ear to tell her troubles to. After Kat had gotten over the shock of Zoe's little tryst in the woods, she'd be calling back with advice. Zoe only hoped it wasn't months from now.

'What are you smiling at?' Sheryl demanded. 'I can't serve this. It's cold.'

'It's called gazpacho. It's supposed to be cold,' Zoe explained. 'It's very good. I promise the customers won't be disappointed. It has tomatoes, peppers, vinegar, olive oil, onions, garlic –'

'Hmm.' Sheryl shook her head, lifting the ladle to let the diced bits of vegetable plop into the large, black soup kettle.

'I'll call it "vegetable" and heat it up in the microwave if anyone orders it.'

'What?' Zoe gasped, appalled. 'It's supposed to be served cold. It won't taste right if –'

'Bob would never have served cold soup,' Sheryl interrupted. She dipped her finger into it and licked the tip. 'It needs hot sauce and some dried onion. I'll get it.'

'No.' Zoe held out her hands to stop the woman. 'Don't touch the soup.'

'Fine.' Sheryl's darkly lined brows arched in defiance. 'But I'm telling everyone you're responsible for this.'

'Fine by me,' Zoe said, biting off her words and fighting the temptation to wring the woman's neck.

'And don't you expect any orders for that trout-with-hazelnut-sauce business you call a special. Hazelnut is for those fancy coffees you grind in the grocery store, not fish.' Sheryl sniffed. 'Now, I need five orders of pancakes with bacon, three with scrambled eggs, one with poached, one over-easy.'

'But –' Zoe moved to look past the heat lamps, through the pick-up window. The restaurant was empty.

'Regulars will be here soon and don't make them wait. If your nonsense starts cutting into my tips, you'll be sorrier than a dirty dog covered in fleas.' Sheryl walked out to the pie case, unpacking and pre-cutting the pies she'd brought from home. The woman didn't talk to her again as she went about her duties.

Frowning, Zoe turned on the griddle and an oven. When Sheryl glanced at her, she forced a smile she didn't feel. Under her breath, so the waitress couldn't hear, she said, 'You'll be the sorry one when I don't make your stupid meatloaf special tomorrow.'

*

Zoe's muscles ached as she dumped the almost full contents of the kettle of gazpacho into the trash – minus the one bowl she had eaten for lunch when she had a two-minute break in orders and a second bowl a local man had insisted was salsa. It nearly killed her to watch him dip tortilla chips into her soup. Not one person ordered the trout and she heard Sheryl making comments like, 'You won't want that soup, Harry, trust me. Have I ever steered you wrong?' and 'Yeah, hazelnut like the coffee. My mama always said to never trust a skinny cook. And have you seen that one?' The insult stung as she'd always been self-conscious about her slight weight. The customers just let Sheryl get away with her attitude, listening to her like she was some kind of waitressing queen. When she was busy, they actually got up from their tables and refilled their own coffee, going into the wait station so as to not bother her as she took orders.

The only other employee who came in was a younger kid named Travis who bussed tables and washed dishes. He smiled shyly at Zoe and stared when he thought she wasn't watching him. Sheryl left with the last customer and Travis stayed long enough to help Zoe clean up some of her area. Wanting to be alone, she urged him to go home as she finished up. When she was finally alone, she took off her jacket to work in her black tank top with built-in bra.

'Is that my profits you just dumped into the trashcan?'

'Ah!' Zoe screamed, spinning around to glare at Jackson. 'Do you have to keep doing that?'

Jackson laughed. He looked decadently comfortable in his untucked button-down shirt with French-style cuffs. Subtle purple, blue and white stripes lined the material. A white T-shirt showed from beneath the spread collar. Khaki twill-front flat trousers hung loose around his legs, yet moulded seductively to him when he moved. 'You must have been deep in thought. I slammed the back door.'

Her heart pounding from being startled, she went back to cleaning the kettle out in the deep steel sink. 'Have you come to check up on me?'

'Yes.'

The simple, blunt honesty of the admission surprised her. 'Afraid I'd give the customers food poisoning?'

'According to Sheryl, you tried.' Jackson chuckled.

Zoe's eyes rounded in shock and she fought the sudden urge to weep. She'd been so nervous, worked so hard and the exhaustion was starting to get to her. 'She called you about me?'

'Several times, in fact.' Jackson crossed over to the trashcan and looked at the red soup coating the contents. 'Is that the deadly vegetable soup?'

'It's gazpacho,' she grumbled, scrubbing the kettle harder.

'You know, I pay Travis to do that.'

'I sent him home.' She scrubbed harder, even though there wasn't anything left to wash off. 'I can't believe you know the bus boy's name.'

'I went to high school with Travis's aunt. She called me to get him the job.' Jackson strode to the large walk-in refrigerator and opened it. He glanced inside before doing the same with the walk-in freezer. 'Gazpacho is an interesting choice for this clientele. Gazpacho manchego might have been a less bold move if you were going to try something different.'

'Why? Because it's hot?' Zoe didn't let her hurt show. The way he said 'interesting choice' stung worse than a slap across the face.

'Perhaps you should run the rest of the week's menu by me,' Jackson said, instead of answering.

'I thought I had free rein to cook what I wanted for the specials.' She gave up on the pretence of cleaning the kettle and rinsed it out. If he was going to take away that one little freedom, this job wouldn't be tolerable.

'Do you think you can do better than today? I don't like to see food wasted. Daily specials and soups usually account for most of the sales.' Jackson placed his hands on his hips.

'If you can get your waitress to stop sabotaging me,' Zoe answered. 'She told everyone my hazelnut sauce didn't belong on trout. I found the old cook's orders. I know he had a lot of seafood and fish specials by what he ordered. What I planned was not a far stretch of the imagination. Besides, it's only been one day. I'm only using the ingredients already stocked in this kitchen. The hazelnut oil looked a little dusty, but it's still good.'

'You must have really said something to set her off. It wouldn't hurt you to remember that folks around here are a little more sensitive than you New Yorkers.'

'More sensitive?' Zoe snorted. Sheryl sensitive? Sarcastically, she drawled, 'Please.'

'You think the trout was a good call, then prove it. Make it for me.' He tilted his head to the side, watching her every move.

Zoe felt all the bravado about her culinary skills slowly drain out of her. 'Right now?'

He nodded.

'We're closed.' She picked up a wet washcloth.

'I'm hungry.' The challenge in his gaze was unmistakable.

'All right.' Zoe tossed the rag back down. This was the

opportunity she wanted and if she could do anything, she could cook. Going into the walk-in fridge, she grabbed a zucchini, one of the trout fillets she'd cut earlier and an array of vegetables.

When she came back out, Jackson was leaning against the counter near the range. 'Why do you want to be a chef?'

Zoe smiled, setting the ingredients down before grabbing a knife. 'All the best moments in life seem to happen over food. Men propose, families get together, old friends meet. It's nice to have a small part of that. I love the look on a person's face when they eat something new, something surprising. And I always had a knack for creating new dishes or embellishing on old ones.' Lifting the knife, she showed it to Jackson. 'The restaurant really could use a better set. These are horrible.'

He grinned, but didn't comment.

'What about you? Why did you become a millionaire?' She chuckled.

'Who says I'm a millionaire?' He reached over, grabbing a piece of raw carrot from the maple-topped worktable.

'About every restaurateur and industry magazine out there.' She cut an extra carrot and slid the pieces over toward him with the side of her blade. 'Seriously, though. Did you always want to be in the restaurant business?'

'No, I thought I'd be a horse rancher or work in the stables. When I was younger, I had no real ambition.' He scooped the carrot pieces into his hand, cupping them in his palm. 'I found out that one of the old ranchers was going to sell his property. I convinced him to let me work the stables for a share of whatever business we created. He gave me one year. I borrowed money from my family to buy a stud horse. The business took off with his expertise, my dumb luck and a very high-producing horse.'

'Then how did you make the leap from rancher to restaurant genius?'

'Are you trying to kiss up?' His playful expression lightened his words.

'Just answer the question, Mr Levy.' Zoe felt giddy. Cooking always relaxed her and when she had something to do with her hands she became less fidgety and nervous. As he spoke, she mindlessly worked – simmering the fish in a pan and blending the hazelnuts and chives with lemon juice and hazelnut oil.

'Six months into it, the rancher's son came home from the military. He bought me out to work with his father and I bought into the neighboring ranch. It did well and seven months later, I sold my share to the original owners. I took that money and bought this diner. Everything I touched just seemed to work. With the money I made here, I invested into a restaurant in Columbia. The owner of that bought me out and then some businessmen paid me to design them a restaurant. I did, and it's still in business. From there, I got another job, then another, and it just kept building. Not a single one failed.'

'Must be nice.' Zoe inhaled, moaning slightly at the wonderful smell coming from the blender. She motioned for Jackson to do the same.

He came close and she trembled at his nearness. Instead of smelling, he dipped his finger into the sauce and licked it slowly. She watched his mouth, transfixed by the way his cheeks moved as he sucked. 'Mmm, delicious.'

All thoughts evaporated from her mind as she looked at him. The memory of what had happened in the forest haunted her flesh and seeing him, smelling him, only made the remembrance all the more potent. 'Thank you.'

'So tell me about the specials you have planned for this

week.' He leant closer, his lids dropping lazily over his eyes.

'Ah, for the soups, I thought I'd do a vichyssoise.' She grinned.

'Another one served cold?' Jackson chuckled, a deep, sexy sound that reverberated along her flesh. His head tipped to the side.

'A cold cucumber, chilled beet, chilled creamed broccoli.' She didn't pull away.

Jackson moved so his lips were a hairs-breadth away from hers. The faint trace of liquor wafted on his breath. 'You're begging for trouble, aren't you?'

'No, trouble is when I don't make meatloaf my special tomorrow.'

Jackson pulled away. 'I wouldn't joke about the meatloaf.'

'Crap, the fish.' Zoe moved to take the fish off the heat, but Jackson stopped her, tugging her hard against him. His lips crushed against hers as he poured all his passion and lust into the kiss. He maneuvred her against the worktable. Jackson cupped her breasts, then ran his hands over her sides and chest and along her waist to pull up her tank top. He reached her naked lower back and she gasped when he skimmed the tender scratches left from the tree bark against her flesh.

Jackson drew his mouth from hers, his eyes questioning as he nudged her hip to spin her around. Her palms fell on the table, pressed flat as she leant forward. The cool juice from some of the vegetables wet her hands and she slid one to the side to push the sharp knife lying on the table further away. His tender fingers traced her scratches as he examined her. Warm lips brushed her side and she inhaled deeply.

'I'm sorry about this.' His words were so soft she barely heard them. He kissed her hip, moaning as his tongue glanced over her skin.

Self-conscious, she tried to turn. 'I should shower. I've been working all day.'

Jackson stood and pressed his hips against her ass. The full length of his cock nudged between her cheeks, working in tiny thrusts as he rubbed against her. 'Why? You're just going to get sweaty again.'

Jackson's hips bumped her hard and he held her shoulder, the action ensuring she didn't stand up straight. He continued to rock against her, the firm outline of his erection digging at her through the material of his pants and her uniform.

'You're tense.' He groaned, urgently tugging at her elastic waistband, taking both her white silk panties and pants down at the same time. 'Relax.'

Zoe tried, but couldn't. She worried about what he must think, worried that someone might walk in on them, worried that having sex with the one man who could make or break her career was a bad move, worried that if she didn't he would punish her, worried that he would know just how badly she wanted to fuck him, how hot her pussy was, how she fantasized about screwing him all over this very kitchen. The sordid thought had just seemed to pop into her mind all day. When she walked into the large fridge, she'd imagine him sneaking in to warm her from the chilled air. When she cut vegetables, she'd imagine him coming behind her and fucking her just as he was now. Dripping ranch dressing on her finger made her think of sucking him off, of drizzling him in some flavorful sauce just so she could lick him clean.

The sound of a zipper coming undone made her shiver.

Naked, hot flesh replaced the material as he massaged his naked dick into the cleft of her ass. He didn't move to enter, only working his hips in a slow, tortured rhythm. The fish continued to simmer on the stove, very close to being over-cooked, but she didn't care. His voice hoarse, he said, 'You're so tense. Talk to me about food. I want to hear your voice.'

Zoe thought the request strange, but obliged. 'Wednesday I thought I'd make cannelloni al forno.'

'Oh, yeah?' He reached around her hip and a thick, warm finger slipped along her wet slit. 'What else?'

'Maybe a tagliatelle with Bolognese sauce or spaghetti with olives and capers.'

'That's it, keep talking, it relaxes you for me,' he urged, drawing the tip of his cock down. He pressed her shoulder so she lay almost flat and nudged her legs apart. She heard a wrapper being ripped open and glanced back to see him spit a condom wrapper to the side. With one hand he brought it to his cock. She couldn't see, but could tell by his actions that he was quickly unrolling it onto his erec-tion. 'Come on, be my naughty little chef. What are you going to make for me?'

'Oh, um,' Zoe gasped, her hands working against the worktable. 'Lima bean and, ah, pesto, um, cous cous.' It became hard to think. The head of his cock rubbed along her slit, parting the folds. 'Vermicelli with lemon.'

Jackson thrust, prying her open. 'Ah, I want to fuck you. I want to ride you so hard, stuff you full of my cock. One look at you and I can't seem to control myself. I got to be inside you and when I can't, I masturbate to the thought of you. I've come so many times today already and it still isn't enough.' He pushed deeper, as if forcing himself to go slow, to torment himself by denying his needs. 'My balls ache and my dick is always hard. And then you start talking about cooking and you get that little excited light in your eyes. It drives me insane, it's so fucking sexy and I can't help hoping you'll get that same light when you kiss me and let me fuck you.'

Zoe didn't know what to think of the admission. Jackson shoved deep, growling loudly behind her. Her breasts rubbed the worktable and her nipples ached for better stimulation. His finger stayed on her clit, pressing down hard. Grunting, he pumped his hips, increasing his speed until he plunged in and out at a furious pace.

'Ah! Shit,' he swore, breathing raggedly. 'Damn it, you feel so good! You should see this, your body taking me in, my cock glistening each time I pull out.'

Zoe made a weak noise, helpless to do anything as he controlled the whole situation. She couldn't gain leverage to thrust back, so instead she let him ride her. The tension built and she came, her muscles contracting violently as he continued his frantic pace. His hand didn't let up on her clit as he forced her orgasm to draw out.

'Fuck! Fuck!' he cried, almost desperately. He jabbed forward, harder. 'You are so fucking sexy like this. I want to take you home and tie you up so I can do this whenever I want.'

Suddenly he tensed, finally coming. His grip on her tightened and he jerked his release. Gradually he pulled out, releasing his hold. Her body weak, Zoe pushed up from the table, unable to believe what had happened between them. His passionate words spun in her head, making her dizzy. No one had ever said such things to her before.

'Wow,' he said under his breath. 'I must have had more to drink than I realized. My brother is getting married and we were out celebrating.'

Zoe pulled her pants up and adjusted her tank top. Disappointment filled her as she realized everything he had said was just drunken sex talk. He hadn't actually meant any of it. The words were a heat-of-the-moment thing. She told herself not to dwell on it. It wasn't as if he had declared love for her. Affairs strictly of the flesh were new to her and she needed to remember these things didn't work the same way relationships did.

The smell of burning food broke into her thoughts and she gasped, rushing to the stove. The trout was ruined and she took it off the heat, pushing it aside. Jackson's arms wrapped around her and he kissed her neck.

'Leave it until tomorrow.' His lips brushed her ear and he bit her lightly. 'I want you to come and stay with me tonight.'

The tension crept its way back into her limbs and she shook her head in denial. 'I can't. I have to be here early. The meatloaf isn't going to make itself. Sheryl made a point of laying the old chef's recipe out so I wouldn't mess it up.' Jackson laughed, his breath tickling her neck. Zoe artfully wriggled out of his embrace. 'I should lock up.'

'All right.' The slow words made her glance at him. Jackson frowned, his gaze piercing her as if trying to read her thoughts.

The lights in the main lobby were already turned off, so she picked up her chef jacket and the keys off the back desk. 'Good nigh –'

'I'll see you home,' Jackson interrupted.

Her desire to run away from him was only slightly outdone by her relief not to be out walking alone in the strange small town. The city streets didn't worry her. She was used to them, but being alone in these darkly lit, abandoned streets, so close to the woods? The thought made her tremble in fear.

'Thank you. I appreciate that. I'm not used to the quiet. Even the air feels ... less charged.' Zoe didn't like leaving a mess behind, but she didn't want to stick around to clean it up either. Jackson grabbed the trash bag and Zoe held open the back door for him. Locking it, she waited for him to throw the trash in the dumpster.

There was no fast way to the front of the building, so they walked down the gravel alley. Moonlight guided their steps. Zoe played with the keys in her hand, letting them hold her attention so she didn't keep looking at the man next to her.

Jackson didn't know what to think. Zoe was unlike anyone he'd ever known. She fell passionately into his arms, yet acted as if nothing had happened as soon as they reached climax. Had he gone too far when he talked about his obsession with her? He did want to take her to his home, did want to keep her locked away there until he could force her to notice him, to feel a tenth of what he did when he was around her. She did something to him, turned him around, confused everything he knew to be true about relationships. More than a one-night stand, she was less than a girlfriend. It wasn't the way he wanted it, but it was the way she made it through her actions.

He felt himself falling into a deep pit that he wasn't sure he would ever escape from. A big part of him wanted to connect with her, wanted to know her, but the only time she ever opened up was when they talked about food. Even that first night in the bar, she'd only given him the time of day because it could help her career. Yet there was something about the way she looked at him, a shyness, that didn't seem characteristic of a career-driven woman. She lacked a certain ruthless quality.

'Do you need anything for your kitchen?' It wasn't what he wanted to talk about, but any conversation was better than none. They came to the end of the alley and turned toward the main street. A large tree on the corner cast a shadow across her features as they passed under it.

'Nothing I can't order. You've already done enough giving me the opportunity.'

Now he really felt like an asshole. The whole reason she was in Dabery was because he had got drunk and wanted to teach her a lesson. Now she was here and he wasn't sure what to do with her. 'You know, on Friday a group from California is coming to check out some of the Thompsons' stallions. They'll probably be at the restaurant.'

'Is there a special request to go along with that information?'

'Just thought you'd like to know when you're planning your menus.' Jackson glanced up the street to the bed and breakfast, not wanting the conversation to end. 'Back in New York, you mentioned you had sisters.'

'Yes, four.'

'Any brothers?'

'No, just two brothers-in-law,' she answered. 'Megan, the oldest, is a police detective. She's married to Ryan, a crime scene photographer. Kat's a photographer married to a bug scientist. She's pretty well known for her entomology photographs. Sasha has been in college for years, I don't know if she'll ever graduate. And Ella is in the navy. We don't hear from her too often.'

'And your parents?' Jackson smiled. It seemed he had found something else her eyes lit up for – family. In that they were the same. He wasn't nearly as passionate about food, but he did care deeply about his family.

'My father is a retired English professor and my mother is ...' She made a weak noise. 'She's, ah ...'

'I'm sorry, is she gone?' Jackson reached for her arm.

'What? Oh, no, nothing like that. She's a flake. She thinks she can read our futures in tea leaves. We can't do anything without her pulling out the kettle. It's actually a little embarrassing. She used to make our dates in high school drink a cup and then would try to predict our relationships. Of course, they never lasted much longer after she pulled that.'

'You think that's bad?' Jackson took heart in the fact that she didn't pull away. As he talked, he slowly moved his arm to hook it into hers. It was a small gesture, but she didn't complain. 'My gramma is superstitious as they come. She has so many rules in her house you have to be born into the family to know them all. I swear anthropologists could write a book about the things she says. She believes things like putting a knife under a bed will cut childbirth pains in two and you'll never get married if someone sweeps under your feet. And, at midnight on New Year's Eve all the doors in the house must be opened to let the old year out unimpeded. Oh, and a food one just for you, eat black-eyed peas on New Year's Day to ensure good fortune in the coming year.'

'My mother once told me the tea leaves said to cut my hair.' Zoe giggled.

'Did you listen?'

She motioned to her chin-length style. 'Apparently, if I didn't cut it, the locks would have gotten caught in equipment at work and I would have lost my fingers.'

'How do you know it would have happened?' He stepped closer to her.

'How do I know it wouldn't?' She looked at him, her expression playful as she arched a delicate brow. 'I cut my hair and I have all my fingers.'

'That's hardly scientific proof.' Jackson let go of her hooked elbow, only to slip his arm over her shoulder.

'Do you eat black-eyed peas on New Year's?' They stopped in front of Marta's house. The blue moonlight caressed her face, highlighting her face with a pale, ethereal beauty.

'Every year.'

'And how do you know that's not the reason for your good fortune in business?' She faced him and his arm slid from her to his side.

He reached to brush a wayward strand of hair from her face, his finger tracing down her cheek to the side of her mouth. Jackson began to speak, but she stepped back before he could get anything out.

'Good night, Mr Levy.' She gave the briefest smile and he couldn't tell if it was genuine or simply humoring him.

As she walked away, he answered in kind, 'Good night, Chef Matthews.'

'Kat, I don't know the first thing about doing this.' Zoe paced the length of her room, only to turn around and pace the other way when she hit the white, slanted ceiling leading down to the painted white walls. The polished pinewood floor gleamed in the lamplight, reflecting a blurry image of her as she walked around the room. A delicate white lace comforter lay over the king-sized bed. When she left that morning, the bed had been a mess. Marta must have cleaned up after her. 'I don't know how to be a mistress.'

'Zoe, sweetie, just calm down,' Kat's tired voice urged through the phone.

'I can't calm down. I don't know what to do. He kisses me and I lose all rational thought.' She paced faster, tossing her hands up as she moved. 'And if I stop sleeping with him now he might fire me, right? But, even if I want to sleep with him, I can't keep this aloof act up. I don't know how to act around him so I end up babbling about food.'

'You always babble about food,' Kat teased. 'It's why we love you.'

'Do you remember that time I was interviewed for the high-school TV station about mystery meatballs?'

'Oh, no, Zoe, please tell me you aren't that bad? Half the school thought you'd been struck down with some sort of weird disease from working in the kitchen.'

'I know. I made mom burn the tape.' Zoe took a deep breath, not wanting to remember the embarrassing incident. She'd been so pale and had ended up spouting incoherent sentences for nearly two minutes. 'Kat, I'm telling you, it's that bad. So I shut up and say nothing and end up looking like some kind of psycho whore who sleeps with a man and then pretends nothing happened.'

'OK, calm yourself. First off, I'm glad you're getting laid. I think it's about damn time. Second, not all sex has to mean something. The fact does not make you a whore. Third, you're a smart, intelligent, beautiful woman – wait, you're being safe, right?'

'Yes, he has condoms.'

'You mean, he already had them when you two –'

'Yes,' Zoe broke in before her sister could say whatever choice phrase she'd come up with to describe her carnal acts.

'Now that's interesting.' Kat hummed softly.

Zoe froze, catching her pale reflection in the window glass. 'Why is that interesting?'

'He planned, or at least hoped that he was going to get you in the sack. Do you know what this means? He's thinking about you when you're not around. We know he likes you. He even came on to you in the bar before either of you knew who the other one was. I'll bet that's why he brought you to the diner. He wanted a chance to get to know you and I'll bet he wants you to get to know him. That's why he brought you to his hometown.'

Zoe shook her head in disbelief, knowing Kat couldn't see her. 'I think that theory is a little far fetched. This is what he said it is – a position he had open and a chance for me to prove myself. Even tonight he said that some important ranch clientele from California would be coming down to check out some horses. It's why he'd need a chef in a diner, to take care of the rich clients when they come. They'd expect more than diner cheeseburgers and greasy fries. It's my job to make sure they're satisfied. The rest of the days are just filler cooking for locals to keep the place running.'

'You should make that creamy ranch for them.'

'I can handle the cooking. It's the man I have no clue on.' Zoe tore her eyes away from her reflection. 'I think he's just interested in me because I shot him down at the bar.'

'Why would you say that?'

'Because I'm awkward and too skinny and –'

'Shut your hole right now, Ms Zoe.' Kat sighed into the receiver, the sound like a stout wind against Zoe's ear. 'You are beautiful and men want you all the time. You just never see it.'

Not wanting to get into a debate, Zoe changed the course of the conversation. 'You know what Megan would say, don't

94

you? She'd say the romance novels I read give an unrealistic view of love and men. Maybe she's right. I expect them to be this alpha hero who's utterly perfect, but I'm not some kick-ass heroine who deserves to be with them.'

'OK, you're talking crazy now. Megan is hardly one to give relationship advice. She sees too many gone wrong on the job. We both know Ryan's some kind of glutton for punishment for even being with her.'

'That is so wrong. He loves her.'

Kat giggled. 'Yeah, but Megs is a handful.'

Zoe flung herself on the bed, bouncing on the noisy springs before settling. 'Tell me what to do. How do I handle this?'

'I don't know Jackson, but I do know you. Take a chance. Let him see you, let him see beneath all your shyness to the wonderful woman you are deep inside. If he's worth anything, he'll notice how magnificent you are.'

'What if I don't want him to notice? What if I just want this to be an affair?'

Kat burst into laughter, gasping and wheezing so hard she couldn't form a coherent sentence.

'What? I don't know how I feel about him,' Zoe tried to interrupt.

'Oh, Zo, I can't breathe.' Kat panted. 'That was too funny. My eyes are watering, that was so funny. Of course you like him. You slept with him. There is no way you could even kiss a man without really liking him on more than a physical level.'

'But how do I know the attraction is real and not just some strange misplaced affection because of who he is and what he can do for my career? I mean, I've been feeling pretty down and desperate lately. I'd do about anything for a shot.'

'That's a tougher one,' Kat admitted. 'But really, who knows where true attraction and affection start? I know you, sis, and you're not a user. Besides, it's still early. You don't know him all that well. Give it time and be yourself.'

Zoe really wished she was more like her sisters. All of them seemed so confident and sure. She'd always been the reserved one, over-thinking every little detail.

'So tell me, how's your room? He put you up in a nice place?'

'It's a little country, but not bad. Reminds me a bit of that place we stayed at in Montana – décor-wise.' Zoe looked around, staring at a sepia print of a little girl in a bonnet next to an old-fashioned car. 'Honestly, it's a little creepy here. It's so quiet, I can't sleep. There are these bugs that just chirp all night long. I never thought I'd say I missed the sound of traffic.'

'Want me to mail you a tape?'

'Kind of.' Zoe laughed. 'I tell you, what I could really use is some street clothes. I thought I'd be in a fine-dining restaurant, so I have mostly chef uniforms with me. I underpacked when it came to T-shirts and jeans. Send me some?'

'Sure. I have movers going to your place tomorrow to take your stuff to storage. I'll grab some then.'

'You're the best.'

'I know. I rock.' Kat chuckled. 'Now get some sleep and don't lose heart. You just keep doing what you do and that little town will wake up and take notice.'

'If Sheryl will let them wake up,' Zoe grumbled. 'Night, Kat.'

'Bye, sweetie.'

Zoe hung up and dropped the phone next to her on the

firm mattress, turning her head to the window without getting off the bed. Her damp hair felt cool against her skin. The rough texture of the bedspread lightly scratched the backs of her thighs and her arms when she moved against it. The pink pyjama shorts and tank top offered little protection, but were perfect for the warmer South Carolina weather. White lace curtains framed the darkness outside. Stars and tree limbs filled the view of the night sky. Even though it made her nervous, she could appreciate the open beauty.

'Jackson,' she whispered. Despite her sister's comforting words, Zoe knew what it was between them. What would a man like Jackson want with a desperate chef? She didn't have money, only had a job because of him and had nothing to bring to the relationship but herself. What they had was an affair, pure and simple. She would be a fool to wish for more.

Rolling onto her side, she grabbed a pillow and hugged it to her chest. She was most definitely a fool.

Chapter Six

Through the pick-up window Zoe anxiously watched the rich California couples sitting at a booth. The women both had blonde hair – one with sleek short locks and the other with flowing curls. Their designer wrap dresses stood out in the small-town atmosphere, as did the long fake nails, high heels and fancy jewelry. The men were Hollywood-refined, slick players with golden tans and lightweight cotton-knit shirts.

All week, she'd not sold one special – except for meatloaf Tuesday when the restaurant went through an inordinate amount of ground beef with baked ketchup topping. She'd followed the old cook's recipe to the letter, doubtful when she started that they'd go through over thirty pounds of baked beef. It was only at the end of the day that she learnt Dabery was the self-proclaimed meatloaf capital of the world. They took their loaf seriously and even though she made it exactly to recipe, she felt their suspicious glances as they ate.

Now, as Sheryl carried the four balanced plates to the Californians' table, she held her breath. They were the first in this town to try her original dishes. Knowing they were coming, she'd made a list of seven options. It also helped to use up some of the foodstuffs she'd ordered but hadn't used during the week. Predictably, the women picked salads – one fresh corn and pine nuts and the other a ginger chicken with melon. The older man with graying temples ordered aged steak with wild mushroom and baby asparagus and the younger chose a salmon rigatoni with parsley sauce.

Zoe held her breath, ignoring the hamburgers cooking on the grill. Their loud sizzle had become a constant background to her days. The restaurant was half full of customers. A few regulars sat at the counter, drinking their bottomless cups of coffee like they did every day. After several hours, they'd each leave a 25-cent tip for Sheryl and a newspaper. For the most part, no one talked to her. It was as if most of them came for the sole purpose of checking her out. To make matters worse, Jackson had disappeared. After he'd walked her home, she hadn't heard from him again. He hadn't come to the restaurant, hadn't shown up outside the bed and breakfast and hadn't called – not that she'd expected any calls. The most she'd had was a manila envelope filled with employment papers with her name on it left on the back desk of *Renée's* kitchen.

Swallowing down the hurt, she kept her eyes on the Californians. The ladies both took tiny bites of their salad. Zoe leant forward, trying to read their expressions from the sides of their faces. Suddenly, Sheryl appeared before the pick-up window, blocking her view. Zoe stood up straight, wrinkling her nose at the grumpy woman.

Sheryl slammed order tickets down on the pick-up window's countertop. 'Two of those steak things and a corn nut olive salad.'

The waitress turned to go, clearly annoyed. Zoe reached her hand through the window, trying to grab her. The hot metal burned a little because of the overhead heat lamps. Whispering, she said, 'Wait, wait a second. Come here.'

Sheryl arched a brow, but slowly made her way to the

metal door. Coming back to the kitchen, she crossed her arms over her chest. 'Yes?'

'Really?' Zoe asked.

'Really, what?'

'Other people want my specials?' She could barely contain her excitement.

'I placed the order, didn't I?' Sheryl moved to go.

'Wait!'

'What?' The waitress sighed heavily.

'We can't do any more of the pine nut and corn salad after this one.' When Sheryl raised a brow, Zoe explained, 'I only bought a small packet of pine nuts from the grocery store to make it. I didn't think anyone else would try it outside of that group from California. No one's tried one of my specials all week.' She couldn't help her giddiness. 'Who ordered it? Those guys at the counter? Or was it the farmer? I bet he took a steak, didn't he? Or –'

'Girly, I'm only going to say this once,' Sheryl broke in, holding up a hand to stop Zoe from saying more. 'Get a hold of yourself. It's just a piece of cooked meat, not the second coming. I've got customers to tend to. Don't make them wait.'

Zoe's smile faded some. She glanced at Travis, who ignored her as he slowly loaded a rack to get it ready to go into the industrial-sized dishwasher. It sucked not having anyone to share these things with. Then, thinking she finally had customers to wow, she hurried back to the grill to flip the hamburgers and move them aside to make room for the steaks. Checking the orders, her grin returned. Her time had finally come. She was her own chef.

Zoe grinned. Nothing could take the smile off her face or the bounce from her step, not even the giant bag of heavy trash she slung over her shoulder. She'd sold fifteen of her special dinners. Fifteen! Fifteen people ordered off her menu, ate it and paid for it. Not one complained. She was finally a real chef in her own restaurant.

Throwing open the lid to the blue dumpster, she wrinkled her nose and tried not to breathe in the horrible smell of trash that came from inside. Garbage service had yet to pick up the week's load. Light from inside the restaurant shone over the shadowed alley, giving her enough to see by. With a grunt, she lifted the bag and tossed it over the side. It landed with a loud bang. As she turned, she saw movement on the ground.

'Ah!' Zoe screamed. The sleek body of a long black snake gleamed in the light. It spread its neck horizontally as if ready to strike. It hissed violently and the loud sound made her spring into action. She leapt for the closest high point – the dumpster. The snake lurched forward. Zoe jumped, digging her feet in as she scurried up the side of the large metal container. The reptile hit her leg and she screamed again, jerking her feet up.

Zoe lost her balance and fell head first into the bin. She bumped her head on an empty tin can inside a black garbage bag. Moaning, she pushed up on the unstable pile, trying to right herself. The acrid, rotting smell made her gag. Her entire body shook as she frantically searched her leg for where the snake had hit. A dark splotch stained her white pants and she felt a sharp sting where it had bitten her. Whimpering, she peeked over the side. The snake thrashed its body on the ground, writhing around in what appeared to be agony. Its mouth hung open and the tongue hung lifelessly out of the side, picking up dirt as it convulsed. Finally, it rolled on its back and died.

Zoe stared at the light belly of the animal, just to make

sure. It didn't move. She tried to make her limbs work, but they shook badly. Keeping her eye on the snake, she hiked a leg up.

'Hello?' Jackson's voice came from inside the kitchen. 'Zoe?'

'Here, help!' she yelled.

His figure appeared at the door, haloed by light. 'Zoe?'

She moaned, not moving to get down. The snake hadn't moved. Jackson's laughter rang out as he came out of the kitchen. 'Did you accidentally throw something away you shouldn't have?'

'Snake. It bit me.' She held her position. 'I had to get away.'

'A rattler?' Jackson's expression fell.

'I think my blood killed it.' She nodded at the ground. Inside, her muscles were so tense they felt like rocks beneath her skin. 'It just started shaking and flopped over. Where's the hospital? I think I might need anti-venom.'

This time, his laughter was louder. 'That's an Eastern Hognose. They're not poisonous and it's playing dead. You'll be fine. Are you sure it bit you?'

'My pants ...'

Jackson walked over to the snake and picked it up. It dangled from his hand as he carried it away from her. Zoe kicked her leg over the side, and landed hard on the ground. She stumbled, falling onto the gravel before quickly righting herself. Her eyes on the ground for more snakes, she limped toward the kitchen.

'Hey, easy. The bites usually aren't bad and they rarely attack humans. They prefer eating toads. You just scared it and the snake just reacted to your presence.' Jackson jogged over to her and slipped a hand under her elbow. He urged her to sit on the step. 'Let me see. Where did it bite you?'

A tear slipped down Zoe's cheek. 'My leg.' She turned her calf to the side where the snake had hit her. A large red spot marred the once-white uniform pants. An awful smell came off her clothes and she wanted to sink into the earth in embarrassment. She hadn't seen Jackson for a week and this was how he found her? Covered in trash and bleeding?

Jackson pushed her pant leg up. His fingers ran along her skin, probing. She closed her eyes tight, waiting for him to hit the wound.

'You're all right. It's just sauce,' he said. 'You're not bitten.'

Zoe tried to speak, but instead she just let out a small sob. He looked so handsome in the dark-blue crewneck shirt and light denim jeans. This was not the impression she wanted to make. Her sweaty, dirty chef uniform was now covered in the last week's worth of trash. She'd missed him, missed the sound of his voice, the touch of his flesh. She'd missed him in a way that should not have been possible in the little time she'd known him.

'Hey, what's this? You're all right. It was just a snake.'

'Today was one of the best days of my life. I was going to celebrate and now I smell like garbage.' Zoe swiped at her eyes. 'And when I go home, Marta is going to kill me. She's fanatical about keeping the bed and breakfast clean. I doubt she'll even let me in the front door. Every time I leave, she cleans my room – washes my sheets, mops, even scrubs the bathroom the second I'm done in the morning. After she makes me eat breakfast, she's waiting with a dishrag to clean up the second I finish the last bite. If I go there looking like this ... you don't understand. Marta yelled at me for my shoes the other night after the spring shower and has been giving me dirty looks ever since.'

'OK, this is an easy fix.' Jackson stood. 'Relax. Come inside. I'll lock up the restaurant and take you home with me. You can get cleaned up there. Tyrant Marta will never know.'

Zoe began to protest, but in the end nodded in agreement. Unbuttoning her jacket, she slid it off her shoulders and went to put it inside an empty trash bag.

'Ready?' Jackson locked the back door and motioned toward the front of the restaurant. 'My truck is out front.'

'One second.' Zoe grabbed more trash bags. 'Are you sure you don't mind?'

'I don't really have a choice. I know how Marta can be and I also know she's the only place in town that takes long-term guests, unless you really want to live out by the highway in a small motel room and walk two miles to work every morning? And she told me about the muddy shoes. You're already on probation with her.'

Zoe gasped. 'They were barely dirty!'

Jackson merely laughed. Parked outside, his new black truck was the only vehicle on the street.

'Is it normally this quiet on a Friday night? I thought teenagers would be out and about.' Zoe glanced up and down the barren street.

'Ranch parties,' he answered. 'They pick secret locations around the different ranches to meet. It becomes a game of sorts between the kids and the local police. They hide the parties and then time it to see how long it takes the cops to break them up.'

He opened the passenger door for her. Zoe put the bag with her jacket in the back before laying the trash bags on the seat to protect his leather. Sitting gingerly on the seat, she made sure not to touch anything. Jackson climbed in next to her and started the truck. Zoe instantly rolled down the electric window and sat as far away from him as she could, hoping the breeze filtering through the car didn't carry her smell over to him. He drove past the bed and breakfast, navigating through a residential district before following a winding road outside of town.

'Where do you live exactly?' Zoe leant to see out the window. His headlights illuminated the blacktop road as the houses became further and further apart.

'I have a little spread a couple miles outside of town. Just up this hill.' The winding road forked in two directions and he took the right. They passed through an open wrought-iron gate supported by two red-brick columns. Hanging lanterns lit up as they passed. The drive turned to gravel as they left the main highway.

'Is this it?' Zoe kept expecting to see the house. The gates looked as if they belonged to one, but the road kept going.

'This is the driveway.' Jackson grinned. He rested one arm on his open window, driving with the other hand on the wheel. She stared briefly at his strong fingers, squirming a little in her seat.

The full moon shone over the land in the clear sky. Oak trees lined the drive, spaced equally apart as if by design. Silvery moss clung to their limbs, giving the landscape an eerie feel. Swallowing nervously at the quiet isolation of their surroundings, Zoe said, 'You're not bringing me to a haunted house or something, are you?'

'There have been rumors that the old place is haunted. It was built back in the 1800s. Of course, it's said all of these old houses are haunted. It's a Southern thing. We love it so much we don't leave after we die.' He grinned. It was an incorrigibly handsome look that made her shiver. 'Why? You scared?'

'It's, ah –' she wanted to say creepy, but instead finished, '– quaint.'

After about a mile, she saw the house emerge from behind the trees. 'Little' was not how she would have described the plantation-style mansion that greeted them. The driveway turned to bricks and wound around a central pedestal. Overhead lights came on as they drove up, illuminating a stone statue of a graceful naked woman that stood in the middle.

The red-brick façade matched the stone on the ground. In the center, a two-story section stood high over the drive. One-and-a-half-story wings came off of each side, perfect matches to each other in design and connected to the center part by covered walkways. A low-pitched roof showcased four tall chimneys, one coming from each corner of the main section. Long rectangular windows, arranged symmetrically around the main doorway, had decorative semicircular fanlights over the tops. The frames were painted a stark white with black shutters as accents. Two narrow windows bordered the front door, making it appear even wider than it already was. Over the door, on the second story, an arched Palladian window mimicked the shape of the door. Decorative molding jutted out from the roofline beneath the cornice.

Zoe had her hand on the handle, opening the door before the truck stopped. As it slowed, she stepped onto the brick drive. 'This is amazing. You actually live here? By yourself?'

'For about five years now. I bought it and restored it to its original state. There are some ruins from the old icehouse, dairy, meat house, barns and stables, but they were too far gone to restore. I thought about keeping horses, but I'm not home nearly enough and I don't want to compete with the local ranchers.' He walked around his car, looking over the house as if seeing it for the first time. 'When I was a kid, we used to love to come out here and walk through the overgrown gardens. There's an old grave-yard out back, where the rich landowners who owned most of the land in Dabery used to bury their family members. In high school, we would take girls back there to scare them. Now the gardens are manicured, but sometimes I miss the run-down look.'

'Please tell me you've outgrown scaring girls. I really don't like to be frightened.' Zoe looked at him, trying not to step too close. She tucked a strand of hair behind her ear.

'Possibly.' He grinned. 'I don't really bring girls here any more. Well, except for Rachel and Rita.'

'Rachel? Rita?' Zoe's voice went up an octave as she said the other women's names.

'The housekeepers. I'd be a slob without them.' His feet made small tapping noises as he crossed over the drive to his front door. She followed slowly, unable to stop looking around. 'The house is considered antebellum because it was built before the Civil War, but the style of architecture is called Federal. You can tell by the curved lines and deco-rative flourish. All the bricks you see are original, made on the old plantation in a kiln they kept on the grounds, and inside, the original wood framing came from trees on the property. The stone trim came from a local quarry. This house is pure South Carolina.'

He opened the door, letting her walk in first. She ducked past him quickly. An overhead chandelier illuminated the tall ceiling. At the end of the front hall, a wide staircase led up to the second story. She could see part of the landing. Beautiful dental crown molding lined the tops of the doors and archways. The white frames blended with the slightly off-white color of the walls, a perfect enhancement to the gleaming dark wood of the floors and oversized rugs. Aside from a couple of antique mirrors and a wooden table, there were no decorations in the room.

'On your left is the parlor and behind that the dining room. A covered walkway with a bathroom leads to the south wing, where you can find the kitchen and laundry room. To your right are the living room and my office, another covered walkway and bathroom, the old library with some of the original books and the old servants' quarters turned reading room. Straight ahead, if you pass the staircase on either side, you'll find the back door and a stone porch leading to the gardens.' He motioned to the left. 'Would you like a tour?'

'I would love one, but do you think it would be possible to take that shower first?' She gave a sheepish glance down at her stained pants. 'Please.'

He chuckled, nodding. 'Right this way.'

Jackson let her walk up the stairs first. Zoe could just imagine the stains on the back of her pants and closed her eyes in mortification. Here she was in the most gorgeous mansion she'd ever seen and she smelt like she was homeless. This place was definitely a far cry from her crappy apartment back in New York. Hell, the bed and breakfast was better than her apartment.

The wood banister gleamed, but she didn't touch it as she reached the top landing. More white walls and wooden floors covered in rugs greeted them. What little furniture she could see looked true to the period of the house – all wooden with finely carved details.

'The upstairs is a little different from most Federalist

homes, as far as the layout goes. There are four guest bedrooms named for different Southern cities and one master bedroom. Each has its own bathroom. The master bedroom has balcony access and a sitting room that joins it to what used to be the lady of the house's bedroom.' Jackson walked to the left.

'Which room should I take?'

'I'll let you choose.' He looked at her, his eyes narrowed as if they held some secret meaning. She had to look away. 'But for now you can use my bathroom. Since I rarely have guests other than family, I haven't had the housekeepers stock the other bathrooms with toiletries.'

The master bedroom had the same light walls as the rest of the house, with a dark wooden armoire, king-sized bed with four square posters and a giant wood fireplace. Logs were neatly stacked inside it, ready to be lit, and more were placed by its side. An antique mirror hung over the mantel. The blue-gray and silver comforter matched the thick, open curtains over the large window.

'Your home is lovely,' Zoe said. 'It's better than lovely, it's amazing.'

'It's been a project. For some reason, I always have big projects going. I like having something to do to fill the hours.'

'It seems to be working for you.'

'Bathroom's this way.' Jackson crossed to a door, opening it for her. 'I did have to modernize this room. I couldn't resist a whirlpool tub and a big shower.' The gray-and-white bathroom was understated in its elegance. Stacked black towels and washcloths sat atop a small rack, artfully displayed. Cabinets flanked either side of the large sink and not a single item looked out of place.

Jackson opened a cabinet. 'Help yourself to anything. Extra toothbrushes are in here. Yell if you need anything.' His dark eyes dipped down over her body.

Zoe self-consciously crossed her arms over her chest. 'Thank you.'

'Oh, here.' He crossed to the shower and turned it on, testing the water temperature. 'Or would you prefer a bath? I can –'

'Shower is perfect. Thank you.'

He nodded once, hesitated and then left the bathroom, closing the door partway behind him.

Jackson breathed heavily, only feeling slightly bad about the fact that he was peeking through the crack left in the door at the shower stall where Zoe washed herself. He couldn't see every detail through the thick, blurred glass, but he could make out her movements. Her hands massaged the blur of her chest, then ran down over her legs. The movements were functional, not meant to be seductive – but, oh, for him they definitely were.

He slowly unzipped his pants. With the running water, she probably couldn't hear him, but he didn't want to take chances. He dipped his hand down the front of his silk boxers and adjusted his cock to a more comfortable angle so it could continue to swell. Taking it in his hand, he stroked the turgid length. His eyes stayed locked on Zoe's body, focusing to make out what he could. She bent over and he almost groaned.

Jackson desperately wanted her to invite him into the shower with her. He'd gladly wash her body if it meant another chance at touching it. The knowledge that she'd allowed him to fuck her twice already gave him hope that this night would be one he'd always remember. He hated referring to what they did as 'fucking', but 'making love' didn't quite describe bending her over a worktable or screwing her against a tree.

He'd opened a window and a cool breeze ruffled the curtains, sweeping across the room. Jackson pumped his hand harder, debating if he should pull his pants down just a little for better access. He wanted to be able to right himself quickly when she stepped out. It wouldn't do to get caught with his pants down. Thinking of her coming from the shower, tiny droplets of water beading her flesh like glistening diamonds just waiting to be licked, made his hips jerk and he nearly came. Damn, this woman did something to him.

'Mr Levy?' Zoe's voice called. 'Is that you?'

Jackson bit his lip. He hated it when she called him Mr Levy. It sounded so formal, and in a way made him feel like some creepy boss taking advantage of an employee. Looking down at his cock in his hand, he frowned. Maybe that was exactly what he was.

'Did you say something?' He hoped the words sounded like he'd walked from across the room. Pushing his cock into his pants, he struggled to pull up the zipper. Releasing the erection had definitely been easier than trying to confine it.

'Oh, I just thought I heard you say something.' Her face leant closer to the door and he jerked back. 'I realize I don't have anything clean to put on. Do you mind if I borrow something?'

'Oh, ah, sure.' He scurried into his room, looking for a shirt. Going through a stack of T-shirts, he decided against them. Instead, he grabbed one of his designer dress shirts

– a cornflower-blue button-down he wore under his business suits. The idea of seeing her in it made his breath hitch in his throat.

He heard the shower turn off and went toward the door. Sticking his arm through, he said, 'Will this work?'

'Perfect.'

Jackson glanced at the mirror over the sink, getting a peek at the side of her breast. Not wanting to get caught being the voyeur, he pulled the door closed to give her privacy. Already he felt a little dirty about spying.

Sniffing his shirt, he frowned and pulled it over his head before kicking it under his bed. He retrieved a fresh grey T-shirt out of his closet and pulled some cologne out of his travel bag. Ridding himself of his tight jeans, he slipped on some pyjama pants and left his feet bare. Tonight, he would woo Zoe to his bed and he would make love to her right.

Ever since he'd finished building the house and moved in, he'd felt the emptiness of the vast estate closing in on him. This house was meant to have people in it, to entertain guests. An almost giddy excitement coursed through him to have her in his home. He hadn't meant to go on and on about the house's architectural style, but he'd wanted to tell her about it because it was important to him.

'I'm out,' Zoe called.

Jackson came from the closet to see her standing in his bathroom doorway. His shirt fell to her thighs. She'd rolled it at the cuffs and fastened it all the way up to the very top button.

'Would you like that tour?' Jackson offered, though he really didn't want to show her much more than his bed at the moment.

'It's been a long day. I want to rest.' She glanced nervously at his door. 'Um, is it always this quiet out here? I can't get used to it. My ears keep straining for noises to block out so I can sleep. Instead, it's nothing but silence and bugs so my mind stays awake.'

'I have a television. Will that help? This is the only room with it, though. I mean, if you don't mind sleeping in my room.' He crossed to the armoire and opened it to show her the widescreen television.

'Would you think me a big wussy if I didn't want to be alone out here?'

'Not at all.' Jackson turned on the television, hiding his smile. He understood that she was used to the city. In fact, he was just the opposite. All the noise when he stayed in the city made him edgy and nervous. 'I don't have many channels, but there are some movies you can flip through.' He pushed a few buttons on the remote before handing it to her.

Zoe climbed onto his bed to lie against a stack of his thick pillows. Her gorgeous legs sprawled forward and it took all his willpower just to sit next to her on the bed and not touch her. What was it about her that made him lose all his confidence and charm? He felt like a teenager, sitting next to a girl he liked, desperate to know if she liked him back, agonizing over every move and word, when really all he wanted was to start kissing her legs and work his way up to taste her pussy.

'Call me Jackson,' he said, tearing his eyes from her feet.

She gave a small laugh at the request but nodded. 'All right, Jackson.'

He pretended to watch the screen as she flipped through movie titles. 'You said you were celebrating tonight. What happened today?'

Zoe made a weak noise. 'Oh, it's ... you'll think I'm silly.'

'Try me.'

'I sold some of my specials tonight.' She looked at him through her lashes.

'More of that salsa? Roger was raving about your salsa the other day when I ran into him on my way out of town.'

'It wasn't salsa!' Zoe exclaimed. 'It was gazpacho.'

'He said it was good. Isn't that what matters?'

'Well, today I sold specials that were eaten like they were meant to be,' she said. 'So you were gone this last week? I wondered why you didn't stop by the restaurant.'

Jackson slowly moved his way closer to her without making it obvious. 'Did you look for me?'

'Oh, look, I love this movie, have you seen it?' Zoe lifted her arm and pushed a button. He caught a glimpse of a foreign title, but couldn't read the words. 'I hope you don't mind subtitles, because it's in French.'

Jackson really doubted he could concentrate enough to read anything at the moment. His cock throbbed and he adjusted his hips as he lay back on the pillows. The soft feathers of his comforter molded to the backs of his legs. 'Are you avoiding the question?'

'What question?'

'Did you look for me this week when I was gone?' Why was he probing? Insecurity wasn't like him.

'I wondered,' she answered, as if carefully weighing her words. 'It is your restaurant after all.'

'So you didn't miss me?' Damn! He'd done it again.

'I was, ah, too busy to notice. I spend all day in the kitchen cooking for your customers.' Her tone changed ever so slightly. 'Where did you go?'

'My nephew had a birthday party. My sister packed a lunch and we took him to Columbia to the zoo. From there I flew to Seattle.'

'Oh? New project?' She glanced at him.

'I thought there might be, but didn't like the terms. I passed.'

'I'm sorry.'

'Don't be. They'll call back in a week and give me what I want.'

This time she looked fully at him. 'And what is it you want?'

You. Jackson shook the answer from his thoughts, instead saying, 'Creative freedom to do things the way they should be done. I've been in the business too long to have my hands tied by businessmen who think they know the market because they took a college course ten years ago.'

'They'd be foolish not to listen to you.' Zoe turned her attention back to the screen. 'Everything you touch turns to crème brûlée.'

At that he laughed. 'I don't know about that.'

'Please. Have you ever had a business fail?' She shot him a challenging stare.

'Business, no.' He glanced toward the television. Opening credits waved over the screen, flashing between images of a river. He hoped she didn't ask about his personal life.

'I went to your New York restaurants. The fine-dining, elegant ones are great, but the truth is the train-themed one is my favorite. I loved how you had it set up like a luxury dining car from the early 1900s.'

'Ah, the *Railroad.*' He nodded. 'We came up with it because of the space. With traffic patterns we knew the location was perfect, but the building was very narrow. Most of the decor came from an actual old dining car.'

'Your visions are truly magnificent.' She gave a shy smile and turned her attention away from him. A slight flush crept over her cheeks. 'And I'm not just saying that to kiss your ass. I mean it.'

As the opening credits rolled by, the soft music faded into melodic whispers. The foreign words meant nothing beyond the rise and fall of their rhythm on screen. Zoe laughed at something one of the actors said and he automatically smiled on hearing the light sound. Her lips parted slightly as she stared forward, a half smile curving her mouth as she watched the show.

Jackson rested his hand to the side, brushing it up against hers. At the touch, she turned to him. Her wide eyes took his in and drew him forward. She glanced away. He'd seen the shy look on her face before.

'How can a woman as beautiful as you be so shy?' he asked, not pulling back.

'I had two beautiful older sisters. Megan had that mysterious, dominant thing guys were attracted to. Kat was the free spirit and I . . .'

'And you,' he prompted.

'Well, I just kind of faded into the background. I turned to books.' When she looked up at him again, the corner of her lips curved upward. The look nearly drove him mad with desire.

All voices in his head died as he moved to kiss her and when she met his lips, not protesting, his hands sprang into action. He ran his palm up her thigh, pushing up the shirttail, needing to know if she wore panties underneath. When his fingers met the wet folds of her naked, exposed pussy, he groaned. Zoe arched into his hand, sinking down on the bed so she lay more beneath him than beside him.

Jackson explored her sex, parting the velvet folds with his finger to discover her hard clit waiting for him. She tugged at his shirt and he let her undress him. As he threw the shirt aside, he grabbed the sides of the designer shirt she wore and ripped it apart to bare her breasts. Buttons flew but he didn't care. He'd gladly ruin a million shirts in order to touch her naked flesh as he'd been dreaming of doing for days.

Kissing a trail down her chest, he forced her legs open. She made a weak noise and her legs tensed as if she wanted to protest at what he was doing. Much stronger than she, he pushed her legs further apart and licked her pussy. The sweet taste exploded in his mouth and soon he was probing deep inside. He reached for her breast, massaging it as he dined on her sex.

His aching cock needed attention so he braced his weight on his knees and reached down between his thighs to free it. The waistband of his pyjama pants slid down over his ass, leaving it naked. Zoe tensed, crying out as she came against his lips, flooding him with her essence. With her taste on his mouth, he surged forth, bringing himself between her thighs. The heat of her pussy met his cock and he gasped as his tip dipped inside her.

Zoe squirmed, her legs open and inviting. Her attractive body sprawled beneath him – the swell of her breasts, her hard nipples, her wet hair plastered to the side of her stunning face. Jackson tried to hold back, knowing he couldn't let this go any further until he'd put on a condom.

Zoe reached her legs around his hips and pulled him to her. His cock inched deeper, the warm heat unlike anything he'd experienced before. He'd always been responsible when it came to sex but the wet heat, uninhibited by latex, made him throw caution to the wind. He had to fill it fully, at least once. Jackson thrust, filling her to the brink with his cock. Tight, moist, velvety soft heat surrounded him.

He tried to pull out, but found himself thrusting forward. Each time he said just once more and each time he found himself pushing back into her blissful hold.

Zoe's legs dropped to the backs of his thighs, her toes curling against him. She clawed at his chest, digging her fingers into his flesh as she came a second time. Fiery tension built in his gut and he groaned, having enough presence of mind to pull out as he came onto his comforter.

Zoe moaned, her body sated. Jackson fell next to her on the bed, untangling himself from her thighs to pull her into his arms. As she'd showered, she'd thought of being with him in a bed. Not that the forest and kitchen hadn't held some element of fun, but there was something to be said for a soft, warm bed and the security of four walls.

Kissing her temple, he whispered, 'I'm sorry, I should have treated you better.'

She snuggled against him, loving the feel of his naked skin against hers – so intimate, so unlike the other times. Her mouth opened to answer, wanting to tell him that it was all right, that next time he disappeared for a week just to tell her before he left. She didn't get the chance. His words interrupted her.

'I promise, next time I'll use a condom.'

Chapter Seven

Zoe awoke to the sound of a phone ringing. Sunlight streamed in from outside, too golden to be much later than early morning. Birds sang, their song filtering through the open window. She stretched her arms, skimming them over the soft mattress and feather comforter. Jackson wasn't on the bed, but she could hear his voice from inside the bathroom.

'I'm sorry you were worried, Marta. Some guys flew in with me from Seattle and I needed Chef Matthews to cook this weekend since she's off at the diner. It was late and I didn't want to wake you,' 'Actually, you could do me a favor. She needs clothes. Would you mind packing a few outfits for her? Yes, thank you, Marta. I'll be by later this morning to pick them up. Yes, I'm sure my associates will be very pleased with her cooking. I know, muddy feet. I'll be sure to warn Rita about that. OK, Marta. All right. I have to go, they're waiting for me.'

Jackson appeared in the bathroom doorway, already dressed. The flat-front khaki trousers hugged his trim waist. A white undershirt showed along the open collar of the button-down dress shirt. Light-blue faded stripes ran vertically over the white linen. He'd showered and shaved. His short brown locks were combed neatly back to dry.

'Morning.' Suppressing a yawn, she gave a slight smile.

'Morning. I have a web conference in fifteen minutes

down in my office. Feel free to wander around the rest of the house and grounds. The housekeepers will be here soon. If they inquire, you stayed in the Charleston suite. It's the blue room right down the hall on the other side of the house. I messed up the bed to make it look like you slept there.'

'Oh.' Zoe's smile faded as she hugged the comforter tightly to her chest. 'OK.'

Jackson crossed to his closet and came out holding some clothes. 'I found these. The jeans belong to my sister. She left them last time she stayed.' He set them on the end of the bed. 'If you're hungry, help yourself to whatever's in the kitchen. I should be done in a couple hours.' Jackson leant over, gave her a quick kiss on the corner of her mouth and left. The subtle hint of his cologne stayed behind.

She slid out of bed. Her stiff legs made it hard to walk as she stumbled to the bathroom. Since her hair was damp when she'd fallen asleep, it now stuck up over her head at odd angles. Zoe immediately began smoothing it, as if by doing so she could change the fact that Jackson had seen her all messy just moments before.

Thinking of him, she stopped. What did he mean by hiding what they'd done? Logically, she could assume he didn't want anyone in his small town to know about them. Though whether that was for her reputation or his, she didn't know. A tiny whisper came from the back of her mind, saying that in truth he was ashamed to be with her, embarrassed, so instead he lied and told everyone she was the help. Or had he planned all along for her to come to his house to cook for his business guests? Were they even now sleeping in some of the guest rooms? Blushing, she tried to remember if she'd made much noise the night before.

Unsure how much time she had before the housekeepers arrived, she turned on the shower. The easiest way to do her hair was to start from scratch. She wasn't sure what Jackson had planned, but by his words to Marta it looked like he wanted her to stay the entire weekend.

As the water hit her skin, she wished her sister were with her in Dabery. She could really use Kat's judgment on the situation. Zoe didn't know the first thing about conducting a casual relationship where love and sex were separate entities. Already she felt her heart being pulled into the mix. But were her feelings genuine or was it just because she'd allowed him to sleep with her? There was no way to call her sister for quick advice on how to handle this weekend. Zoe had left her cell phone at the restaurant, in the desk.

'Don't think of the future, just take it as it comes,' she told herself, hoping that was the advice Kat would have given her because it was what she was going to try and do. 'No point in looking for trouble, because trouble always has a way of finding me on its own.'

'Are you enjoying your stay in Winterwood?' asked Rita, a stout woman with a cheery disposition. Her identical twin sister, Rachel, looked at Zoe expectantly. The women wore charcoal-gray slacks and white, short-sleeved shirts.

Zoe raised an eyebrow at the housekeepers. 'I thought I was in the Charleston suite.'

Rachel laughed. 'The plantation – Winterwood.'

'Named because of the old, dead trees that populate part of the land,' Rita added. 'There will always be plenty of heat in the winter because of them.'

'Not that it matters now. Winterwood has central heating and air now,' Rachel said.

Zoe smiled. The housekeepers were friendly, once they had learnt she was in the kitchen to cook and not order them around. Every modern appliance was hidden beneath a period look – from the brick oven taking up the majority of the wall to the nickel-plated turn-of-the-century range with the words 'Glenwood Home Grand' embossed on the front door.

'Don't worry.' Rachel pointed at the range. 'It's been converted. Works perfectly.' Then she crossed over to a cabinet and pulled open the door to show Zoe the microwave. 'Here's this if you need it.'

Zoe wrinkled her nose. She avoided microwaves whenever she could. About all it was good for was melting things.

The housekeepers left, carrying window-cleaning fluid and dusting rags. Zoe pulled at her borrowed pants. They were rolled at the waist to keep them up. Jackson's T-shirt would have fitted him, but hung loosely on her thinner frame. A white phoenix, wings spread, had been airbrushed over the black material.

Too preoccupied to cook breakfast, she helped herself to a demitasse cup of coffee from the antique gold vacuum coffee brewer. The brewer was mounted on an Italian marble base and adorned with hand-cut crystal with a matching creamer, sugar pot and golden spoon.

Everything in Jackson's home bespoke perfection and taste. Many of the rooms had wood fireplaces, from the guest rooms to the dining room. The minimalist approach to decorating made the home uncluttered, but the pieces that *were* there were stunning in their elegance. Antiques and replicas made her feel like a lady of the estate, or perhaps even some Southern belle. She could easily see grand parties in the front hall, or formal dinners at the large wooden table with gentlemen in suits and ladies in hoop skirts, carrying delicate fans.

Taking her cup with her, she went to the covered walkway next to the kitchen. Large ferns hung in the windows. Seeing a door to the backyard, she found herself walking outside, onto the stone porch. It wrapped around the side of the center section with a balustrade along the edge. Stone stairs led down into a fairy-tale garden. Manicured shrubbery, magnolia and cypress trees and flowers encased benches, statues and fountains. The ruins of a brick wall provided the perfect anchor for some vines. Walking paths wove along them, disappearing behind flowering bushes.

'There you are.'

Zoe turned on her way down the steps, shading her eyes as she looked up at Jackson. He'd unbuttoned and untucked his shirt, letting it hang open over the white T-shirt. Even casual, he looked like a man of power and influence. 'Business all done?'

'For today.' He smiled. The morning sun shone on the brown waves of his short hair. 'Did you get breakfast?'

'Wasn't hungry.' She held up the demitasse cup. 'Found the coffee.'

'I have bigger mugs.'

'Was I not supposed to use these?' She looked down at the nearly empty cup. 'I'm sorry, the housekeepers said I could help myself to it. I didn't think to –'

'It's fine,' he interrupted, chuckling. Jackson joined her on the steps, glancing back toward his home before cupping her jaw and leaning in to give her a quick kiss. He held her face in his hand for a brief moment. 'Good morning, Zoe.'

'Morning,' she said, feeling breathless.

His hand dropped away and he continued down the stairs. When he reached the end, he looked up at her expectantly. 'Coming?'

Zoe looked down at the cup.

'Leave it on the steps,' he told her. Obeying, she set it down and joined him on the walking path. 'I wanted to show you the ruins.'

'Am I working this weekend? I mean, here? Am I working here?' She couldn't stop the question from coming out.

Jackson looked at her in surprise. 'No. Why?'

'When Marta called, it sounded like you meant for me to cook this weekend. It's fine, if that's why I'm here.'

Jackson again glanced back at the house before touching her face lightly. His hand dropped to her shoulder and then slid along her arm to rest near her elbow. An intensity shone from his dark gaze, piercing her in a way she had come to recognize in him. 'A gentleman doesn't spread rumors about the woman he's seeing.'

'Are you seeing me?' she whispered, suddenly feeling very shaky and weak.

For a moment, he didn't speak, merely searching her expression. She tried not to give too much away, scared of what he'd find. Then, almost playfully, he leant closer and said in a soft tone, 'I'm looking at you right now.'

It wasn't an answer. Or maybe it was.

Keep it light, she told herself. *Light and fun. This is an affair, not a relationship. Remember the difference. Don't get too attached. Don't be one of those women.*

'Show me the ruins.' Zoe didn't lean in to kiss him, as she continued to tell herself to play it cool.

Trees added shade as they strolled. Gravel crunched under her white sneakers. She'd managed to clean the shoes in the bathroom sink that morning. For the first time since meeting him, she managed to make light conversation, telling him of her family, her work, her childhood. Jackson talked of Jefferson, his engaged brother, and how they would be having the wedding right there on the plantation. Jefferson volunteered at the fire department and worked on one of the ranches. He'd met his fiancée at a horse show and it was love at first sight. His sister, Callie, worked for him so she could stay home with her sons. Zoe liked the look Jackson got on his face when he spoke of his family. It was a gentle, loving look, one she never expected him to turn on her. But knowing he was capable of it made her heart physically ache with longing.

Keep it light, Zoe, keep it light.

'And your parents?' Zoe asked as they left the fairy-tale gardens for a tree-lined walk.

'My pa died when I was eleven. My momma and her sisters, Aunt Sonia and Aunt Natalie, work in the diner on the weekend. They like having something to do.'

'And it's a way you can help them out while still letting them keep their pride,' Zoe concluded. She could tell by his look her assumption was right. 'What's your mother's name?'

'Renée.'

'You named the diner after her. That's sweet. I once named something after my mom.' Zoe chuckled. 'I was nine and I created this awful strawberry, mandarin orange, chocolate chip, maraschino cherry cookie. I called it a Beatrice. No one could eat them.'

'Flattering,' Jackson drawled, laughing.

'I was nine. She had just grounded me because I said her tea leaves were stupid and she was even stupider for believing in them.' Zoe shrugged. 'It's something that's been passed down from generation to generation. I think some-times she's hurt because none of us girls ever took it up.'

'People around here believe in all sorts of things – spirits, tarot cards, palmistry, folk remedies and psychics. I've never seen anything I'd call paranormal, but that doesn't mean there isn't something to it. I don't think science and modern reason can explain everything.'

'So, Mr Levy, are you telling me you believe in ghosts?' They had neared a small private graveyard. The weathered tombstones had dates etched into them from the late 1800s. Unlike the gardens, the grasses had been allowed to grow longer within the fenced area. An old cypress, with long hanging branches, created the ideal supernatural back-drop.

'I told you to call me Jackson.'

'Do you believe in ghosts, Jackson?' She leant against the wrought-iron gate surrounding the graveyard.

He looked over her shoulder and stiffened. His mouth opened and no sound came out. Startled, she quickly turned, backing away from the tombstones at the same time. The second she did, hands grabbed her arms and Jackson growled. She screamed in fright, jerking away from his hands. Jackson laughed, a deep, hearty sound.

'I should have known.' She hit at his arm. 'You warned me about liking to bring girls out here to scare them.'

'Yeah, I forgot how much fun that was.' His handsome grin widened.

'Oh, yeah, fun.' Zoe tried to keep a straight face. 'You just watch your back. I owe you one.'

Jackson led the way down a narrow path to a fallen brick structure. 'When the house was first built, this was the kitchen. They made them separate in case there was a fire. Being a chef, I thought you might be interested.'

Zoe passed under the arched door. Time had eaten away at the old frame and dust had settled within. A small tree grew in the corner and much of the roof had long since blown away. The remains of a fireplace, some broken pottery and what looked to be a partially buried kettle were all that was left. Diffused light came through the broken roof, dancing like reflected crystals over the entire area.

'I don't think I'll be cooking you dinner here anytime soon.' She ran her finger along the old fireplace.

'Hey, come here.'

The hoarse words made her look at him. This time when he cupped her cheek and kissed her, it wasn't quick and polite. His tongue delved into her mouth, instantly deepening with passion. He moaned, tugging her close to his body. Their heads moved, angling one way and then the other. Zoe ran her hands into his hair, wishing she could touch him everywhere at once.

Inside, her heart beat a frantic rhythm. It always did when he was near. Outside, the world faded away. Nothing mattered but this moment, his lips on hers, his body pressed tight. All of this seemed like a fairy tale – the wondrous house, the handsome man.

He pulled back, his mouth open as he breathed hard. Tiny specks of light moved over his features as the overhead leaves moved in the breeze. 'I've wanted to do that all morning. I can't seem to resist you. Stay the weekend with me.'

Zoe nodded. Birds sang, adding music to their hideaway. Her hard nipples rubbed against his chest, sending small jolts to her stomach. Cream gathered between her thighs, eager to welcome him once again. His smoldering expression said he felt it too. She begged herself not to fall for him, but it was too late. Zoe could no more resist him than she could stop cooking. The knowledge washed over her in bittersweet agony. What she wanted could never be and she knew she should run away, leave his home, his town, his restaurant. She couldn't. All her dreams, all her hopes were right here, in her arms, wrapped up in Jackson Levy.

'You're very beautiful.' Jackson made a weak noise of pleasure, his gaze hot with passion as he moved to kiss the tip of her nose. 'What are you thinking about when you look at me like that?'

Zoe swallowed, knowing that answering, *Falling in love with you* wasn't an option. So, instead, she answered, 'Cooking.' It wasn't a lie, just not the greater truth.

He pulled back slightly, but didn't let go. 'Cooking?'

She wanted to slap herself for the answer. It sounded conceited and stupid and she wished she could swallow it back.

'At least you're honest,' he said. His expression became guarded. 'I can respect that.'

Now she felt worse. 'I don't always think about cooking.'

Jackson laughed. His fingers trailed over her neck, slipping over the rapid pulse that beat there. 'I should hope not. If you do, I need to work harder.' His fingers slipped down over her chest, through the valley between her breasts. They drew a haphazard pattern over her stomach before landing on her rolled waistband.

'Jackson,' she hesitated. 'I'm ... We ...'

'I know.' He put his hand to her mouth. 'You don't have to tell me.'

Zoe wasn't sure what he thought he knew. She'd been going to say she was no good at this sort of thing. Maybe it was better if he stopped her from speaking until she had a chance to plan what she would say.

'Kiss me,' she whispered, offering her mouth up to him. 'I like it when you kiss me.'

Jackson didn't want to hear her say that there was nothing between them but sex, so he stopped her from speaking. There was so much he wanted to say to her, but when he tried, when he tested her responses to his admissions, her look stopped him. He'd asked her what she was thinking when her wide eyes looked up at him, searching his face. He'd wished for some deep answer, hoped for a hint of more, and would gladly have settled for the tiniest bit of encouragement to explore a commitment between them.

But did she think of him? No. She thought of her career. Never in his life had he thought he'd have to compete with food. Sadly, food was winning hands down.

Her eyes lifted to meet his, her soft words still between them. *Kiss me. I like it when you kiss me.*

His heart hammered in his chest. He'd never felt like this with a woman before. Desire and longing had distracted him in his conference and driven him to end his meeting early so he could run to find her.

His choppy breath echoed all around him, shutting out all other sounds. Her eyes captured him. Why couldn't he read her? Why couldn't he figure her out? Why couldn't he walk away? From that first night, drinking in her bar, he hadn't been able to walk away. He'd even convinced himself that he was punishing her by bringing her here, but really he was punishing himself.

Jackson opened his mouth to speak, but he still couldn't find the right words. Smiling slightly, he tugged at her T-shirt, lifting it so he could feel her smooth stomach with the backs of his fingers. He didn't grab her, didn't force her to stay against him. A breeze drifted through the kitchen ruins, kicking up dust.

'Let me take you somewhere else.' Jackson wished they were back in his room, but the housekeepers had full run of the house. He didn't want anyone thinking they knew something. Rumors spread fast in Dabery, especially about him. He didn't want the entire town pushing and questioning a relationship he was trying to have.

The erotic feel of his closeness made Zoe's flesh itch to be free of her clothes. Instead of allowing him to take her from the ruins, she lifted herself up on tiptoes and kissed him. 'Here is good.' Her mouth captured his and a wave of potent desire shot from her mouth to her breasts and pussy. Heat flooded her sex, hot and moist. His firm mouth worked against hers, his tongue dancing and twirling in her mouth. He'd worked his fingers into her shirt and groaned as he found her breasts. The erect nipples were waiting for him, already puckered and sensitive. As if he knew their torment, he pinched them between his fingers, rolling the delicate buds. Her hips jerked in response.

She pushed his long-sleeved shirt off his shoulders. The tight movement of his muscular chest took her breath away. Everything about him was perfect, even the little flaws.

Moaning, she sucked on his tongue, the way she suddenly wanted to suck on his cock. The taste of him was like a potent sex drug that made her want more. Zoe pulled at his shirt, wanting to look at him. He lifted his arms and she trapped them over his head, holding the shirt so he couldn't get it off. She kissed his chest, licking at his small nipples. Jackson groaned as she explored every inch of him with her mouth.

Letting go of his shirt, she ran her hands over his strong

sides to his hips. Already she could see the bulge protruding from between his thighs. Jackson tossed his undershirt aside while she unzipped his pants. Zoe didn't consider herself particularly skilled at giving blowjobs, but suddenly she wanted to try and give him such pleasure.

She kissed his stomach, slowly going to her knees. Jackson let loose a long breath. Her hands shook slightly as she pulled the pants from his hips, taking his boxers down with them. She brushed her lips along the trail of hair leading down to his thick erection. An animalistic lust took over and she became more aggressive. Her mouth watered as she lightly kissed the blunt tip of his shaft.

Zoe's breath caught in the back of her throat. She didn't stop to think as she flicked her tongue out to taste him. Her gaze raked over his chiselled body before looking into his eyes. He watched her intently, somehow begging and commanding in the same expression. Entranced by her nearness, she sucked the tip of his cock between her teeth.

She ran her hands over his stomach, massaging his hips as she drew him deeper into her mouth. His hands threaded into her hair, not pulling or pushing, just holding. It was impossible to take him fully, so she brought one hand to help as she inched forward and back, sucking and licking.

Her hips worked in small circles and her pussy ached to be filled. She cupped his balls, rolling them in her palm. Her teeth nicked him, bumping along his shaft. Jackson tensed. Zoe moaned low in the back of her throat. Her head bobbed faster. Suddenly, the grip on her hair tightened and Jackson jerked her off of him. He turned, bracing his weight against the fireplace as he spurted onto the ground.

Zoe pushed up from the dirt floor, brushing the dust off

her jeans. When he looked at her, his eyes were still hot with passion. The words a breathy growl, he said, 'My turn.'

Zoe gasped as he grabbed her arms and spun her around so her back was pressed to the falling stone wall of the ruins. He gripped her ass before tugging on the pants. They fell without needing to be unbuttoned. Jackson was instantly on his knees before her, lifting her naked thighs up as he pushed at her T-shirt to slip his head beneath the material and get to her sex. He put one leg on his naked shoulder and grasped her hips. She panted at the wet, hot feeling of his probing tongue. With one hand she pinched her own nipples, running the other down to touch him where she could through the T-shirt. She wiggled and his grip tightened. He pulled her slit against his mouth, sucking her clit as his fingers parted the moist folds to probe the depths of her pussy.

It was all too much. Her body stiffened and her hips jerked. The muscles of her sex clamped down on his fingers, racking her with pleasure as she came against his hand. Jackson milked her body for all it would give. When she could take no more, he pulled away, coming from beneath her shirt to grin up at her. The intimate sight of her cream on his lips held her attention. He licked them slowly, standing before her. Jackson kissed her and she tasted herself on him.

'I'm starving,' he said. 'Let's get dressed and go in. Rita normally brings me something for lunch. We can take it out on the stone porch.'

It didn't take her long to pull up her pants and roll them to fit. 'I can make us something if she hasn't.' Zoe still wanted to cook for him, especially since the first meal of burnt trout.

'No, you're off this weekend.' He buttoned his pants and pulled the T-shirt over his head. The white cotton had dust on it and Zoe reached to brush it clean. Shaking out his long-sleeved shirt, he slipped it over his arms. 'I have a couple more meetings this afternoon, but after that I'm all yours.'

Rita smiled knowingly as she set down a pitcher of iced tea on the wrought-iron table covered with a white table-cloth. The housekeeper had set out torn-leaf salads with grilled chicken, walnut and apple slices and thick wedges of white chocolate cake for two. Though the woman looked friendly, there was a slight standoffishness to her demeanor now as she served. Zoe wondered if it was because she now thought of Zoe as a guest and not an equal. Not liking the invisible barrier, she reached forward and took Rita's hand. 'Join us. You and Rachel. Please.'

Rita looked surprised and shook her head. She poured tea into the glasses.

'I insist. You've been working all morning. Please, join us.' Zoe smiled invitingly. Jackson appeared at the table, a news-paper in his hand. He'd changed his clothes, and was now wearing a black cotton dress shirt with sateen pinstripe and dark dress pants. Zoe tugged at her oversized T-shirt, wishing she had her own clothes with her. Jackson was acting like nothing had happened between them, but how could the maids not suspect? She was eating dinner with him, dressed in his shirt and ill-fitting pants. He sat down and nodded at Rita, not giving the woman much thought.

'Another time,' Rita said softly. 'I don't want to interrupt your business meeting.'

Jackson glanced up. The housekeeper walked away. 'She keeps making me salads for lunch. I eat them, but would prefer a thick steak.'

'Salad is healthier for you.' Zoe picked up her iced tea and took a sip. She coughed in mild surprise at the flavor. Peaches and sugar sweetened the strong brew.

'There is that.' Jackson opened the newspaper. 'Do you follow the market?'

'Don't own stock,' Zoe answered. 'Don't trust the market.' Silently, she added, *Don't have money to invest*.

'Do you understand the market?'

Zoe arched a brow, frowning. 'Do you mean to be condescending?'

Jackson laughed. 'No. Was I?'

Zoe spread her thumb and forefinger and lifted it to him to signify 'a little.'

He leant across the table, taking her hand briefly. 'I didn't mean to be.'

'It's all right.' She lifted her salad fork as Jackson went back to his paper. The vinaigrette dressing had a distinct garlic and herb flavour and she guessed it came out of a bottle. He didn't speak to her and she found herself watching him eat, almost entranced by the movements of his hand, the slow chewing of his mouth.

Zoe wasn't sure what she expected lunch to be, but this wasn't it. Clearing her throat, she took a sip of tea. 'I thought about trying Cajun salmon fillets this week or perhaps blackened sea bass with long-grain wild rice and pine nuts or an eggplant with penne and mint pesto.'

'The salmon should go over well.' Jackson glanced up briefly, but kept reading.

'You don't sound convinced. You think I should make something else?' she asked.

'Make what you like. That's why I hired you.' He finally set the paper down and studied her.

'You're testing me, aren't you? My whole probationary

period. But you haven't told me what you're looking for. I assume I'll be judged on sales figures?'

He continued to study her. 'Numbers can tell you some things, but the restaurant is established. So long as the numbers stay steady and don't decline, I will call that a plus. There is only so much market in Dabery.'

'Then, I'll be judged on customer surveys?'

'Are you worried?'

'Have there been complaints?' Zoe set down her fork.

'Would you really like to know?'

Zoe bit her lip. No, she didn't really want to know, not from him. But, if people were talking, she needed to know what they had said to him. 'Yes.'

'Roger Cumberland raves about your salsa. Sheryl has several complaints –'

'Well, that's not my fault. She's ...' Zoe forced herself to take a breath. 'She's a complicated woman.'

Jackson laughed. 'A diplomatic answer. I'm well aware of what Sheryl is.'

'What other complaints?'

'Jenny Stuart offered to come help you with the meatloaf because it was a little dry. Louise Baker said you didn't return her smile.' He fingered his glass. 'And Fred Louis said his steak wasn't pink enough –'

'The guy who wanted it raw?' Zoe shook her head. 'I gave it to him medium rare. Any good chef will tell you that's the perfect –'

Jackson held up his hand. 'The point is he wanted it very rare.'

Zoe lowered her eyes to the plate. His tone made her feel like a scolded child. 'So you're saying the customer is always right, even if they want me to make something that is not to the best of my ability.'

'I'm saying it's your job to cook for the customer.' Jackson sighed, as if considering his words. 'Part of being a chef is giving the public what they want. When you're a big name, cooking in New York or Paris, they want whatever you want to give them. When you're in Dabery, working in a Southern diner, what do you think the customers want? Blackened sea bass with long-grain wild rice and pine nuts? Trout with hazelnut?'

'I don't think that just because these people are small-town Southerners they can't enjoy finer foods than bacon and grits,' Zoe defended herself, struck by the fact that she was also defending his family and friends.

'I'm glad you see that.' He nodded in approval. 'And it is what you have to decide how to handle. I won't tell you what to cook. It is up to you to predict and serve the people you are cooking for.'

Zoe frowned. His words made sense, but he wasn't really helping her. Handing her a menu would have been better. But then, she wouldn't really be a chef making her own decisions. She'd be a line cook. 'I won't let you down.'

He lifted his glass of sweet tea in the air, silently toasting her before taking a drink. Zoe hoped it wasn't a lie.

Chapter Eight

'That is a ridiculous sum,' Jackson said, frowning at his computer screen. The image of Contiello's agent stared back at him.

Mr Duncan, a thick man with a moustache that overgrew his upper lip, cleared his throat and pretended to study his blue silk tie before smoothing it down. 'We both know my client is worth twice that.'

Jackson laughed. 'A bold claim, especially since we both know that little Las Vegas scheme he had brewing is falling through and his current employer is speaking with a bankruptcy lawyer.'

The agent's eyes shot up and his mouth worked before he caught himself and frowned. 'I don't know where you get your facts, Mr Levy, but I assure you my client has many options open to him.'

'And I, Mr Duncan, am not interested in hearing about every two-bit franchise that will hire him after he manages to spell his name right on an application.' Jackson knew he was being harsh, but he was tired of dealing with Contiello and his insufferably greedy agent. The chef was still one of the best options to fill his client's needs. If he bided his time, Contiello and his agent could come around. 'My assistant faxed you my offer. I suggest you take it to your client.'

'It would help if you told me which American city it was in,' Mr Duncan said.

'And confidentiality with my client forbids it at these preliminary stages. You know how cutthroat business can be. Though, if it's any consolation, my name is on the project.' Jackson kept his smile slight and his eyes hard. He knew he didn't need to say anything more. Mr Duncan knew what that meant.

'I'll speak to him,' Mr Duncan said at length, 'but we're looking at many other options at this time.'

'Naturally.' Jackson lifted his hand, as if he expected no less and didn't care. 'But, I should remind you, this offer is not exclusive to your client. We do want him and his talents, but we will not wait forever.'

'Good day, Mr Levy,' the agent said, nodding once.

Jackson returned the gesture. 'Mr Duncan.'

He turned off the webcam, glad the meeting was over. Looking down at the list in front of him, he sighed. Only five more conferences to go and then he could get back to Zoe. Jackson would much rather be with her than in his office taking meetings.

He looked at the door, as if feeling her near. Of course, it had to be his imagination. There was no logical reason to believe he could really sense her presence. Every part of him wanted to blow off his meetings and call her to him, though he was too responsible to do such a thing. His mind was only too happy to offer an alternative. What if she were there with him, under his desk as he did business? The men on the other end of the computer connection couldn't see his legs. They would never know.

'Except when I start grunting and thrusting into her mouth,' he mumbled, adjusting his hips as his cock instantly lifted. 'Shit!'

He wondered where she was, what she was doing, what she was thinking. So far, this weekend wasn't going as romantically as he had planned. At lunch he hadn't been able to think of what to say to her so he'd rudely buried his face in his newspaper, not really reading it. When she'd finally talked to him, he'd ended up lecturing her on her job.

His mood suddenly foul, he reached for a file and opened it, quickly reading over the personal details of the man he was about to talk to. Even as he committed the words to temporary memory, Zoe stayed on the edge of his thoughts.

Zoe wished she had her cell phone so she could call her sisters. She'd even settle for calling her eccentric mother. As far as she could tell, Jackson didn't have a phone in his house, just the cell phone he carried. After dinner, Jackson had gone back into a meeting and left her alone in his house so there was no borrowing it from him – not that she would waste his minutes when it wasn't an emergency.

Zoe spent the day avoiding the housekeepers, treating it almost like a game of hide and seek as they moved from room to room like efficient robots. She explored the library with its old bound books. There was a distinct musk to the room, the smell of old pages and dust, even though it looked spotless. Old painted portraits in oval frames hung from corded ropes on the wall, the faces dour in their turn-of-the-century clothing.

Jackson's office door stayed closed and she didn't wish to walk in on him during his meeting. She did tiptoe by a couple times, trying to eavesdrop. But the oak door was too thick and not a sound came from within.

Upstairs, the guest bedrooms were each decorated in distinctly different accent colours with a matching under-lying style. She found the blue guest room right where he'd said it would be, far away from his own bedroom. It boasted a darker shade than Jackson's room, with gold accents. The large bed had a scrolled wooden bed frame and a golden comforter with thin threads of blue running through it.

On top, she found a box with her name on it. She instantly recognized Kat's artistically flowing handwriting. Next to the box was a floral suitcase she didn't recognize. When she opened it, she saw a couple of her chef uniforms, a pair of jeans and one of her tank top undershirts. The floral suitcase must have belonged to Marta. Zoe made a face. She didn't really appreciate the woman going through her things, not that she had anything to hide, and not that she hadn't already suspected that Marta had gone through them the first moment she'd left the bed and breakfast.

The box was addressed to her via Marta's. It must have come the day before, when she was at work. Mildly surprised not to find it already opened, Zoe pulled on the clear packing tape. It came up easily and she found older, cut tape beneath it. The box looked too new to be a reused one and her sister always taped packages like they carried gold bricks inside them.

'Nice, Marta,' Zoe drawled sarcastically. The woman had evidently gone through the package. On opening it she found a letter from her sister on the inside. It lay flat on the top, free of creases and envelopes. Eagerly, Zoe read it. 'Dear sis, these should get your boss's temperature rising. Don't be a good girl and you just might snag you a rich man like me. Kat.'

Zoe held her breath and read it again. If Marta had opened her box and read Kat's note, she wouldn't know her sister was joking. The soft folds called to her and Zoe climbed on top of the giant bed. She let her body sink into the feather comforter, only then realizing how exhausted she felt. Closing her eyes, she let the tension drain from her limbs. She didn't want to think and worry any more. What the future held would come regardless.

Jackson stood at the end of Zoe's bed, watching her sleep. She'd kicked off the jeans and they were now a crumpled pile on the floor at the foot of the bed. The T-shirt covered her down to her upper thighs and, since she rested on top of the covers, the long lines of her bare legs spread out over the gold comforter. Warm sunlight streamed in through the window, past the brightness of midday but not yet heavy with shadow. A box and a suitcase sat on the edge. He'd sent Rachel to town for Zoe's clothes before taking his meetings. His web conferences were finally over, having lasted two and a half hours past the time he'd allotted. It was well after six o'clock and the housekeepers had left for the day. On Sunday they had the day off and he'd have Zoe all to himself.

He set the tray of food he carried down on the floor and crawled onto the bed with her. Lying on his side along her back he lifted his hand, hovering it over her body without touching her as he traced his fingers over the gentle swell of her hip. Jackson inched closer to her, part of him willing her to wake up and turn to him, while another part of him willed her to sleep so he could have this moment next to her. It struck him how lonely his life could be. He had his family, business associates and friends. Anytime he wanted a party, there was one. Anytime he wanted company, he'd find some. But what about the times in between?

What about the times when he'd had a hard day like today? He had nothing in particular to complain about, but it was just tough and long all around. What about the nights? When he didn't want sex? Who would hold him then? Who would whisper secrets, laugh with him, spontaneously dance around the house? Who would bring him soup when he got sick? Who needed him in a way that had nothing to do with money or power?

As she slept, it was easy to imagine she could be that woman. But his mind, always logical, refused to buy into the fantasy. He knew what Zoe wanted. She'd made it clear enough. Before she'd found out who he was, he hadn't got one kind word from her. She was with him because of who he was and what he could do for her. Jackson lowered his hand, touching her smooth outer thigh. He might as well get something out of this, too. Pleasure.

Zoe wiggled her hips, moaning softly. Jackson scooted closer to her, spooning his body to hers. His arousal met the soft cleft of her ass.

Reaching for his waist, he unbuckled his belt and unfastened his pants. With one hand supporting his head, he pulled up her T-shirt and pressed against her once more. His silk boxers caused him to slide against her as he rocked his hips.

Zoe inhaled a deep breath, her sudden movement attesting to her alertness. Jackson slid his hand up to the soft folds of her pussy. The warm lips parted to his gentle probing and he easily discovered the hard bud of her clit buried in the velvet hold. Intimately massaging her, he felt moisture pooling around his fingers. Her butt held his cock tight against it, moving along with his circling hips.

She arched against him, her voice heavy with sleep as she whispered his name. 'Jackson.'

He increased the pressure of his exploring hand, letting a finger dip inside her. The walls of her pussy enclosed him, contracting lightly. Jackson pressed his face to her hair, smelling his shampoo in the locks. Licking the back ridge of her ear, he continued to fuck her with his hand, becoming more aggressive the more she responded. Zoe reached around, grabbing his ass to hold him along her back. The soft pants and weak cries washed over him in bittersweet torment. He wanted her so badly, wanted to pull her into his chest and never let go.

Her ass rocked harder and he let the pleasure of it overtake him, not holding back as the tension of release built inside his cock. His tender balls ached and he found himself bucking hard against her. Zoe came against his hand, jerking violently. It was enough to send him over the edge and he came inside his silk boxers.

Zoe let go of his hips, turning to face him. His boxers stuck to his cock, glued to his flesh. She placed her hand over her mouth, clearly blocking her breath. His fingers slipped from inside her, still wet with her cream.

'You're done with your meetings. How did they go?' Her lashes dipped lazily over her eyes as if she were still only half awake.

'Fine,' he answered, brushing a strand of her hair back from her forehead. 'Are you hungry? I brought up food.'

'Mmm,' she moaned, smiling. 'I thought I smelt something.'

Jackson rolled off the bed. Leaning to pick up the tray, he said, 'I didn't have much to work with in the refrigerator. Rachel and Rita normally only leave me enough to snack on while they're not here.'

'You cooked for me?' She honestly looked surprised.

'I might not be a world-renowned chef, but I have picked up a few things over the years.' He set the tray next to her and grinned. 'A very gourmet roast beef sandwich on wholegrain gourmet sliced bread. Gourmet chips fresh from the grocery store bag.'

Zoe laughed. 'Gourmet tea straight from the pitcher?'

'No, I milked a tea cow for that.' He grabbed a potato chip and popped it into his mouth. 'It's a lot more difficult than you think.'

'You know –' Zoe picked up a chip '– I've heard that.'

Jackson laughed, trying to ignore his sticky boxers as he buttoned his pants. 'I'm going to go change out of my work clothes.' As he walked to the door, he added, 'There are some days I really want to hurt the person who invented webcams. Before that, I could wear whatever I wanted for phone conferences and the client never knew the difference. I even stopped wearing my cowboy hats around the same time everyone went to webcams because everyone expected me to be some kind of eccentric cowboy when they finally met me in person. I got tired of being taken to strip joints and being offered cigars.'

'Thank you for the sandwich,' she called after him as he left the room.

Jackson went straight for his shower, his steps lighter than they'd been before.

Despite the fact that it was later in the day and she had nowhere to go, Zoe wanted to look pretty. So she shed the oversized T-shirt and slipped on one of the dresses her sister had sent to her. The cobalt-blue wrap was simple, comfortable, and definitely more feminine than baggy denim jeans. White piping along the hems gave it just enough accent to make it stylish, as it fell to her knees. The deep V of the neckline worked well with the new bra-and-panties set her sister had sent with it. Kat had even included shoes, cute little blue pumps with open toes and a low heel.

She stepped out of the room and began walking down

the hall. As if by some divine timing, Jackson's door opened. He wore a pair of fleece exercise pants with a dark-red strip down the sides and a black, tightly fitted V-neck muscle tank.

'Wow,' Jackson said, taking a couple of steps toward her before stopping. 'Hold on, I'll change.'

'Wait, no.' She lifted a hand to stop him, though she was too far away to make contact. The tight shirt looked really good on him and she saw no reason for him to change. 'It's fine.'

His gaze called to her and she willingly answered. They walked toward each other, their eyes dipping unashamedly over the other's body as they met at the top of the stairs. Zoe stared at his body, from his strong, naked feet to his damp hair. She wanted him, always wanted him, but it was more than just a physical attraction. She wanted to know him, to connect to him, to understand him. But she was afraid of what taking that route would mean for her career and their relationship. Jackson hadn't so much as hinted at anything serious with her and who was she to start that kind of conversation? To do so might make her lose what she did have with him. Besides, if she said she wanted more, how could she do so without making him think she was into him because of who he was?

He smiled at her, an adorably handsome look as he nodded down the stairs. 'I thought maybe we could go horseback riding tomorrow. The Thompsons have a new stud I'd like to check out.'

'Oh, OK,' Zoe answered, biting her lip.

'Have you ever been?'

'Ah, once. They had pony rides at Central Park. I was pretty young and the horses went around in circles. I always felt so bad for them, walking around and around all day long, carrying child after child. I used to have fantasies that I could sneak away and free them.'

'Yeah, those horses never look happy.' Jackson nodded. 'They really don't belong cooped up in the city. They need open fields and grazing pastures, fresh air.'

'You can tell they're not happy?' Fascinated, she glanced at his mouth as he spoke.

'Each horse has a different personality, but normally you can just see it in their eyes.' They reached the bottom step and Jackson lifted her hand, placing it on his shoulder. Holding her close, he began dancing with her in the front hall. There was no music beyond the soft sound of his voice as he talked. 'Their coats can lose a bit of their sheen, they lose interest in things around them, pin their ears back whenever someone comes near, they can pace, not eat. In many ways they're just like humans. If you know how to hear them, they will tell you what they're feeling.'

Zoe swayed against him. Jackson led her around the room. His effortless movements attested to his ease on the dancefloor.

'Do you think that is why you're so good at reading people?' She laid her head on his shoulder. Could he read her? Did he know the thoughts she tried to push from her mind?

'Perhaps. I'm sure it helped. Working with horses you learn to look for signs that aren't clearly stated.' He twirled her away from him and Zoe laughed at the sudden move.

Zoe became entranced by the euphoria of his nearness. They didn't need music. Her head became filled with a secret song only they could hear as they danced their own private ball.

Jackson danced with her along the hall, bringing her toward the covered stone porch in back. Evening started to darken the sky and a few stars began to show. A cool breeze stirred the air, carrying with it the sweet scent of flowers. Insects hummed in the background. Jackson twirled her around the porch, continuing their dance.

Zoe laughed, carefree feelings washing through her. For the first time, conversation flowed between them. They spoke of food, of restaurants, Jackson's many travels, of art and music. What they didn't talk about was what was happening between them.

'Are you done rebuilding?' Zoe asked, glancing at the view from the porch.

'Why?' He laughed. 'Does the house look unfinished?'

'No, but you look happy when you talk about horses. Maybe you should rebuild the stables.'

Jackson shook his head. 'I don't want to compete against the local businesses.'

'Then don't. Why does something you so clearly love have to be a business? Why don't you just do it for yourself because it makes you happy?' Zoe stopped dancing. The movements of his body against hers were arousing beyond measure and she needed to put distance between them to catch her suddenly choppy breath. 'You redid the house because you loved it. Why not the stables?'

'I might,' he said, as if considering it for the first time.

'If you think the other ranchers will worry, buy your stock from them, invite them over for a stable-warming party, like a house-warming for your horses, and assure them it's for personal pleasure.' She pretended to study the horizon when really all her attention was focused to the side where Jackson stood next to her. 'Or, if you want to make extra cash, bring clients here and showcase your neighbors' horses as well as your own. Or, make deals with them to help you out when you're gone, to breed together, something so everyone wins.' She finally looked at him. 'From what I've seen you can't do anything wrong in the eyes of this town. I doubt they'd have hard feelings about you rebuilding a historically important part of this plantation.'

'You make a pretty persuasive argument when you want to.' Jackson slid closer to her so his arm touched her as they both held onto the stone rail.

'I have four sisters. Persuasive arguing is a necessity.' She moved her little finger to touch his. 'I can also do math in my head.'

'Hmm, can you now?' He turned to lean his hip against the rail as he studied her. 'What's twelve plus twelve?'

'Are you mocking me?' She crossed her arms over her chest. 'Ask me a hard one.'

'342 multiplied by 763?'

Zoe closed her eyes for a few seconds, visualising the numbers, before grinning. '260,946.'

Jackson cupped her cheek. 'I have no idea if that is right, but I will tell you a secret. I prefer to use a calculator.'

'You like pushing buttons?' Zoe tilted her head coyly.

His hand trailed down her throat, stopping to rest between her breasts. 'If they're the right ones.'

The moonlight caressed his face, shadowing the hard planes. Her heart beat fast and hard and she knew he could feel it against the backs of his fingers. She waited to see what he would do. When he merely stood, she lifted her hand to mimic his movements, drawing the back of her hand down his cheek and neck to rest on his strong chest. His heart beat as fast as hers.

'Would you like to take this inside? I could open a bottle of wine and light a fire.' Jackson dropped his hand from her.

Zoe knew what he was asking, what he thought would happen once he got her inside by the fire. She couldn't blame him. It wasn't as if she'd protested against sex so far. The truth was, she wasn't about to start protesting against it now.

'It's a little warm for a fire, but the wine would be nice. I like reds if you have one.'

'Sure. Coming right up. Do you prefer Cabernet Sauvignon, Chianti or Merlot?' He paused, holding open the door that led into the front hall.

'Sauvignon would be fine.' Zoe followed him inside, stopping to kick off her heels in the front hall. She left them by the stairs.

'Here we are.' Jackson returned from the wine cellar, carrying two empty wine glasses in one hand and an open bottle in the other. 'It's only fifteen years old, but I think it'll do.'

Zoe smiled. He crossed toward the library, prompting her to follow. Her bare feet padded across the cool floor. In the library, he dimmed the lights and moved to a large, over-stuffed chair near the barren fireplace. He set the wine down on a small round marble-topped table and pressed a hidden button in the fireplace's mantel. A soft orange glow emitted from within, minus the heat of an actual fire.

Zoe approached as he poured then lifted a glass to her. She swirled the wine in her glass, noting the room temperature of the liquid. Too many people tried serving red wine cold, which only made it taste bitter. Too hot, and the taste of alcohol would overpower the flavor.

Sipping it, she smiled. 'Who makes this?'

'It's good, isn't it?'

Zoe nodded.

'It's a winery right here in South Carolina. I try to buy from locals whenever I can. My brother worked there for a while. He used to be a wine technician and taught me more than I ever wanted to learn about drinking wine.'

'I didn't realize they had wineries here.' Zoe took another drink, letting the liquor warm her stomach.

'There is a whole world outside of New York.' He sat down in the overstuffed chair as she came around the side.

'How about we stop with the New York snob jibes and I'll not call you an uneducated hick? Deal?'

Jackson reached for her outer thigh, not getting up. 'Deal.'

He worked her skirt up to touch her flesh. Lashes dipped lazily over his gaze as he watched his hand on her leg in the soft light. Zoe took another long drink, finishing her glass before handing it to him. He placed it on the table and she walked around to the front of the chair. With the light at her back, she pulled at the belt of her wrap dress. Two small buttons kept it in place. She looped the belt behind his neck.

'Take off the dress,' he ordered, resting his hands on the chair arms.

Zoe's figure shadowed him as she stood in front of the fireplace. She reached for the buttons, undid them and slowly pulled open the flaps of her dress. It slithered off her shoulders, leaving her standing in her lacy blue bra and matching panties.

'Turn around. Let me see.' Jackson moaned as she obeyed, gradually moving in a circle before facing him again. 'Mmm, beautiful.'

Zoe knelt on the floor, between his spread legs. She gripped his thighs, massaging them through the fleece pants. Jackson sank down into the chair, inching his hips closer to her. Soon his cock was in her hand, hard and ready for her. He lifted himself up and she pulled down the waistband, freeing his erection.

Jackson made a small sound of pleasure as she stroked him. Her lips followed, her tongue rolling over the tip. He tasted good, salty and sweet. She rolled his balls in her hand. There was something primal in the way his body moved and tensed against her fingers and mouth. Her teeth grazed against him and he groaned. The more she grazed, the louder he cried out. His hips pushed up, nearly choking her with his cock.

Still, he didn't touch her. His hands worked against the arms of the chair, gripping the brown suede. The muscles of his arms flexed beneath his tight flesh.

'Take off your panties and come here,' he ordered.

Zoe pushed up from the floor, slipping the lace off her hips before going to him. She didn't mind being naked with the lights on, because she could see what looking at her nakedness was doing to him. The potently masculine smell of him filled her nose and she moaned in desire. She kissed his stomach and chest through the muscle tank top. He panted for breath, as if fighting for control. She continued to kiss his magnificent body, wanting it, needing it. Jackson did something to her, made her want him.

Her breasts seemed to swell against the lacy bra and her nipples ached. Cream gathered between her thighs, her pussy wet and ready for him, eager to be dominated by his cock. She wanted him inside her, wanted him to fuck her good and long. Straddling his thighs, she maneuvred her body to take him in. Jackson reached into his pocket, and took out a condom. With expert ease, he slipped it over his arousal.

He took her hips and pulled them forward to bring her

over his body. Impaling her on his cock, he groaned. Zoe tossed her head back as he filled her. Once she was fully seated on his lap, Jackson tugged her lacy bra down to free her breasts over the top of the cups. His mouth devoured her breasts, sucking and biting the nipples until she was writhing on top of him.

Gasping, she pulled her weight up before seating herself on him again. He leant back in the chair, watching her move as she took control of the rhythm. She stared at his gorgeous face, the tense lines around his mouth trembling as she went torturously slow. It felt too good. She began to move faster as the tension built, until finally she rode him wild and hard.

She grabbed the chair next to his head. Jackson arched up, straining to meet her pussy. He groaned noisily. Zoe tensed, climaxing hard. Jackson gripped her as he met a jerking release. He pulled out and hugged her to his chest, holding her against him, not letting go for a long time. Finally Zoe pushed up, putting space between their sweaty, glistening bodies, and adjusted her bra to make it more comfortable. Leaning to the side, she grabbed the bottle and refilled their glasses.

'Let's go upstairs.' Zoe stood, setting down her wine long enough to slip her dress over her shoulders. Jackson pulled his pants over his hips, keeping her belt around his neck. As he grabbed the bottle and his glass, she took her panties off the floor. He didn't bother to turn off the fireplace as he led the way through his home.

As she passed them, she picked up her shoes and held them to her chest. Her eyes roamed over his firm ass as he took the stairs. She followed mindlessly, sipping her wine as she looked her fill of his strong back beneath the muscle tank, and the long line of his muscular arms.

'I should sleep in the guest room. I wouldn't want the maids to find me in your bed.' She watched the side of his face for a reaction.

Turning, he pulled her across the landing toward his room. 'Mmm, no, they don't come in tomorrow. You can stay in my room. I like having someone to warm my bed.'

Zoe laughed. 'Then you've definitely picked the wrong woman. I'm always cold at night. I'll suck up all your heat.'

He lifted a brow and glanced down toward his cock. 'Sounds good.'

She lightly hit his arm with her shoes.

'Oh, like it rough, do you?' He continued to chuckle. An impishly playful light entered his eyes. Hauling her to his chest, he kissed her hard and walked her with him into his bedroom. His lips tasted like the wine, his kiss just as intoxicating. When he let go, Zoe took a long drink, finishing the glass.

Jackson held her from behind, unbuttoning her dress only to pull it off her shoulders. Next, he unfastened her bra, tugging it so it fell to the floor with the dress. Naked, she stood before him, letting his hands roam over her. He cupped her breasts, pinching her nipples before exploring every inch of her flesh. Hands dipped between her thighs, down her legs, up to her ass, over her back. Reaching her hair, he pushed the back of her head, urging her to lean toward the mattress.

Zoe bent over. In the corner of her field of vision, she saw his shirt flying toward the end of the bed, followed by the unmistakable whisper of his pants being taken off. His cock brushed her slit from behind and she moaned softly. Jackson smoothed his palms over her back, drawing his fingers down her spine until she shivered. The world melted away – careers, the townsfolk, the diner, New York and Dabery. Such concerns didn't matter, not here, not tonight. Time itself slowed when he touched her.

Small noises washed over her as he vocalised his pleasure. He grabbed her hips, keeping her from pushing back fully onto him. His cock dipped in but stayed on the edge of her slit, teasing and tormenting, driving her crazy with lust. Zoe gasped. Why was he teasing her? She'd already come before, but felt the need again as urgently as the first time. Almost desperate to have him inside her, she groaned.

As if the frustrated sound were what he'd waited for, he thrust forward, filling her up. The position caused her to stretch wide and she moaned, gripping the covers of his bed. He kept the movements slow and the sensation was more erotic, more real, more vivid than anything she'd ever felt. Every inch of his cock caressed her sex. She tried to stand, but it was impossible to move as he had complete control over their joining.

'Oh, yeah, baby,' he grunted. 'You like that, don't you?'

'Mm-hmm,' she agreed. But the moment she did, he pulled out. 'What?'

'Lie on the bed.' He pulled her belt from around his neck, where it rested against his naked shoulders. His cock stood tall from his thighs, glistening with her body's cream. Jackson disappeared into his closet. She shivered, crawling to lie down on the bed. When he came out, he carried her belt and three silk ties. 'Give me your wrist.'

Zoe hesitated.

'I said, give me your wrist now.'

The hard, demanding tone of his voice both frightened and excited her. She obeyed, watching the surreal sight of him binding the limb to one of the posters of the bed with her belt. He walked to the other side, holding his hand out expectantly. Zoe again hesitated before letting him bind that one as well, only this time with one of the silk ties. Now trapped, she wiggled on the bed.

Jackson lifted the wine bottle, and took several long pulls from it. Setting it down, he crawled on top of her, straddling her waist with his thighs. His erection bumped her stomach as he leant over to cover her eyes with the second tie. He knotted it behind her head.

'Jackson?' she asked, her voice shaking.

'If you get uncomfortable,' he whispered into one ear before switching to the other, 'say "bordello."' His tongue flicked at the sensitive lobe before she felt the bed shift. 'You're gorgeous.' A finger skimmed her chest, encircling a nipple. 'I like to watch you come.'

Cool material whispered over her stomach and she could only guess it was the third silk tie. It danced lightly over her flesh, tickling her. He skated it over her breasts and stomach, along her neck and shoulders, down to her legs and feet. By the time he had covered every inch of her front she was gasping for breath. The silk brushed against her pussy, tweaking the little curls she had there.

'Seeing you tied up and helpless, subject to my whims, makes me want to fuck you.' Silk moved over her mouth, smelling of her cream. 'I want to stick my cock in your mouth and make you suck it.'

Zoe gasped, her mouth opening. The silk traveled over it.

'Today, in my meetings, I wished you were naked under my desk giving me a blowjob as I talked business. I wanted to come down your throat.' The bed shifted, but she couldn't tell what he was doing. 'I've wanted to fuck you since I first saw you in that bar. My cock actually ached to be inside you, just as it does now. I see you cooking and I want to dump sauce all over your body just to lick it up. I see you bend over and I want to sink my cock in that sweet ass of yours. I want to fuck you in every room of this house. I want you on my desk, on the dining-room table amidst the fine china. I want to fuck you on the kitchen floor, in the shower, in every guest room.'

Lips brushed her mouth and she leant up to kiss him. Her legs worked frantically against the bed. 'Jackson, please . . .'

'I want to keep you tied up, your body naked and ready whenever I feel the need to sink my cock inside you.' His tone was husky and dark. 'You like it when I talk dirty to you, don't you? I can tell. Your pussy is so wet.'

'Jackson,' she breathed. No one had ever said such things to her.

'Tell me, Zoe.' He lifted her hips, shoving a pillow beneath them. 'Have you ever been fucked in the ass?'

She shook her head.

'Mmm,' he groaned. Jackson pushed her legs apart forcibly, coming between her thighs. Her legs clamped down on his waist but it didn't stop him. 'Don't worry, baby, I'll make sure you're nice and slick when I pry you open. I promise you've never come like you will when I fuck your sweet ass. You'll be begging me to do it.'

She couldn't breathe. Darkness surrounded her and she felt the world spinning. His cock brushed her thigh and she jerked, gasping loudly.

'I'm just going to get wet.' He thrust inside her. 'That's right, make my cock nice and slick.'

After several thrusts, he pulled out and drew the tip of his cock down. Her cheeks parted and she clamped her legs tighter. The pillow angled her hips up, allowing him access to her anus. The tip pressed against the rosette. Heat flushed her face. She couldn't catch her breath. He was gentle with her, taking it slow as he eased her to his size. Nerves she never knew she had tingled.

'Ah, tight,' he groaned in approval.

As she accepted him fully, he began to quicken his pace. Jackson rubbed her clit. Another orgasm tore through her, her muscles contracting violently around him. He cried out, loud and long, tensing against her as he came.

He pulled out of her, gently kissing her mouth as she gasped for breath. Her heart hammered in her chest. Jackson pulled the pillow from beneath her hips and began untying her. Zoe weakly pulled the blindfold from her eyes, blinking hard in the light. When she finally saw his face, he smiled at her.

Jackson lifted her off the bed and carried her to his shower. There, he worshiped her body as he washed her flesh. Water and soap slid between them and by the time they were finally clean, he was kissing her against the shower wall, building her passions to a scorching peak once more. When he carried her to the bed, she was as eager as he. They made love slowly, their orgasms less violent than before, more a gentle washing of emotion that ran over them and left her body so weak she couldn't move. Completely drained, she fell asleep in his arms.

Chapter Nine

Zoe couldn't help but smile as she looked across the truck at Jackson. That morning, she had awoken to his kisses and breakfast in bed. The toast and eggs hadn't been anything fancy, but the fact that he'd got up early to cook for her made her all giddy inside.

They traveled to the Thompson Ranch to see a new horse. She'd overheard several people talking about it at the diner. There was no doubt that horses were big business in Dabery.

Wide open fields spread out behind bright white fences. Horses grazed, their long tails swishing back and forth in rhythmic motion. Most of them were brown and black with a couple of spotted white mixed in.

'Look at all this space,' Zoe said, more to herself than Jackson. She thought of her cramped old apartment.

'This ranch sits on about four thousand acres.' Jackson turned the truck up a dirt road. Cars lined both sides of the road, parked along the fence. He pulled up behind them, taking his place in line.

'What's going on?' Zoe asked, looking down the long line of vehicles. Parents walked with their kids, the children running around.

'In the summer, everyone comes out to the ranches on Sunday to see the stock and sometimes picnic. The Thompsons have the newest stallion so everyone's here.'

He walked with her along the road. Her low white heels had been a pretty choice when she'd put them on, but now, as she walked through the dirt, she knew she'd made a mistake. At least she was wearing denim jeans and a comfortable pink floral baby-doll shirt with a thick ruffle along the bottom hem.

Jackson's cowboy boots crunched over patches of gravel. He too wore denim jeans, though his were faded compared to her dark-blue ones. His brown T-shirt looked new. Looking up at his head, she suppressed a grin. The dark felt cowboy hat matched the shirt and boots. It didn't look new but suited the chiseled lines of his features.

They walked nearly a quarter of a mile before reaching the large stables. The red barn stood two stories over the field, opening up to a gate that led to the pens. Many of the townsfolk stood along the fence, gesturing at the large black horse being led around by a man in an off-white straw hat.

'This one's going to need a firm hand,' one man said to another.

'Ole Thompson said he's a wood chewer,' the second man answered.

'Small animal in his stall will keep him from doing that,' the first said. The man glanced back, stopping his conversation as he nodded at Jackson and eyed Zoe. He frowned slightly in her direction and turned back to watch the horse in silence.

Zoe continued walking next to Jackson, not making public claim to him by holding his arm or hand. She waited for him to make the first move. He didn't.

By the time they'd made it to the stables, she felt the cold stab of eyes on her, burning a hole through her face with their hostility and suspicion. Was it because she was with their golden boy? Because she was a lowly cook and he their town hero? Because she was a city girl and he their country boy? Zoe didn't know and couldn't ask. Jackson didn't seem to notice their reaction.

He introduced her as the new chef at *Renée*. The news met with silent nods, a few grumbled greetings and one enthusiastic hug. Though the hug did come from a five-year-old girl who seemed to be hugging everyone, so Zoe wasn't sure that counted as a true welcome.

The hours sludged on painfully slowly and a strange sort of coldness and discomfort grew between Jackson and Zoe. She didn't know what to say to him, how to act. She tried to take her cue from him, but the standoffish way in which he walked beside her and talked about her wasn't promising. By the time Jackson suggested leaving, she nearly tripped over her heels to get back to the truck. She felt miserable and alone and she wanted nothing more than to get to the restaurant and grab her cell phone so she could hear a familiar voice. She'd even settle for calling her mother and listening to her give a tea-leaf reading over the phone.

'Maybe I should have her read my future,' Zoe mumbled. 'I'm not doing a very good job at arranging it.'

'What was that?' Jackson asked, opening the truck door for her.

'Nothing,' she lied. 'I just said it was a beautiful horse.'

Jackson offered to drive her back to his home for dinner, but Zoe declined. Her bags were already in his truck and she needed to get back to reality. Giving the slightly untrue excuse of needing to plan a menu for the upcoming week, she had him drop her off at the bed and breakfast.

As she opened the door, he said, 'Thank you.'

Blinking, she stared at him. 'For what?' The words came

out harder than she'd intended in her nervousness. She didn't know how to act and he wasn't giving her any clues.

'For this weekend. It was …' He looked as if he were struggling for the right word, only to finally settle for, 'diverting.'

Diverting? Like some trampy sexual diversion? She was something to pass the time and relieve stress? Zoe felt the color draining from her face at that single insulting word.

'Glad I could be of service,' she quipped angrily. She moved to get her bag and the box out of the back. Jackson was right there, helping her.

'When can I see you again?' he asked. His tone was low with obvious meaning. It was a meaning she refused to get.

Almost flippantly, she answered, 'I work for you, boss. You can see me anytime you come into the restaurant.' Before he could clarify himself and make her feel worse, she hurriedly added, 'I should get going. I have menus to plan, recipes to research.'

She grabbed the box from him, silently refusing his help to carry her things as she marched toward the door.

Diverting?!

Irritation and hurt kept the box locked under her arm, as if by sheer force of will it wouldn't drop from its uneasy position. In the other hand, she carried the floral suitcase. Somehow, she made it up the stairs to the porch without falling. Marta was at the door as soon as she walked in, eying her like some high-and-mighty schoolmarm. Zoe glanced at her, biting her tongue to keep from asking about the opened and resealed box. She didn't feel like facing the woman. Not now. Not when she felt like complete and utter crap. Instead, Zoe nodded once and went upstairs to rest.

Jackson walked around to get in his truck, stopping as he saw Marta in her bright-pink dress coming to greet him. He forced a smile he didn't feel, trying to put on a pleasant face for the meddling gossip. It didn't take a genius to see Zoe had hated every second of their afternoon at the stables. She had barely talked to anyone, no matter how many people he introduced her to, and she'd made a point of keeping her distance from him – a clear statement to anyone watching that they were absolutely not together.

What could Jackson do? Force her to take his arm? Force her to smile just once at him in encouragement? He'd watched her closely, waiting for a sign that she liked him, wanted him closer. She'd given him nothing.

What the fuck was wrong with him?

Any other time he was confident and strong. He swept women off their feet with one look, swept them into his bed with one glance. He controlled what amounted to a culinary empire, had a deal on the table to produce a bunch of cooking shows, had chefs lining up to give him whatever he wanted, new restaurant proposals given up like some sort of temple-god offering for his approval. But one petite, achingly beautiful, incredibly sexy woman knocked the wits right out of him. Zoe left him tongue-tied to the point where he doubted himself, and he *never* doubted himself. He found himself watching everything he said and did, and analyzing every one of her actions.

'Hi, Marta,' he called, lifting his hand in greeting.

'How was your weekend?' the woman asked, her eyes darting to the side as if she could see around her head back toward the front door where Zoe had disappeared.

Jackson frowned. The woman was up to something. 'Fine. Lots of business. Keepin' busy.'

'Mm-hmm.' The dry tone sounded like a parent scolding a child. 'Fellows at your house, were they?'

Instantly understanding what she was about, he shook his head. Clearly, when the housekeeper had picked up Zoe's clothes, she'd told Marta that no one else was at his home. 'No, they canceled.'

'Oh.' Her dour face cleared with a look of surprise and she relaxed a little. 'I thought that might be the case.'

Jackson let her have her lie. 'I let Chef Matthews stay as my guest for the weekend so we could go over menu changes at the diner.'

'Mm, good idea. I've heard things.'

Jackson didn't encourage her. 'I have all those guest rooms so I might as well get some use out of them. Callie and the boys don't seem to make it out as much as I'd like.'

'How is your sister?'

'Just fine. I'll tell her you asked.' Jackson made a move to get into his truck. Marta pursued him. He paused, one leg inside. 'Was there something else?'

'You're a good boy, Jackson. You've done a lot for this town and for me, so I feel obligated to warn you. That Chef Matthews is looking to cook up more than a fried chicken steak if you know what I mean.'

Jackson dropped his foot down on the ground. 'I'm afraid I don't.'

'She's after your money,' Marta said.

'That's ridiculous.' Jackson laughed. 'Have you been watching soap operas again?'

'A letter came from a woman named Kat, postmarked New York. It indicated that this Kat is Chef Matthews' sister.'

Jackson nodded. He knew that. Zoe had told him all about her sisters.

'She indicated that she'd sent some fancy clothing to help draw your notice so Chef Matthews could snag a rich man like this Kat had done.' Marta reached out to touch his arm. 'You should be careful.'

'Kat wrote you this?' he asked.

'No, she wrote it to her sister.'

Jackson lifted a brow at the admission.

'What?' Marta demanded. 'You can never be too careful when dealing with outsiders. You have to protect yourself. I need to know what type of person is staying in my home. What if she were some kind of criminal? Or a murderer? You know women can be murderers, too.'

'Marta,' Jackson stopped her, his tone urging her to focus.

'She's after your wallet, Jackson, and having her out at your house, alone, is a recipe for disaster. No good can come of it. What if she gets you drunk and seduces you and then says she's pregnant. You can't imagine what some girls will do to trap a rich –'

'Marta,' Jackson said, ending the woman's tirade before it could get going into a full rant. 'Thank you for your concern and your information. I can assure you there is nothing to worry about. I hire chefs to cook all the time and know how to handle them.'

'I know you do.' Marta patted him again. 'You're a good boy, Jackson. Say hi to your momma for me.'

'Will do.' He climbed into the truck, automatically starting the engine and putting it into drive. He knew Marta to be a gossip, but she was a good person and wouldn't deliberately make up stories to hurt someone. Zoe had succumbed to him rather quickly. Was it all part of an act? He knew she wanted a career, a career he could give her. Did she see him as an opportunity for more? Or was the career enough? He'd known she wanted something from him, but he hadn't wanted to think too hard on it.

Feeling Marta watching, he took his foot off the brake and let the truck roll down the street. He didn't look back as he took a long route out of town, needing time to think.

Zoe waited until she saw Marta outside by the clothesline hanging sheets before sneaking out the front door. She'd changed her shoes, opting for flat sandals. After heels on uneven dirt, her feet ached and the comfortable footwear was a welcome change. While she was inside the day had turned humid, causing her undershirt to stick as she walked down the block.

Nearing the restaurant, she slowed. Cars lined the street in front of it. Through the window, she saw every seat in the place was full. Almost hesitantly, she opened the front door. Lively talk assaulted her, punctuated by laughter and the sounds of people dining. As the bells rang over her head, eyes turned toward her and she imagined everyone stopped talking for the briefest of seconds.

Zoe nodded at the room in general, but for the most part everyone went back to ignoring her. She slowly made her way back to the kitchen, pausing when she saw Sheryl sitting at one of the booths with a couple of her regulars who came in during the week. The woman frowned at her, leaning toward those at her table to whisper something. Ignoring her, Zoe went back into the kitchen.

Rich smells wafted over her as she went through the door. It was hard to pinpoint exactly what was cooking, but she detected the aroma of fresh bread, beef and sautéed mushrooms. A woman came from the storage room, holding a bag of flour. Her short dark hair framed her pretty face. Small wrinkles lined her eyes and mouth. Her burgundy T-shirt and blue jeans were protected by a full white apron with little cherries embroidered on the right hip.

Seeing Zoe, she stopped. 'Hello.'

'Hi.' Zoe held out her hand. 'I'm Zoe Matthews, the new weekday chef.'

'Ah.' The woman nodded, laughing softly. The sound was amused, but not cruel. She pointed at her chest. 'Constance. I'm the weekend cook – this weekend anyway. Next weekend I'll be out of town and Maybelle will be here filling in.'

'What is that delicious smell?' Zoe asked, unable to keep from walking over to the range. Mushrooms sizzled in a brown sauce. She took a deep long breath.

'Smothered steaks are warming in the oven. Big pot is goulash.' Constance put the bag of flour on the counter where she already had ingredients in a mixing bowl. 'And over here I'm making dumplings, which I'll cook with the beef stock and mushrooms over there for dinner.'

'Do you mind if I watch?' Zoe asked, as Constance dumped flour into the bowl without measuring.

'If you're in the kitchen, you'll have to make yourself useful. You can start by peeling potatoes.' Constance motioned to the end of the table where a bag of potatoes waited. 'We're going to need a lot of them. I don't cook like Bob.' She paused. 'That's the guy you replaced. His secret was to mix instant potatoes with the mashed so the real potatoes went further. My momma would roll over in her grave, rise up and smack me if I were to do that.'

Zoe chuckled. 'I would've liked your mom.'

'Well, these are all her recipes, passed down my family line. If you want to learn, you best watch because I'm sworn to silence on them. Only my daughters will be told the secrets.'

Zoe smiled, up to the challenge of figuring it out. 'Got an extra apron?'

'Twenty-seven missed calls.' Zoe frowned, reading her cell phone as she walked from the restaurant back to the bed and breakfast. The first twenty numbers belonged to Kat and the last seven belonged to her mother.

Cooking all day with Constance had been a crash course in Southern cuisine. Though the woman had stayed true to her oath and hadn't revealed any family recipes, she'd been more than willing to share local ones. She'd gotten so busy learning, she'd forgotten all about calling her sister. Dialing voice mail, she put the phone to her ear.

'Hi Zoe, did you get my box? Just checking in,' Kat's first message said.

'Hey, Zoe, I've been trying to get you all day. Where are you? Call me.' The second message from Kat was a little more insistent.

Kat sounded frantic by the third. 'Zoe? Seriously, it's been two days. Where are you? I'm starting to worry. All these backwoods murder scenarios are going through my head. I need you to call me.'

Number four was simply, 'Don't make me fly down there, Zoe.'

The last message was from her mother, Beatrice. 'Zoe, honey, this is your mother. Kat's worried about you, but I did a reading and know you're fine. Make sure you call her. It's not good for new mothers to worry. Oh, and by the way, how is your weekend going? I see here it's going to be a really telling one.' Zoe grimaced, knowing her mother had been looking at an empty teacup as she'd spoken. The knowing tone made her shiver, though Zoe was used to her mother's purported premonitions and cryptic comments. 'Do tell me about him when you call me back and don't worry, I won't say a word until you do. I'll talk to you later, honey.'

To anyone else, the message would have sounded dead-on like some sort of love-life fortune reading. But Zoe knew her mother kept it just vague enough to be read into – or at least that's the conclusion she and her sisters had come to. Though there were times when Zoe wondered.

Not wanting to worry her sister, she hit the speed dial and called. Getting Kat's voice mail, she left a quick message telling her sister she was all right and hadn't called because she'd been without her phone. Flipping it closed, she walked several steps before opening it again. Zoe pushed a few buttons, looked at her mother's name, shut the phone, felt guilty and then opened it once more to call her.

'Hi, honey!' her mother said, sounding like her normally enthusiastic self. Very unconventional, Beatrice Matthews had always marched to her own peculiar tune. Yet there was something about her that drew others in. She could find someone to talk to no matter where she was and she'd learn their entire life story in one setting. 'I'm so glad you called, though you're a little late. Everyone just left.'

Zoe had completely forgotten that today was Sunday, the day her family always got together at their parents' house.

'Well, almost everyone. Ella is home. I think something is wrong with her, but she won't talk. I don't know if the navy is working out for her. She went out with some friends this evening.' Beatrice paused.

Zoe took the opportunity to get in, 'Hi, Mom.'

'Hi, honey,' Beatrice said. 'Did you call your sister? She's really worried.'

'Yes, but she didn't answer. I left her a message. I'm fine, everything's fine –'

'I know, honey, I –'

'Ah, Mom,' Zoe groaned. 'I'm tired. Please don't.'

'Tired?' Beatrice asked. Her tone became higher-pitched. 'Any reason?'

'I've been cooking.' It wasn't a lie, just not the whole truth. But there was no way she was telling her mom about her torrid weekend at a Southern plantation. Whenever she got back to New York, the entire city would know about what she'd done with Jackson.

'You know, your father would really enjoy going to South Carolina. He's heard there's fishing there. Any chance there'd be a reason for us to come down and visit you?'

Knowing her mother was probing, Zoe sighed. After so many girls, their parents had given up on ever having sons – though they remained hopeful for five sons-in-law. With Kat and Megan's marriages, plus the recent birth of Mariah, it stood to reason that their parents should have been content. But it wasn't so. Her father, Douglas, was a retired English professor, as serious as his wife was flighty. He'd worked at several private schools, most prestigiously Harvard. He never overtly said anything about sons-in-law, but left the prodding to his wife.

'Um, not really,' Zoe said, hiding her laugh as she gave her mother an answer she wouldn't want to hear. At the very least, Beatrice would have expected her to say something along the lines of, 'You never need a reason to visit me, Mom.' And Zoe would have, too, if she hadn't known her mother would be on a flight down the very next morning with even such little prompting.

Clearly disappointed, Beatrice's tone fell. 'Hmm, all right, have your mystery for now.'

'I have to go, Mom,' Zoe lied. Marta was sitting on the porch, sipping a cup of tea, her hawk eyes staring at Zoe as she neared the front sidewalk leading up to the house.

'I love you, honey,' Beatrice said.

'I love you, too,' Zoe answered, and flipped her phone to end the call. Glancing at Marta, she mustered a smile. 'Hello.'

'Talking to your boyfriend?' the woman asked, rocking back slightly on her chair as she held her teacup in front of her chin.

Zoe gave a short laugh, not feeling any humor, especially when she thought about the woman going through her box from Kat. 'Goodnight, Marta.'

'Goodnight, dear.' The woman continued rocking.

Zoe went inside to hide out the rest of the evening in her room. With any luck, her racing mind would shut off long enough to help her sleep.

Zoe started her second week as *Renée*'s new chef with a renewed sense of purpose. Instead of foisting her 'city girl' fine dining on the country folk, she was going to give them what they were used to – only better. With Constance's words in her head, she planned her menu as she prepped for the day. As she'd promised, the weekend cook had left a recipe book of Southern classics on the back desk for Zoe to look over. Monday would have to be trout, because that's what she had in the walk-in fridge. Luckily, though, the grocery would bring whatever else she needed for the rest of the week.

She decided on trout with a simple butter and garlic seasoning, breaded with cornmeal and sautéed to flaky perfection, homemade garlic mashed potatoes and green beans with bacon and sea salt for flavour. By the time Sheryl arrived, she had breakfast prepped and lunch well on the way. The waitress snorted a greeting, saying nothing as she went about her work. Monday breakfast wasn't too busy – mostly coffee drinkers ordering pancakes and eggs with the occasional toast. Every time the front door bell rang, Zoe found herself looking to see if it was Jackson. She didn't expect him, had no reason to, but after their weekend together she had strange fantasies of him stopping by, of him sending flowers, of calling – something – but got nothing.

Mid-afternoon, she called an order in for the rest of the week. Lunch and then dinner rolled by, not terribly busy but with some special orders of her trout. She gave generous portions to get rid of all the fish in stock. As the last customer left, taking Sheryl with him, she stayed alone in her kitchen spending extra time cleaning, hoping Jackson would show. As she took trash out to the dumpster, she searched the alleyway for his truck, hoping he'd offer to help so she didn't have to go near where the snake had been. He didn't and she was forced to face the fear, kicking her feet to make noise as she ran to the bin, threw in the trash, and ran back to the kitchen.

Finally, unable to make excuses to wait any longer, she locked up and made the trek back to the bed and breakfast. Almost hating how pathetic she was being, she found herself watching the street for headlights. A few teenagers rolled by, their music as loud as their laughter. One of the boys yelled to her, his words lost in the fast whiz of the passing engine.

Three days and still he resisted going to see her.

Jackson tilted his beer, taking a long pull from the bottle

as he stared at his backyard. Everywhere he went in his house, he imagined Zoe. Fantasies of her danced in his head, teasing his senses and making his cock fill with hard desire. Distraction caused him to zone out during important meetings. Desire made him scream into his pillow in frustration, even as he tried to work a release out for himself. And something he couldn't quite describe curled inside him, making him fear what Marta had told him, making him desperate to see Zoe and terrified that he would go to her.

That was something he shouldn't do. Each time he looked at her, he felt himself closer to saying something he would only come to regret. Thinking of it, his hand shook and he balled it into a fist, while continuing to grip his beer with the other one. He couldn't face her just yet, not until he knew he could control what he would say to her.

His eyes drifted to the folder in front of him. Inside was an article that had been faxed to him the night before by the editor-in-chief of the premier culinary magazine *Chef d'oeuvre*. The article called Chef Matthews a culinary diamond – but it wasn't finished. They wanted a quote from him about her cooking, why he had hired her, why he hadn't told anyone he was doing it. The author of the article, Josine Gray, referred to Zoe as his secret up-and-comer. Her list of questions for him speculated that he had big plans for his little diamond.

If it had been anyone else, such news would have made him proud because he had discovered a new talent, but Zoe? Why couldn't he muster any happiness for her achievement? She'd earnt it with her cooking, all on her own and in less than a week. Perhaps all she'd needed was a shot, her chance, and he'd given it to her. All her dreams were starting to come true, with that article right there in its blank folder – if he just gave Josine the right answers.

Jackson took another drink, finishing his beer, hating the part of him that wanted to say that what Josine had eaten was a fluke; Zoe was only a diner cook, a nobody going nowhere. No one would question his word. The article would go away. Zoe would never know and then she couldn't leave Dabery, not yet, not until he was ready to let her go.

Jackson closed his eyes, leaning his head back in his chair as the warm night air whispered around his features. The insects seemed too quiet, especially for such a fine evening. He wouldn't go and see her tonight.

Zoe sighed. The third week was half over and though she spent her days in a building with an endless stream of people, she had never felt so alone. Taking Jackson's advice, she tried to smile at everyone through the pick-up window. It worked because a few smiled back. None made conversation and Sheryl didn't count because nothing she said was much better than a curse. Travis tried, but he was just a kid and they had no common ground on which to converse.

Where was Jackson? Why hadn't he come? Why hadn't he called? A week and a half had passed since he had contacted her. A week and a half since the weekend they'd shared.

She hit her hand against the table, gripping the chicken bones. She'd prepared a broth to make chicken and dumplings for Thursday's special. She'd boiled them all day, making them easier to debone. She took the meat and threw it into the big stockpot.

Fuck him. She didn't need to see him anyway, not if he was going to treat her like some whore who he screwed and then discarded until he was horny again. With venom, she threw one bone into the trash and grabbed another piece to tear at it in frustration.

But did she have a right to be mad? It wasn't like she'd demanded a relationship, demanded he'd treat her like a girlfriend or even a lady. She'd gone to him eagerly, desperate to touch him, to have him inside her. The memory of his touch made her body ache. Her nipples swelled against her tight undershirt with the built-in bra, and her pussy nearly wept with cream at the thought of being filled. Even now, she could remember his smell, the taste of his wine-tinted kiss.

'I need you to cook for me.'

Zoe nearly screamed with fright at the demanding words. She would have recognized his voice anywhere, even hoarse as it was now. Turning, she placed her hand over her heart to glare at Jackson's face through the pick-up window. Unable to answer right away, she turned back to finish deboning the chicken. The metal door swung open.

'Kitchen's closed. Try coming back during business hours,' she answered, scooping up the last of the meat and throwing it into the pot using a little too much force. Liquid splashed out of the side, running onto the table. With a brush of her hand, she swept the bones into the trash can.

'Are you upset?' he asked, sounding surprised.

'No, of course not,' she lied. Zoe told herself not to tell him, to play it cool like Kat would, to be confident like Megan. She failed. 'I often spend an entire weekend fucking someone only to be ignored for weeks afterwards.'

'I'm sorry?' His words weren't an apology so much as a request for clarification.

'Yes, you are,' she mumbled, her temper beginning to

flare. At least when she'd got pissed at Contiello, he hadn't acted surprised. He'd known he'd been an asshole and deserved her rage. Jackson had the gall to stand there with a stunned look of shock on his handsome face.

'Did I miss something?' He glanced around, as if that would help answer his question.

Zoe picked up the pot, struggling under its heavy weight as she carried it to the stove. She hadn't planned on heating it back up tonight, but the task gave her something to do with her hands, gave her a way to channel her frustration so she didn't turn the full force of it on him. 'I guess not,' she answered sarcastically.

'Will you stop for a moment and talk to me?' he asked.

'You ordered me to cook, boss,' Zoe said, turning the stove on with an angry jerk of her hand. 'So I'm cooking.'

'You're mad because I didn't call.' He leant against the table, arms crossed over his chest.

The obvious statement made her quirk a brow. 'No, I'm mad because you . . .' Zoe frowned. The not-calling part was most of it, but she wasn't in a mood to agree with him at all. 'You didn't treat me very well.' She picked up a rag and began cleaning furiously, wiping up the mess she'd made with the chicken.

'What do you mean?' Jackson demanded. His stricken look as she brushed past him made her pause in her tirade. Lifting the lid to check the stock, she absentmindedly threw down the rag. 'This isn't the 1800s, you could have called me. Should I be offended by the fact that you didn't try to get a hold of me?'

'That is beside the . . .' Zoe glowered at him in frustration. 'You're the man. It's your job. Besides, you're my boss. Like I'm going to call you socially.'

'My being your boss never came into play when we were

together. I never pressured you to . . .' He took a deep breath. 'I never forced you. Don't you dare cry –'

'Don't you dare finish that insulting sentence,' Zoe warned, lifting her finger. She paced to the counter to finish cleaning it and frowned when she couldn't see her rag.

'I'm sorry, that wasn't fair. A man in my position has to be careful about women who try to –'

'Don't you dare finish that one either.' Zoe frowned, eyeing the floor. To herself, she whispered, 'Where in the world did I put it?'

'I don't understand what it is we're fighting about or why,' Jackson said. 'I only came here to ask you to cook for me. I realized you'd never actually cooked a meal I could eat and I came to rectify that. If I'm to tell people about your cooking, I should be able to tell them I've sampled it.'

'Fine. Tomorrow's special is going to be chicken and dumplings – homemade, thanks to the recipe book Constance left for me. I'm afraid the roast I made for today is all gone. Sold every single last piece of it.'

'Really?'

'You don't have to sound so surprised.' Zoe frowned. 'Will tomorrow work? I'm tired. It's been a long day.'

'Of course. We'll do this later, during business hours.' Jackson looked as if he wanted to say more. 'I'll leave you be.'

He turned to go. Zoe felt an acute disappointment that he hadn't even tried to seduce her. She missed his touch, ached for it, and he was just going to leave? Not that she'd given him any reason to stay.

Stopping at the door, he pointed at the stove. 'I might have to miss tomorrow. You threw your rag in the pot.'

Zoe gasped, hurrying to her stock. On opening the lid,

she saw that the cleaning rag dancing atop the rolling boil. She cursed, hurrying to fish it out, even as she knew the stock was ruined and she'd have to start over. By the time she threw the rag into the trash, Jackson had left and she felt no better for having yelled at him.

After closing up, she went back to the bed and breakfast. A clean towel awaited her in the bathroom, having been laid out in one of Marta's nightly rituals. The woman had never once said Zoe had to bathe after work, but the small implications were there. Zoe didn't mind. She liked to shower the day's work off before bed.

As the hot water hit her flesh, she closed her eyes. She wished she could take back how she'd handled Jackson. Her words hadn't been lies. She had been hurt by his neglect over the last few days. That hurt had caused her to strike out in anger.

The soap trailing over her flesh caused her nerve endings to tingle as she thought of him. Why had she fought him? If she'd just played it cool, acted like she didn't care, she could have been with him right now, satisfying the fire burning deep inside her.

Touching herself was a bittersweet sensation next to the memory of Jackson's flesh, and no matter how she stroked her clit, dipping her fingers inside her slick pussy, she couldn't make herself come like he could. When she climaxed, the weak pleasure it gave caused her to cry out softly. Tonight, he hadn't even tried to make it better between them and it was quite possible that it'd be several more days before she saw him again.

Chapter Ten

'I like her. She's got spunk. Your dad would have liked her too.' Constance Levy eyed her son. 'A good, clever mind, too. Willing to learn and accept different things. I think you've done very well for yourself with this one.'

Jackson eyed his mother in turn, glad she was finally back in town so he could see her and ask her about Zoe. She'd been in Louisiana visiting relatives for the last week. He would have called her, but he'd wanted to have this conversation face to face, so he could read her expression. 'I don't remember asking for your advice.'

'Please.' She laughed, waving him to sit beside her at the glass table on her wooden deck. It was the house he'd grown up in, the first house his father had bought for them when they moved to Dabery. Jackson had helped add a couple of rooms onto it for his mother – a craft room and a dining room. He'd never offered to buy her a new home. She'd never take it. This was where the family's memories lived and it was where she would stay until the day she died. 'The first words out of your mouth the second you came out here were, "So you met the weekday cook," not a "Hello" or an "I love you, Momma" or "How was your trip? Did you enjoy yourself? How's the family?" You came here for the sole purpose of getting my advice about Zoe.'

'Marta says she's a gold-digger after a rich husband and I know for a fact that she's interested in me because of what I can do for her career.' Jackson sat and his mother automatically poured him an iced tea from the pitcher on the table. He didn't even try to deny her claim a second time. He was there for advice.

Besides the shorter cut of her hair and a few wrinkles, Constance looked as she had when they'd first moved in. There was an ageless beauty to her, a vitality and a quiet strength. She was a good mother and a fantastic grand-mother, spoiling his nephews terribly.

'Marta is a gossip. What evidence does she have of this besides her own boredom? The woman means well and must be tolerated for it, but I raised you smarter than to take someone like Marta's word as fact.' Constance sighed. 'As for Zoe's career, good for her.'

Jackson laughed. 'You want a woman to be with me because of what I can do for her?'

'Don't pretend you stole a frog's brain this morning. You know I want the best for all three of my children. But think of it this way. She is honest, told you about her career. Your father knew I wanted to work when we first met. He never stood in my way and I loved him for that. If there was a way he could help me, by God he did it.'

'She doesn't fit in here,' Jackson said.

'Maybe so, but if she fits with you does it matter? Jackson, ever since you were a boy you were too big for this town. I don't know why you always fought it. You had this natural curiosity. Remember those grand adventures you'd take Jeffery on?' Constance reached across the table and held his hands in hers. 'I know you love Dabery and it will always be home but, no matter how hard you try, the outside world will always call to you. No matter how many businesses you fix up, how many houses you refurbish, your wander-lust will come and bite you where the sun don't shine.'

'I don't think she'll ever fit with me. She doesn't seem interested and I don't want a woman who sees me as second to her career. Dad might have supported you working, but you never put him or us second to your careers.' Jackson smiled to himself. His mother had had many jobs over the years. He pulled his hands away and took a drink. The sweet flavor reminded him of being a kid, playing in the backyard with his brother, stealing sips out of his mother's glass when she wasn't paying attention. Changing the subject, he asked, 'Have you talked to Jeff? Are the wedding plans coming along? The photographer called me saying he wasn't answering his phone.'

'Why did he call you?'

'I hired him to take some photographs of the house a few months back,' Jackson explained. 'What's happening with Jeff?'

'There was a small hiccup.' Constance shook her head. 'Madelyn found out from the doctor that she can't have children. She told me she wanted to have herself checked out. You know about that accident when she was a kid. The doctors told her she could have a hard time conceiving because of the scar tissue.'

Jackson didn't speak, feeling terrible for the couple.

His mother continued, 'She tried to break it off to free your brother from such a fate. He whisked her away for a few days to convince her he didn't care.'

'Jeff always wanted lots of children,' Jackson said. 'Poor Madelyn, she seems like she'd be a great mother.'

'And perhaps they shall be parents yet. There's always adoption.' Constance pushed up from her chair and set her glass on the tray by the tea pitcher. 'Have no fear, the wedding will go on as planned. Have you asked Zoe to go yet?'

'What?' Jackson frowned, taking a big drink to hide his surprise before putting his glass on the tray. It was a mistake. He choked and ended up coughing violently. His mother merely laughed at him. Breathing hard, he asked, 'Why would I ask her to a family wedding?'

'To let the rest of the clan meet her. To stake claim, or whatever it is you men do. To take her out on a date. To let her know you take her seriously, aren't ashamed of her.' His mother lifted the tray and walked toward the sliding-glass door to the house.

Jackson thought of the fight they'd had. 'Did she talk to you about me? What did she say? Is this when you gave her the recipe book? Did she know you were my mother?'

Constance chuckled. 'You already know I met her. She came in a couple of Sundays back to pick up her phone and stayed to help me, plying me with questions about "Southern cuisine."' Her laughter deepened. 'I don't know about cuisine, but I described to her some of the local dishes and a few Cajun ones I'd learnt from your great-aunt Eliza. She's got what your gramma would have called a natural instinct in the kitchen. You did good giving her a chance and giving Bob some time off. It's good for Callie and the boys to get away. And, no, I didn't feel the need to tell her I was your mother.'

'Did she say anything to you about me?' Jackson asked, insistently.

'She said you gave her a chance at her dream and she's very grateful for it. You are helping her, aren't you? Because when I spoke to your sister, she said you were making some odd decisions.'

'Callie told you my plan, didn't she?' Jackson should've known. 'Why didn't you say anything about it?'

'What is there to say? So, are you going to do the honorable thing by her and help her out? Or are you still on your drunken mission to teach her a lesson?'

'Fine, it was a stupid idea.' Jackson didn't have many of them and he wouldn't admit it when he had to just anyone. 'And you know me, once I have an idea I don't back down from it. I got her down here and I gave her the job. I don't think I've really punished her, though. She wanted to cook in one of my restaurants and that's what she's doing. It'll look good on her résumé.'

'You are helping her out, aren't you? Not just dumping her in the diner for a few months while Bob's on vacation. What's next after Bob gets back?'

'That's up to her.'

'You are helping her.' This time it wasn't a question, but a motherly order.

'She helped herself. A couple of guys from California came into the diner with their wives. They were here to acquire horses for a movie and one of the wives just happened to be a reporter and critic for *Chef d'oeuvre* magazine. She impressed them. Apparently their cover story flopped and they needed a new angle to replace it. The reporter is pushing through an article about Zoe in the summer issue and the editor faxed me a preliminary copy to comment on. They called her a culinary diamond.'

'And what did you call her?'

Jackson sighed heavily. Part of him still didn't want the article to come out, but he refused to stand in her way. So finally, at three o'clock in the morning a couple of days after receiving the fax, he'd sent off his answers to Josine's questions. Simply, he replied, 'A chef.'

'Good for you, dumplin'. Can you believe what that jerk Contiello did to her?' Constance clucked her tongue.

'Shameful behavior. You think twice before ever considering hiring that man.'

'What did he do?' Jackson had to admit that he'd been curious, but it seemed a very touchy subject with Zoe. He doubted she'd tell him if he asked. Though to know she'd volunteered her story to his mother, a stranger she'd known less than a day, caused a great pain to wash over his chest.

'You don't know?' Constance came to the table and set the tray back down. 'Contiello tried to buy some of her original recipes. She told me about them and they sound great – especially the ranch sauce. I suggested she write her own cookbook. She said she has a journal she keeps them in, everything she's created since she was a little girl.'

'That's it?' Jackson's brow furrowed in question. 'He offered to buy her recipes?'

'I guess he offered an insultingly cheap price, like ten dollars a recipe, and when she said no, he got angry. He treated her like dirt, making her come into work early to take care of janitorial duties, making her clean the bathrooms while everyone else cooked for some big event, threatening her job. It all rings of blackmail if you ask me.'

'So he fired her?'

'From what I understand, she blew up at him and quit. I say good for her, but she says that it ruined her chance of getting another chef position until you came along.' Constance smiled at her son. 'I am so proud of you. You did a really good thing with Zoe. It's not fair that she lost everything because of one jerk.'

'To hear Contiello tell it, she tried to steal recipes from him.' Jackson had never really trusted Contiello's word.

'I don't know this Contiello, but I trust Zoe to be telling the truth.'

'How can you be so sure? You don't know her.'

Constance laughed. 'Because I raised three kids and I know when one of them is lying. She's about as bad at it as Callie is.'

'What did she lie to you about?' Jackson asked.

'I wouldn't say she lied so much as she wanted to lie. Instead she blushed profusely, babbled a little incoherently and quickly changed the subject.' Constance smirked, again lifting her tray to carry it inside.

'What was the question?' Jackson asked, getting up to follow his mom.

'What exactly it was she felt for you.' Constance grinned, sliding the door shut in her son's face. He reached for the handle, but his mother latched it, smirking at him through the glass.

'Momma?' he yelled as she walked away, leaving him in torment on purpose. He knocked on the door. 'Mother?! Mother! Get back here. Why did you ask her that? What happened?'

She didn't come back.

'*Mother!*'

'I'm here to pick up a pie.'

Zoe glanced up from the recipe book Constance had lent her, surprised to see someone standing in the kitchen who wasn't Sheryl, who pointedly ignored her anyway. The voice had the soft Southern charm expected of any belle, delicate and very feminine with a quality that made it impossible to tell the owner's age. The lady who carried it was young, thin and utterly débutante-perfect in her pink dress suit with white trim and matching high heels. Her dark hair swept up at the sides to fall in large curls down her back. Wide brown eyes looked bigger with the shading of eyeliner along the outside corners and her full lips bowed in a permanent pout. Zoe half expected to see delicate white gloves in place of the perfectly manicured hands. Two diamond rings graced her fingers, their gold bands as delicate as the lady wearing them.

'There is pie for me, isn't there? I don't know what I'll do if there isn't pie. Connie didn't come, did she? I thought she was running behind, that's why I'm here. Though, honestly ...' The woman had an unladylike laugh, a wild look coming to her eyes as she crossed deeper into the kitchen toward Zoe in the back. Her hands began to move frantically. 'I don't know what I'm doing here. I shouldn't be getting pie. I should be in some loony bin. Have you ever had one of those days?'

Zoe was almost afraid to answer. She was saved as the woman continued.

'I'll bet not. You look so collected. I've heard you're very collected. I'm a mess.' Suddenly, the woman's eyes welled with tears. 'Please tell me there's pie. I can't think straight and there has to be pie tonight. It's been planned for months.'

'Ah.' Zoe stood, grabbing a tissue from the box on the desk. She handed it to the woman. 'Do you need me to call someone?' *Like a psychiatrist?*

'What? No. I'm sorry, you're Zoe, right? I'm Maddy.' The woman looked at her like the name should mean something. It didn't.

'Let me check the walk-in for you,' Zoe said, thinking that maybe Sheryl had left something for the woman to pick up. It would be in character for the waitress not to tell her, just to make her look incompetent.

'Oh, thank you, shug,' Maddy said, following her. She toyed with her diamond earring, turning it slowly. 'I am normally not this frazzled, but I'm ...' Her eyes welled up again. 'I'm having one of those months. I'm supposed to be happy, but I – I don't need to bother you with this.'

'Found it,' Zoe said, uncomfortable with the situation. 'Found two, actually. Cherry crumb and strawberry rhubarb, is that right?'

'Yes, perfect! Thank you.' Zoe carried them out to the front of the diner, hoping the woman would take the hint and leave. 'Would you like me to carry them to your car?'

'Would you? You are such a peach.'

Zoe forced a smile, concentrating on making it look polite, but the truth was she was too tired to deal with some lady who'd forgotten to take her happy pills that morning. Maddy held the door open and led the way to a pink sports car parked out front. Zoe put the pies on the passenger seat.

'It's too bad you couldn't have gotten off today like Sheryl or I'd invite you to the party too.' Maddy waved, unaware of the bombshell she'd just dropped, and slipped into the driver's side of the car. As she pulled away from the curb, Zoe frowned. Sheryl was at a party? The waitress had told her she had to go to a doctor's appointment today.

'That bitch,' Zoe swore under her breath as she went back inside the quiet diner. It was Friday, one of their busiest nights, even though at the moment the streets were really quiet. Sheryl had left after the lunch crowd, abandoning Zoe to man the entire restaurant by herself for dinner. She wasn't looking forward to it, but she would manage. Most of Sheryl's customers were used to filling their own drinks anyway. They probably would have no problem picking up their own orders from the window.

Either that or she'd send Travis out to work the floor.

She headed to the back of the kitchen, sat down at the desk and picked up her pencil, preparing her orders for the following week. As she wrote, running her finger down the recipe for split-pea soup, she whispered, 'Parsley, celery, bay leaf, dried split peas ...' Next, she flipped to the earmarked page for potato soup and began the process again. 'More celery, more parsley, lots of potat –'

'Zoe?' Jackson's voice startled her and she dropped her pencil.

'Jacks – on.' Her breath caught as she looked at him. A bouquet of what looked to be two-dozen pink roses rested in one fist along his thigh. She slowly stood. Her gaze traveled down to the flowers and then up over his fashionable dark suit and silk blue shirt to his perfect eyes. 'What are you doing here?'

'Did Madelyn stop by?'

Zoe's eyes again went down to the flowers. Pink. Just like Maddy's dress, like her car, like her shoes. Jealous, she snorted softly, before turning back to her list to pretend to write. 'You mean the crazy lady? I hope you brought a straitjacket. You're going to need it.'

'Are you joking?' he asked, unsure.

'Look, if you like her that's great, but she is either on drugs or insane.' Zoe wrote the words 'drug,' 'insane' and 'bitch.' Anger boiled inside her. How dare he come here to meet up with a date? How dare he flaunt roses in front of her? 'Unless you like that sort of thing.'

Jackson stared at Zoe's back, unable to believe how mean she was being, and without cause. Sure, Madelyn had been a little upset and scattered lately, but she was a bride-to-be and that was normal under the best circumstances. He looked down at the flowers in his hand. The florist had only had pink because of his brother's wedding this weekend. Whatever Madelyn had ordered for decorations, Jackson had doubled it, slipping the florist cash in private to give his brother the fanciest wedding possible. He'd done the same for his sister and knew the man wouldn't tell. Jackson wasn't looking for acknowledgement; he merely wanted the best for his siblings. And Madelyn had had such a rough time of it, especially lately, that he wanted his new sister to feel like a true princess on her wedding day. Even now workers were at his house, setting up banquet tables along his stone porch and a gazebo in his backyard for the couple to get married under.

Now, looking at Zoe's turned back, hearing her horrible words, he gripped the flowers tighter. Irritation rolled through him at her words. He'd planned on giving the roses to Zoe and asking her to go with him, on a real date, to his brother's wedding. He wanted to show his family, the most important thing in his life, that he was serious about Zoe. And he wanted to show her that he wanted her in his life.

'She's had a rough time of it lately,' Jackson said through gritted teeth.

'If you say so.' She didn't look up as she continued to write on the yellow legal pad in front of her.

'I'll kindly ask you to stop speaking about my future sister-in-law like that and to show a little sensitivity if you happen to be around her again. Not only is she suffering normal wedding jitters, she just discovered she can't have children.' Jackson didn't know why he was telling her. Maybe because he knew she wouldn't tell anyone else. Her shoulders stiffened, but she didn't answer, didn't look at him. 'When she was thirteen her drunken stepdad ordered her to pick up something he'd dropped on the ground. To get it, she had to walk behind his stallion. It kicked her in the stomach and nearly killed her. I think this news is only the latest development of that long-ago accident.'

Zoe still didn't move.

'She told me a week ago that she wanted to have eleven kids, enough for a whole football team, with my brother. She dreamt of a large family and so did Jeff.' He sighed, tossing the pink roses into the trash can. 'So maybe you can muster up a little understanding.'

'Jackson,' she began, setting her pencil down.

'I came by to tell you I need you to run the kitchen at the wedding on Sunday. It's an all-day event. The food's been ordered. Staff are coming down from Columbia to work it.' Jackson didn't stop the lie, even as he knew he was telling it. Family was everything to him and he wanted her to be part of that, but she had insulted his future sister, a woman with a good heart. Her cutting comments reminded him of the first time he'd met her in the bar. No matter who he was, what he did, Jackson felt as if he'd never be good enough for her. Was it because he wasn't a New Yorker? Was it his accent? His clothes? His manners? He'd been all over the world and the person he was never offended other people, never put anyone off. Or was it something more, something he didn't want to admit? Was it just the fact that Zoe could never come to care for him? To love him?

Love.

The word echoed through him, making it hard to breathe. The pain ripped him in two and left his heart for dead. He loved her. And knowing she didn't feel the same way, not even close, left him numb.

'I'll send someone to give you a ride tomorrow night so

you can go over the menus and schedule and make your plans. Do you think you can handle that?'

'Yes.' The word was soft, but he heard it clearly.

'Lock up and go home. Everyone's at the party. There'll be no customers tonight. Sheryl should have told you.' Jackson left, not really feeling like a party, but as the best man he needed to be there for his brother. He walked away, not knowing why he was tormenting himself. This time he couldn't blame liquor for the rash decision to bend her to his will by using cooking.

'Kat, I need you,' Zoe said into the phone, not knowing why she was whispering but afraid that Marta might be lurking outside her bedroom door, listening. 'I don't know what's wrong with me. I open my mouth and these words just spew out. Every time I look at Jackson I get upset. I try to play it cool, try to act like a modern woman, but I can't do it.'

'You really care for him, don't you?' Kat answered. 'You did the same thing in high school whenever Bobby Henison came around. You had a crush on him so you ignored him and treated him like he was a nuisance if he said anything to you.'

'Bobby? I didn't have a crush on –'

'Oh, please,' Kat drawled. 'You so know Megan read our diaries.'

Zoe gasped. 'How did she find mine? I had it hidden beneath a floorboard under my dresser.'

Kat laughed. 'I'm convinced she hid in our closets and watched us with that little notebook of hers.'

Zoe sighed. 'Fine. I liked Bobby Henison, but this isn't about Bobby. I don't ignore Jackson, I yell at him – twice already. The first time I told you about, when I said he didn't treat me very well because he hadn't called me after we spent that weekend together.'

'Did you call him?' Kat asked, her tone light.

'We've been over this.' Zoe grimaced. 'It was his place to call me.'

Kat chuckled. 'Ah, sorry, babes, but this isn't some historical romance. Girls are allowed to call boys. Did you ask him to call? Indicate that you wanted to see him right away?'

'No,' Zoe mumbled in dejection.

'There you have it. What about the second time? What did you get mad about? You didn't say anything that would cause permanent damage, did you?'

Zoe cringed. 'I got jealous and called his future sister-in-law something along the lines of a crazy escaped from an asylum. And I never make fun of people with mental problems.' A tear slid over her cheek. 'I was just so frustrated.'

'You were jealous of his sister-in-law?'

'Future sister-in-law,' Zoe corrected. 'And it was before I knew who she was. I saw him holding these pink roses and he asked about her. I just assumed he had a date.'

'He brought you flowers?' Kat gave a girly sigh.

Zoe rolled her eyes before resting her gaze on the pattern of the comforter. She traced her finger along a wrinkle, kicking her feet in the air as she rested on her stomach. 'He never said who they were for. He just threw them in the trash and left after telling me I was in charge of the woman's wedding this weekend.'

'He brought you flowers,' Kat repeated, this time as a definite statement. 'Did you take them out of the trash and keep them?'

'No.' Zoe glanced over to the single pink rose on her

nightstand. 'Anyway, it's at his house. He's sending a car around tonight to pick me up.'

'OK, so you're going tonight. That's perfect. More than likely, at least part of the wedding party will be staying out there too. It'll give you a chance to either get in good with his brother the groom or to become best friends with the bride.'

'But I'm not charming like you are,' Zoe protested.

'Shut it!' Kat demanded. 'Listen to me. You are going to go in there and pretend it's like one of those benefits you used to go to for your job. You'll wear that pretty blue dress I sent you and an even prettier smile. If you think of it like work, you'll make the effort to talk to everyone. I've seen you in the zone. You can do this.'

'And how do I handle Jackson?'

'I don't know him, but I do know men. If he brought you roses, it means something. You two fought before that, so he must have been trying to make up. It's unfortunate you didn't listen to what he had to say, but it's not unfixable. The ball is in your court. You're going to briefly apologize and then drop it, instantly changing the subject so it's in the past and can't be dragged out into another argument.'

'Then what?' Zoe asked.

'I can't tell you everything. Try being honest.'

'I don't know if I can risk it. I'm nervous, Kat.' Zoe rolled onto her back, staring at the ceiling. The afternoon light glowed softly across it, highlighting the tiny bumps. She'd spent most of the day in her room, only going down for Marta's breakfast of toast and eggs after the woman's insistent knocking. Lunch had been delivered on a tray to her room – a bowl of chicken noodle soup and a grilled cheese sandwich. The soup had come from a can and the cheese had been a cheap sandwich square with not enough milk and too much oil. With reluctance, she'd eaten every bite. Thinking of it made her stomach ache and she gently rubbed her hand across her ribcage.

'Then be partially honest, but start by being nice to him and his family,' Kat said.

'I wish you were here. I need someone on my side.'

'You'll be all right, Zoe, I promise. You're a good person. They'll see that.'

'I just miss you all.' Loneliness washed over her. 'Everyone here worships Jackson as the town hero. I have no one.'

'Do you need a nap?' Kat sighed heavily into the phone. 'Because you're starting to sound depressed and that is not the Zoe I know. Get some rest before tonight. You'll feel better.'

'OK,' Zoe mumbled. She hadn't slept too well. The nap would probably do her good.

'Oh, and I miss you, too.'

Being back at Jackson's house brought forth a rush of memories, vivid recollections of what they'd done, so potent they made Zoe blush heavily. The surroundings tempted her back into their fairy-tale world, a place where Jackson had been hers, even if only for a short while. As she looked at his front door, her body heated up, cream dampening her panties. A shiver worked its way over her entire being. Would they be alone tonight? Would he seduce her? Would she let him?

The same driver that had picked her up from the airport drove her to his home and dropped her off. She was too ashamed to ask his name a second time, so found herself calling him 'sir.' Turning to lift her hand in farewell, she waited there until he was down the drive.

She knocked on the door, gripping the handle to Marta's floral suitcase. The woman had insisted she use it again. Zoe waited several minutes before the door was answered.

Madelyn poked her head out, grinning. A light haze to her eyes showed that she'd been drinking heavily. Seeing Zoe, she eagerly waved her in. Her white linen dress featured tiny embroidered pink roses. 'Hello, shug! I'm so glad you could make it. I can't tell you how much this means to me. When Jackson said the caterer he'd hired had come down with the flu, I almost had a nervous breakdown. Oh, look at that dress!' The woman's eyes drifted down over the blue, black and green of Zoe's strapless dress. The velvet bodice had a sequin motif with embroidered floral pattern, a sweetheart neckline and boning to form. Beads embellished the inset waist, leading to a printed chiffon skirt with a gold-striped ruffled hem. 'So cute! Is that chiffon?'

Zoe nodded. 'I believe so.'

'It's gorgeous. I love chiffon.' Madelyn waved her hand for Zoe to follow. 'Everyone is in back checking out the decorations. Tonight it's just the wedding party and family.' She paused, grabbing Zoe's arm. 'I can't believe tomorrow's the wedding. I thought I'd be more nervous than I am, but then I've had a lot to drink.'

'It's early yet,' Zoe said. 'You're allowed to party before the big day.'

'I so agree.' The Southern drawl deepened. 'Everything is set. All that's left is to show up. Well, everything is set now that we have you.' Madelyn again stopped, halting their progress near the stairwell. She patted Zoe's arm. 'You are such a lifesaver. I would have panicked, but you seem so competent. Jefferson's mother says great things about you.'

'She does?' Zoe asked, surprised. 'I don't think we've even been introduced.'

'Really? Constance said you two cooked together while she had the shift at the diner.' Madelyn looked confused.

'Constance is Jackson's mother?' Zoe asked, before she could stop the question.

'She didn't tell you?' Madelyn laughed. 'That sounds like Connie all right. Anyway, she says you're capable and that's good enough for me. Plus Jackson likes you.'

It was a small confession, but one that gave her immense pleasure.

'Just as long as you don't try to make something like ground-turkey-based sauce on green noodles. The first caterer I interviewed suggested that. I suggested we try elsewhere. Disgusting. Actually, the menu is already planned. I hope that's all right with you. Everything's ordered and I believe started. Oh!' She covered her mouth. 'There I go again. I promised Jackson I'd let him handle it and I'm babbling like a ninny. Come on, let's join the party.'

Outside, miles of tulle and pink satin covered Jackson's backyard from the distant gazebo surrounded by long rows of chairs, to the stairs and stone banister, over the round tabletops and chairs and the long bar. Light from inside the long windows shone over the covered porch, mingling with the soft play of evening stars and moonlight. Madelyn turned, grinning widely like a little girl just named princess for the day. Her eyes sparkled with excitement and pleasure.

'Zoe, I want you to meet my Jefferson.' Madelyn motioned to a younger, sloppier version of Jackson. Long floppy hair brushed around the man's shoulders and an air of playfulness lined his brown eyes.

'Hey, Zoe, I've heard so much about you.' Jefferson didn't stand from his place at one of the tables near the bar, merely lifting his beer in her direction. Cards were dealt around the tabletop. Next to him sat Constance and a woman who had to be Madelyn's mother. Across from her was an older man who was most likely Madelyn's stepfather. Zoe remembered the story about how he'd drunkenly gotten Madelyn hurt as a child, resulting in the woman's current troubles. It was impossible to tell if he was drinking by the glass of tomato juice in front of him. It could have been a mixed drink for all Zoe knew. Madelyn didn't appear to be holding a grudge for that long-ago event as she went to take a seat next to him.

'Zoe.' Jackson's voice sounded at her side. She felt his hand brush her elbow, guiding her forward. She looked up at him, her heart pounding wildly at his nearness. Shadows crept across his face, but she'd remembered every detail of it and didn't need light to remind her how handsome he was. 'This is my sister, Callie.' He motioned to the woman next to Madelyn's mother. 'And her husband, Bob. The boys are upstairs asleep.'

'So you're the little schemer who stole my job, eh?' Bob said, frowning.

Zoe felt the color draining from her features. 'Ah, well, I ...'

'Oh, Bob.' Callie laughed, hitting him lightly. 'Don't tease. She doesn't know you're joking.'

Bob suddenly grinned, standing to offer Zoe his chair. 'Do you play?'

At Jackson's gentle push at her back, indicating she should join them, she asked, 'What's the game?'

'Bullshit,' Jefferson said. When Zoe shook her head to show she didn't know it, but sat in the proffered chair anyway, he continued, 'We deal all the cards out and the object is to get rid of your hand in the discard pile. One person starts, discarding one or more cards on the pile. The first player discards aces, the next twos, one after threes and it continues around. Since the cards are face down, you don't have to play the cards you are calling out. If another player suspects you are discarding a card out of rank, they yell ...'

'*Bullshit!*' the group screamed in unison, giggling profusely.

Zoe laughed. 'Sounds simple enough. Deal me in. I'll learn the rest as we go.'

'I remember you like red.' Jackson slid a wine glass in front of her on the table. He then moved a chair and sat next to her.

'Ah, Jackson has a girlfriend,' Callie teased, pretending to study the cards being thrown in front of her.

'Callie!' Constance scolded. 'Don't embarrass Zoe.'

'It's all right.' Zoe glanced at Jackson before quickly looking away. 'I have four sisters. I doubt she can say anything to upset me.'

'Don't tempt her,' Jackson said.

'Hey!' Callie took an ice cube out of her glass and tossed it at him.

The game started and Zoe learnt quickly, despite the fast pace at which they played. She took Kat's advice, making a point of smiling at every person around the table. After a couple of hands, she found it easy because they were all very likable. She wasn't sure about Madelyn's father, who she learnt was named Hank, because the red liquid was indeed liquor. As her eyes adjusted in the dim light, she detected the red lines on his bulbous nose, giving away the fact that he was still a drunk.

With each passing hand, each loud bout of laughter, Jackson's leg moved closer to hers under the table. The light touch tested her response and she didn't pull away, letting him know she wanted him touching her. A few times his hand brushed her thigh, moving dangerously close to her sex before pulling back.

'All right, kids,' Constance announced. 'It's getting late and we have a long day tomorrow.' Everyone automatically stood, except Jackson, who busied his hands picking up the card decks and separating them into two piles. 'Oh, don't bother with that tonight. I'll take care of it later.'

'I've got it,' he said, glancing in her direction. 'You all go to bed. Zoe can help me pick up the drinks.'

'All right.' Constance leant over and kissed his head. 'Goodnight.'

A chorus of goodnights and sweet dreams rang around the group as they made their way in, some stumbling, others laughing. Zoe reached for the beer bottles on the table, pulling them toward her.

'You really don't have to pick up,' Jackson said. 'I just wanted to get you alone.'

'I don't mind.' Zoe blushed. Jackson had ensured she'd kept a full glass and, as she lifted the wine bottle he'd set on the table, she realized she'd drunk over half of its heady contents.

'Come here,' Jackson said, pulling her onto his lap. The thick press of his erection nudged her outer thigh. 'As you can see I couldn't exactly stand up when everyone was here.'

'Jackson, I need to apologize to you.' She touched his cheek, looking deep into his eyes. 'I shouldn't have said those things about Madelyn and I shouldn't have yelled at you.'

He opened his mouth to answer, but Zoe didn't let him speak. She crushed her mouth down on his. The almost bitter taste of beer mingled with the wine on her lips. Heat whispered across her cheek when he sighed. His arms wrapped around her waist, pulling her closer.

When they parted, she took Kat's advice and quickly changed the subject, leaving her apology and their fight in the past. 'I like your family. They're very nice people.'

'I have a small confession of my own.' He paused, nuzzling her throat. 'All the guest rooms are taken. Even the library is overrun with my nephews playing camp-out.'

'And where does that leave me? Sleeping in the kitchen?' Her lashes shaded her eyes as she looked at his mouth.

'I think we'll be more comfortable in my room.' He touched her chin, nudging it up so she was forced to look into his eyes. 'No one will know you're staying with me. Everyone is so preoccupied with the wedding they won't think twice about it and you can sneak out while they're getting ready for the ceremony.'

Zoe's nature reeled against the idea, but she wanted to be with Jackson more. Too much time had passed since he'd touched her. 'I don't care if people know. I want to be with you.'

Tension ran over her as she awaited his response. Jackson's smile came slowly, but it did come, curling his sexy mouth with pleasure. 'I want to be with you, too. I've wanted to be with you since I first saw you. I ...'

'Go on,' she urged, relaxed by the wine, seduced by his nearness.

Jackson hesitated. 'Ah ... ?'

'How come, if we're not having sex or going to have sex soon, you hardly talk to me? Like at lunch.'

'What lunch?'

'That afternoon, here, when we dined. You sat there reading your paper.' She pulled back, still feeling his arousal next to her. 'You barely spoke to me. And when you did it was a lecture. Then, at the restaurant, you didn't even try to make it better between us. You just left.'

'Why do you care? After we have sex you act like nothing has happened, like it's nothing to you either way,' he countered. 'Besides, what am I supposed to say?'

'I . . .' Zoe knew what she wanted him to say, but would not force him.

'What am I supposed to say?' he repeated. 'When everything I want to say I can't.'

'Like what?' She held very still, breathless and waiting. Her eyes moved to his lips, in case she missed a single utterance.

'Like . . .' His grip on her waist tightened. The night air fell away, as did the humming insects. 'Like I care for you.'

The soft words made her doubt what she was hearing. 'Really?'

'Yes, damn it.' This time his words were forceful, angry. 'I care for you, Zoe, and I'm tired of pretending I don't.'

'I care for you, too, Jackson.' Their lips met and happiness exploded over Zoe at his admission.

Chapter Eleven

Jackson led Zoe up the stairs, taking her quietly to his room. He gripped her suitcase, carrying it for her. His feet whispered past the closed doors to the guest rooms. They didn't speak, sneaking like hurried teenagers to the master bedroom. As the door clicked softly behind him, he dropped her suitcase and turned to pull her into his arms.

Her lips tasted of wine and the heady liquor only added to his desire to kiss her. Passion had always coursed between them, but this time it went deeper. She cared for him. For the first time with her, Jackson felt hope – hope for the future, for them, for something more happening.

He grabbed her hips, pulling her hard against him, letting her feel the full length of his cock. His erection pressed into her, stiff and aching for release. He rocked his hips in a steady rhythm. Groaning, he said, 'I want to be inside you.'

'I want you inside me,' she whispered.

Jackson couldn't help the smile crossing his lips. Her lids were heavy over her eyes and he slid a hand down to reach beneath her skirt. The warmth of her pussy called to him and he worked a finger beneath the lace he found guarding it. He walked her back until she was trapped against his door. Rubbing her clit in small circles, he moaned as her cream flooded his finger. Zoe gasped, her mouth opening wide as he thrust one finger inside, then quickly joined it with a second. He worked it along her slit, leaning into her to keep her upright against the door.

'You feel so good.' His words sounded gruff, even to his ears. He didn't think, just acted. 'Tell me you want this. Beg me to fuck you.'

Zoe grabbed his shoulders, kneading her fingers hard into the muscle. Her hips rocked, meeting his thrusting hand. 'Yes.'

'Say it. I want to hear you say you want me. I want you to beg me to make you come.' He bit lightly at her neck. 'Talk dirty to me.'

'Yes,' she breathed, pushing harder along his hand so that she rubbed her clit on his palm. 'I want you to fuck me. Take me. Make me come. Give me your big hard cock.'

Her words nearly made him come there and then. Still he resisted pulling down his pants. Her hand slid down his arm, reaching to cup his dick and balls. He groaned, his breathing harsh.

'Oh, yeah,' she moaned, a truly feminine sound that curled his toes. 'That's it. I want you to ...' She hesitated, as if trying to think what to say next. 'I want you to do whatever you like with me. However you like. I'll do anything for you.'

'Mm, that's good.' He moved his cock against her massaging hand. 'You like me taking control, don't you?'

'Yes.'

'First, you're going to come on my hand.' He finger-fucked her harder. 'Next, you're going to undress me and tie me up on the bed with my silk ties. I want you to suck my dick so I can watch.'

Zoe came hard against his hand. Jackson crushed his mouth to hers, silencing her would-be cry of pleasure. He pulled back, taking his shirt off and throwing it aside. Despite what he'd said he couldn't wait for her to undress him, so he made quick work of his clothes himself. She kicked off her shoes before stumbling toward his closet. He grinned, knowing she was going to obey him.

Zoe fingered the rack of ties, from satins to silks, all stylish, all expensive. Pulling a couple of red ones out, she held them in her hand. Unsure of her choice, she carried them to his room. Jackson was already naked and on his bed, limbs spread out in evidence of his over-eagerness to play. The combination of wine and desire made a light fog fall over her senses.

'Are these all right?' She held up the red ties. Jackson nodded. She crossed over to him, binding one wrist and then the other. Since she didn't know how to tie the right knots, she merely made pretty bows out of the ties. When Jackson looked at what she'd done, he smiled. The handsome look nearly took her breath away.

His body sprawled out over the bed, his thick muscles strained like some beautifully carved statue. She didn't tie his legs and his heels dug lightly into the mattress. Zoe watched his eyes, losing sight of his gaze only as she pulled her dress over her head. With her bra and panties on, she crawled onto the bed and straddled his thighs.

Zoe wet her lips and ran her hands along his hips before taking the towering length of his cock in her hand. Guiding the tip to her mouth, she took him between her lips like he'd asked her to, sucking gently, rolling her tongue along him, tasting him. His soft gasps of pleasure filled her head.

'Stop,' he ordered. 'I can't hold out much longer. I want you to ride me. Condom's by my hip.'

Zoe debated whether or not she'd continue. His knees

bent, squeezing along her sides as if he could force her up. Finally, she let up, but only because she needed to feel him within her. She ripped open the condom, fumbling to get it on. Hurrying to rid herself of her panties before crawling on top of him, she brushed her pussy along his cockhead. Dark, beautiful eyes met hers as she slowly lowered her body onto his. The leisurely movement as she rode him made her sex quiver and tighten. She rubbed her clit, sending small jolts of pleasure throughout her body.

Jackson jerked, his mouth opening and his eyes closing tight. Every muscle in his body seemed to tense. Zoe's release followed his. She fell forward, her hands digging into his chest.

Afterward, she curled along his side, running her hand over his stomach. 'I should get to sleep. I would hate to mess up your brother's wedding.'

His head pulled back so he could study her. 'I'm sorry you have to cater tomorrow.'

'It's fine. I'm glad to assist.' She giggled, realising she still had him tied. Reaching for a wrist, she tugged on the bow, easily freeing his arm. 'You can't help it that the caterer got sick.'

'Actually, I fired him.' Jackson moved to untie his other wrist before pulling her into his arms. He kissed her briefly, before confessing, 'I wanted to ask you to my brother's wedding tomorrow, but when you insulted Madelyn I ordered you to work it instead.'

Zoe wasn't sure how she felt about what he'd said.

'Are you mad?' he asked.

'You were going to ask me on a date? To your brother's wedding?' A slow smile curved her lips. She was disappointed that she wouldn't be going in that capacity, but knowing he had been going to ask was almost as good. 'Really?'

'Would you have said yes?'

Zoe nodded. 'I guess it's my fault as much as yours. I did say some mean things to you, things I didn't intend.'

'I thought you were going to be a lot madder at me. I even have a peace-offering gift for you.' Jackson smiled.

Zoe pushed up. 'You do? What is it?'

His grin widened. 'Well, I don't need it now. You're not upset with me.'

'Ah!' She hit his chest. 'What did you get me?'

'I'll give it to you after our next fight.' He pretended to go to sleep, closing his eyes and taking a deep breath.

Zoe hit him just a little bit harder before reaching over to pinch his nipple. His body jerked in surprise at the act and he looked at her again. Forcing a frown she didn't feel, she said, 'You're about to get a fight if you don't tell me.'

'Since you put it like that.' Jackson untangled his arms from her and rolled off the bed. He went to his dresser, and opened the top drawer. Taking out one of the large white-and-blue envelopes used by the United States post office, he handed it to her. 'For you.'

Although aware that she was naked, she didn't bother to hide herself. Jackson pulled back the covers before once more joining her. The envelope was addressed to him from *Chef d'oeuvre* magazine. 'What is it?'

'Just look.'

Zoe chuckled. 'You are giving me your magazine subscription?' she asked, only to teasingly add, 'Smooth present.'

The envelope was already open and she tipped it on its side, letting the magazine slide out. She was about to make a joke about his pretend present when the glossy cover stopped her. It bore a picture of her in her chef uniform.

Her heartbeat quickened. Along the edge, the title 'Culinary diamond in the rough' was printed in large red letters.

'Is this a joke?' Her hands trembled as she lifted it up, holding it gently like delicate porcelain.

'No. One of the women from California who ate at the restaurant works at the magazine as a critic. She contacted me for information about you.'

'Where did they get this picture?' She touched the image of her hair. It was longer than she wore it now. The photo had been taken about three years earlier. Beatrice had read an article about women who worked and had been inspired to have all her girls' portraits done. Kat had taken it one afternoon at their parents' house.

'I'm not sure, but I know they interviewed some of your family.'

'Why didn't they talk to me?' Zoe asked, finally opening it up to the table of contents before flipping to the feature article written by Josine Gray. Smaller pictures of her cooking at the diner decorated the long article. The angle of them came from outside the pick-up window, from the direction the reporter had been sitting in.

'It's not that kind of piece. I offered to get them in contact with you, but they said they wanted to tell the story from outsiders' perspectives. Josine thought it would add to the mystery of your situation.'

'My situation?' Zoe eagerly read the opening paragraph.

In the gentle south of Dabery, South Carolina, a culinary gem lies hidden within the secret tree-lined folds of this small town. Chef Zoe Matthews, relatively unheard-of in prestigious cooking circles, is a star on the rise. There is no doubt for this reporter that she will soon be a household phenomenon, as common as sliced bread.

'Omigod.' Zoe looked up at him, torn between fainting and screaming. She opted instead for breathless wonder. 'How did this happen?'

'You made it happen. I don't know what you made for her, but Josine loves you. She even pushed to have you on the cover.' Jackson brushed a length of her hair off her cheek. 'This hit news-stands today and I've been getting messages for you all afternoon.'

Zoe continued reading. Josine had spoken to her family, all of them except Ella. Megan talked about her original recipes and the journal she still had. Kat raved about her homemade ranch dressing. Sasha commented that it was about time her talented sister got her big break. Beatrice spoke of Zoe's first apron and how she'd been a cook since before she could talk, making everyone meals in her pretend plastic kitchen at the age of two. Her father talked of a feast of burnt cookies and ground-filled coffee from when she was six.

After her past, the article spoke of her present and future. Seeing Jackson's name, she glanced up. He watched her, his eyes shaded as if waiting. Swallowing nervously, she turned her eyes back to the page. It spoke of him discovering her in a bar where he'd had a meeting, leaving out her rudeness and his come-on lines. According to Josine, she'd impressed Jackson with her skills and he'd hired her that same night, bringing her to his secret restaurant in the South where she could perfect her recipes before moving on to bigger things. It was only by chance that Josine had discovered this hidden talent, thereby gaining the knowledge to out her to the culinary world.

'That's not how it happened,' she said. 'I was mean to you.'

'Would you rather I told her I drunkenly came on to you

and was shot down, only to try and punish you by bringing you to this small town to teach you a lesson?'

Her expression fell. 'You brought me here to punish me?'

'I was drunk and it seemed like a good idea. But now I know it was more than that. I needed an excuse to get to know you, to get you down here.'

She sighed. 'I should probably care, but I don't. Whatever the reason, I'm glad you did.'

'Finish reading.' He didn't smile, but neither did he frown as he moved his gaze to the article, urging her to do the same.

Zoe turned her attention to the page once more. Reading aloud, she said, 'Mr Levy, who is known for his impeccable taste when it comes to all things culinary, says, "Zoe Matthews is a lady whose poise is only outdone by her great talent. She is a culinary force to be reckoned with and one I see a great future for. Any of my restaurants would be lucky to have her."'

Tears clouded her eyes at his comment. To have had him say that, publicly, made her tremble.

'You're upset.' The matter-of-fact tone made her look at him.

'I think I love you,' she said, not knowing what had prompted the honest revelation.

The admission shocked him and he gave a nervous laugh. 'Then you like it?'

'It's the single nicest thing that anyone has ever done for me.'

'I didn't do it. You did.' He sat up, his hand brushing hers where it pressed down on the mattress to hold her weight. 'Josine wants to fly you to California for a follow-up piece. I told her I'd ask you.'

'But you never even let me cook for you. Each time it was ruined.' She studied each and every one of his movements, trying to read his thoughts. It was impossible. Her own words echoed in the back of her mind.

I think I love you. I think I love you …

He didn't answer the admission.

'I ordered take-out. I figured it was the only way I'd keep my hands off you long enough to try. I particularly enjoyed your take on the beef dumplings and the lasagne.'

'You're my standing mysterious daily take-out order?'

'What did you use on that garlic bread?'

'It's a secret.'

His eyes widened in challenge. 'I have ways of making you talk.'

He leant toward her naked thigh, but she stopped him. 'That's a way of making me scream and your family is here.'

'Let them hear us.'

She managed to get his face away from her leg. 'It wouldn't be right. Tomorrow's the wedding.'

'Fine,' he said grumpily. 'I'll get the lights.'

Jackson turned the lights off as Zoe set the article aside and got under the covers. Bathed in complete darkness, she felt the bed shift with his weight. Soon, his hands were on her waist, pulling her back tight against his chest.

'I'm glad you're here,' he said, nuzzling his face into her hair so he could kiss the outer ridge of her ear.

'Me, too.' She closed her eyes, not knowing how she'd sleep with Jackson so sweet and so near. Thoughts of the article zoomed through her head and she had never felt so close to her dream. The giddy excitement pumped in her veins.

'Hey, Zoe?'

'Yeah?'

'What is your secret to that garlic bread?'

She giggled, snuggling into him as she closed her eyes. 'Ask me again later when your family isn't in the next room.'

Zoe barely saw Jackson save for glimpses through the crowd during the long day. Her only break came halfway through the wedding, when all her prep work for the dinner was finished. She caught the end of the wedding. Madelyn's white gown seemed like something from a Victorian dream, with thick bell-like skirts and a train that reached back as far as the first two rows of chairs. Six bridesmaids and a maid of honor were decked in pale-pink gowns. The satin Renaissance-style halter gowns had a sash of black at the waist. The women were escorted by groomsmen with matching pink vests over their black shirts, ties and three-button tuxedos. The elegant cut bespoke the richness of taste, from the satin lapels to the longer length of the jacket. Jackson was particularly handsome as the best man, drawing her eyes from the back.

Afterward, drinks and appetizers were served to well over five hundred guests and Zoe was once more stuck in the kitchen. It looked like Jefferson had invited most of the town. Though tired from her sleepless night, she managed the staff with relative ease. They were trained and didn't need much instruction to do their jobs. The only difficulty was one waiter who kept eating half the shrimp puffs off his tray before they even made it out the kitchen door.

Strangely, dinner was at odds with the formality of the event. It consisted of fried chicken, barbeque ribs, thick steaks cooked to order, shrimp kabobs and a variety of buffet-style dishes. One of her assistant cooks manned the grill while Zoe stayed in the kitchen arranging trays and keeping a hot stream of local fare on its way to the tables. A string quartet played as a background to the meal, the sweet melodies classical and upliftingly romantic.

By the time late evening rolled around, the dishes had been cleared, cleaned and repacked for the trip back to Columbia. The quartet was replaced by a DJ who played nothing but classic rock and country music. The wedding crowd got into it, hollering and dancing around the stone porch and yard.

Stars glittered, their brilliance hidden behind the occasional cloud drifting over the night sky. Zoe slowly unbuttoned her chef jacket, letting the cooler air of evening wash over her. She stayed to the side, feeling somewhat of an outsider since she'd been 'the help' for the rest of the day.

'There you are.' Jackson came up behind her, slipping an arm around her waist. 'I'm sorry, I tried to get away earlier, but somehow I've been put in charge of everything.'

Zoe pulled out of his arms.

A look of panic crossed his features. 'What's wrong? Are you upset? I'm sorry, I did try –'

Zoe shook her head. 'I smell awful, like sweat and grease. And you look so handsome in your tux. I don't want to get my smell on you.'

He laughed. 'You think I'm handsome?'

'And possibly slightly drunk.' She eyed him from head to toe.

'Perhaps, a little.' He again made a move to hold her. 'Would it help if I told you this is a rental and I don't care if it goes back smelling like sweat and grease?'

'I wouldn't have you smelling me like this. It's not very appealing.' Again she backed away.

'Everything about you is appealing.'

'Now I know you've had too much to drink.' She backed toward the door leading inside to the kitchens. From there she could sneak up the stairwell to his bedroom. 'If you don't need me, I think I'll go take a shower.'

'Good idea.' His eyebrows rose mischievously seconds before he darted forward to grab her. Zoe screeched in surprise as she was lifted into the air. He tossed her over his shoulder.

'Jackson? What are you doing to that poor girl?' His mother came from the side. Zoe couldn't see her as her feet were angled toward the woman. 'Why don't you bring her on out for a dance?'

'I'm going to go give her a shower and then I'm going to put her to bed.' Jackson's bold claim made Zoe stiffen, even as her body churned with lust at the thought. 'Goodnight.'

'Goodnight, dear,' his mother answered, a laugh in her tone.

Jackson whirled her around, not putting her down as he walked inside. Zoe finally saw his mother's laughing face. Constance winked, not seeming to care. In a lot of ways, she reminded Zoe of her own mother's progressive attitude when it came to relationships. As if his shoes were on fire, Jackson sped through the kitchen, past the lingering staff, through the main hall and up the stairs. He didn't stop until they reached the master bathroom.

Setting her on the floor, he shrugged out of his jacket and pulled at his tie. 'I talked to Josine today. We fly to California in two days for your interviews.'

'What?' Zoe stared at him. 'When did you make these arrangements?'

'This morning, before the ceremony.' He unbuttoned his vest and shirt.

'What about the diner?'

'I gave Bob his job back.' Jackson slipped his vest and shirt off at the same time. Her eyes went to his chest, to the strong lines and well-formed muscles. 'Callie was happy. He's been fixing things around the house and driving her crazy.'

'Bob? Your brother-in-law? He was the chef before me? You fired your brother?' Zoe blinked, slowly drawing her eyes up to meet his.

Jackson shrugged. 'He was due for a vacation. Your working at the restaurant gave him one, but now –'

'You're firing me?' Zoe felt a momentary wave of hurt, even though he hadn't looked malicious as he'd said it.

'Like the article said, you're off to bigger and better things.'

Zoe looked around the bathroom, as if she could find some answer to her unspoken question written on his wall. She wasn't ready to go. They'd just finally gotten to a place where they were talking and getting along. What would happen to them now? She would have no reason to stay in Dabery.

'I'm prepared to give you your own restaurant. The owners were very specific about what they wanted and I think you'd be perfect,' he continued.

'What did they want?' The idea of being offered a better job in one of his fine restaurants suddenly didn't seem so important. What would happen after that? She'd have her dream job, but she wouldn't have her dream man. At best, she could hope he'd come to visit the business he'd built after he turned it over to the people who'd hired him to create it.

'A chef poised for greatness. It's the position I interviewed Contiello for, but the man has proven himself to be unreliable and unreasonable. He makes too many demands and I'm not sure I trust him to have control over this project.' He paused, studying her. 'It's a nice old building in Greenwich Village, not too far from the Phoenix Arms. I need a chef specializing in Italian willing to contract for at least eighteen months. Pays nice. Silverback is a solid investment group I've worked with before. They're fair and honest, but they do tend to take a hands-on approach so you'll have to deal with seven owners. The good news is that they don't cook so you'll have full run of the kitchen. You will just have to explain what you're doing every step of the way.'

'I don't know what to say. It wasn't too long ago that I had no prospects and now you're offering me . . .' Zoe didn't finish aloud, but instead added silently, *almost everything I want.*

He leant over to turn on the shower, gauging its temperature. 'Don't be nervous. You'll be fine. I've contacted a publicist I've worked with in the past. She's arranging several interviews and a tour of guest appearances. We'll get the full details when we get to California.'

'Then you'll be coming with me?' Hope rose within her.

'They wish to interview me as well,' Jackson said. 'I did discover you, after all. And, once you accept Silverback's offer, we'll make that announcement together. They'll be very happy to have the free publicity.'

There were so many questions she wanted to ask him,

but she was too tired and overwhelmed to think straight.

'Is that all right with you?' He stopped, his hands on his waistband.

'Of course. I'll like having you there. I've never given an interview. Well, I did once, but it was for our high-school newspaper.' She gave a small laugh. 'The article was on the football team. It's hardly the same thing.'

Jackson grinned, playfully eying her clothes. 'Strip out of that uniform. We have all day tomorrow to discuss this. Right now, I just want to be with you.'

Her heart fluttered and she couldn't speak as she slowly undressed. His eyes focused on her body and his breathing visibly deepened. She stepped into the shower first, sighing loudly as the warm water hit her flesh. Jackson lathered the liquid soap, using it to worship her body as he cleaned and massaged her. The smell of mint wafted over them and she inhaled deeply to rid her mind of the smell of food. When he'd finished, she bathed him, taking her time to explore every inch of his body.

Soon hands turned into lips, until neither of them could take it any more. Jackson pressed her up against the shower wall, thrusting inside her. His gaze pierced hers, demanding that she look deep into his eyes as their bodies connected. As he neared release, Jackson pulled out so he didn't come inside her.

Towel-drying quickly, they ran to bed. Their damp bodies stuck to the sheets, but Zoe didn't care. Jackson held her close, keeping her locked into his embrace as he spooned her body from behind. Despite being tired, she couldn't sleep. They stayed awake, talking of recipes, of California, of childhood mishaps. Jackson whispered to her, pausing in his conversation to kiss the back of her ear and nuzzle her neck.

'Zoe?'

'Yes?'

'I think I love you, too.'

Zoe giggled, happiness bubbling within her. She turned in his arms. 'Really?'

Jackson didn't answer as he kissed her. His hands ran over her hip, keeping her close. For the time being, everything was perfect.

Chapter Twelve

'You no-talent, lying piece of –' Zoe paused, searching her mind for the perfect insult – 'rotten carp!' Every muscle tightened and she shook violently. Only Jackson's steady hand on her arm kept her from beating the ever-living crap out of Chef Contiello. The smarmy man's smile made her skin crawl, as did the superior look in his eyes. Zoe's nerves had been on edge since she'd flown with Jackson first class to California the day before. After a meeting with the publicist Jackson had hired for them, they'd retired to a swanky hotel on Sunset Strip.

Now, standing on the empty set of *The Josie LaVella Show*, she felt the tension inside her build to a raging fire. Red cushioned chairs were lined up like theater seats, arcing around the stage, which consisted of modern crimson designs. Large cameras pointed toward the front. Strange teardrop shapes curved elegantly behind wide black chairs. Unlike some shows, there was no desk, just the chairs. The studio audience wouldn't come in for another half hour and the show's guests had been encouraged to look around before the live broadcast.

She'd been through hair and make-up and wore a brand-new dress Jackson had had the publicist deliver to the set. The straight-lined cream skirt and jacket looked very professional, with a fun splash of green in the silk shirt. A long beaded necklace acted as the only accessory. Jackson wore a dark suit over blue cashmere.

According to everyone – Jackson, the publicist, her sisters and parents – this was the beginning of her future. The last person she expected to see in that future, standing on the set that was to be her television debut, was Contiello. No one had even mentioned him being there. Zoe had never wanted to hit another person so badly in her life. 'How dare you say I stole from you? I should have my sister arrest you … you … treacherous piece of –'

'Do you see what you have chosen over me?' Contiello demanded, staring at Jackson while waving his hand to encompass Zoe. He, too, had been through hair and make-up. His face tightened, but his voice stayed low. 'A bad-tempered child! Her lies were a mere nuisance when she worked for me, but this is too much! You give –' his voice dropped further as he leant forward, so as not to be overheard '– this scheming bitch my job? My cover article? It is too much! I will not stand for this. I'm here to take what is mine.'

'Back away,' Jackson ordered. 'She is a thousand times more qualified to be here than you are.'

Contiello laughed and sneered at the same time. 'Is that your professional opinion? Or simply a man defending his whore?'

Jackson surged forward, his hand balled into a fist. Zoe instantly grabbed him. This time it was her steady hand that held him back.

'All you have is a lot of talk to cover up the fact that you have no talent,' Zoe said. 'I could out-cook you any day of the week and you know it.'

'Care to put a wager on that statement?' Contiello asked.

'Name it,' Zoe said.

'The recipes. When I win, I want my recipes.' The chef arched a brow, crossing his arms over his chest.

'They're my recipes and you know it.' She glared at him, as she considered letting go of Jackson so he could take a swing at him. Beneath her hand, his muscles had relaxed by a small degree.

'Then what do you have to be afraid of? If what you say is true, you'll out-cook me. Or do you admit that I am the better chef? After all, I've been trained by top culinary geniuses.' Contiello looked her over, snorting.

'You're right, I am at a disadvantage,' Zoe agreed. 'I was partially trained by you. I'll give you your wager. I'm not afraid of you.'

She prayed she knew what she was doing. Contiello grinned.

'Zoe?' Jackson asked. 'You don't have to do this.'

'If I win,' Zoe told Contiello, not answering Jackson, 'you never come into my presence again. You don't talk about me, look at me, think of me.'

'That won't be a problem, even when I win.' Contiello laughed as he sauntered away. He headed toward a group of men who'd appeared on the other side of the set.

'I'm sorry I couldn't warn you. That last phone call was Callie. The producer for *Battle Chefs* called her. Contiello's agent called the show, the magazines, everyone who'd listen, and peddled some story about how you stole from him.' Jackson sighed. *Battle Chefs* was exactly like it sounded – a television show where two rival chefs battled it out in a kitchen. 'This show and *Battle Chefs* is owned by the same people. They want to announce your intentions and your feud with Contiello on today's show. Then, you two will meet in two weeks, with little time to prepare for the culinary cook-off. Callie's waiting for me to call her back to confirm. We have about –' he paused, looking at his watch '– fifteen minutes before the show airs to decide whether or not you accept the challenge.'

'How can I not? I already told Contiello I would, though it seems now his people had already told him about the event.' Zoe swore under her breath. 'Besides, I have to. If I don't, that proves I'm scared of him, and he wins by default. It's time I put that jerk in his place once and for all.'

'You'll be on your own, no help. The best I can offer is making sure the judges are fair and impartial. A man like Contiello will try to get friends on the panel. I'll make sure that doesn't happen.'

'How?'

'By calling in some celebrity chefs. The network will love it. From a publicity standpoint, it's a golden opportunity. They'll put money behind it and you.' Jackson touched her cheek. 'But none of that matters, Zoe, if it's not what you want.'

She slid her hand over his. 'I want my good name, Jackson. And, scared as I am, I want to prove to Contiello, to you, to myself that I can beat him, that I am the better chef.'

'You don't have anything to prove to me, Zoe. I already know.' He brushed his lips to hers, only to stop when a trilling laugh rang out over the set.

'I see we're going to have several announcements to make on today's show,' Josie said. A tall woman with bright-red hair and flawless skin, the talk-show host nevertheless appeared overdone with too much make-up and gold jewelry. Yet the look worked for her and translated well on to television. 'Any juicy gossip for my fans?'

'Only that I'm in love with Chef Matthews,' Jackson said.

Zoe smiled. The words were coming more easily each time they said them.

'What was that, Mr Levy?' Josie asked, her loud voice coming across the set.

'I said, Chef Matthews and I are dating,' Jackson answered, louder this time so Josie could hear it.

Zoe felt a small wave of disappointment at his change of words, but didn't let her smile fade. He'd said he loved her and that counted for something. He hadn't said he wanted to spend eternity with her.

Zoe stopped her thoughts. This wasn't a romance novel. It was real life and in real life men didn't talk like that.

'Ooh!' Josie clapped her hands. 'Perfect! This is going to be a great show.'

The host sat in the main chair, wiggling around in it and taking deep breaths in what appeared to be some bizarre pre-show ritual. Zoe suppressed a laugh as Jackson led her back toward the guest dressing rooms.

'We have five minutes until the show starts and maybe another five before you're introduced,' he whispered into her ear. 'Want me to help you relax?'

'You shouldn't have said that. Now I'll be thinking of jumping you the entire show.' Knowing live television and facing Contiello were so close, she inhaled sharply. 'Omigod, five minutes.'

'Hey.' Jackson pulled her into the dressing room and held her close. Stroking her hair, he said soothingly, 'We talked about this. You're going to be fine, just remember what we practiced last night.'

Zoe arched a brow, thinking of how they'd made love in

one of the hotel chairs, their bodies smothered in whipped cream from the pie room service had brought.

'Not that.' He laughed. 'Though I am suddenly craving banana cream.'

She felt a stirring near her stomach, and pulled back. 'I'm pretty sure you don't want that poking out during the show.'

A knock sounded on the door. 'Ten minutes!'

Zoe again tensed.

'Seriously.' Jackson cupped her face, turning her attention from the door back to him. He kissed her, stealing her breath. 'You know what to say. Just remember to smile and be yourself. If you get nervous, look at me. I'll be sitting next to you the whole time.'

Jackson watched Zoe from the corner of his eye. Somehow, her nervousness kept him calm, as if his body automatically knew she needed him to be strong. Her bright smile only belied the slight shaking in her hands as she clutched them in her lap.

The small microphone attached to her lapel carried her soft voice easily and, though Jackson knew he might be prejudiced, beautifully. On his other side sat Contiello. The man's boisterous attitude was a stark contrast. He knew that Contiello would appear charming and sexy to people watching, but Jackson saw easily through the façade. He could only hope everyone else would as well. Josie stayed impartial during the interviews, though she smiled and flirted with Contiello, who encouraged her behavior with hearty laughs and wide-sweeping gestures.

'I maintain that the recipes are mine,' Contiello said, never losing his smile. 'They were created in my kitchen, under my guidance and supervision. My mistake was trusting her to write them down.'

'Zoe?' Josie prompted.

'We never worked on recipes together. My recipes are mine. I've been creating them since I was a little girl,' Zoe defended herself. 'I would never take his recipes.' Shooting Contiello an annoyed look, she added, 'They're not that good.'

Laughter erupted over the audience, followed by a chorus of, 'Ooooh.'

Contiello lost some of his ease, adjusting his position in his chair. 'Tell that to the thousands trying to get into my restaurant.'

'Ohhhh,' sounded again.

Jackson knew Contiello was exaggerating, but he didn't call him on it. He refused to get into a pissing match with the man on public television.

Zoe gave a small laugh and shook her head. 'This is ridiculous. They're my recipes. I even have notations of when and where I wrote them.'

'Forged. You've had time to do it,' Contiello answered.

'I can tell you what inspired them.' Pausing, she gave the chef a pointed look. 'Can you even name half of them? A quarter? You don't even know what they are.'

'How am I to know what you called them?' Contiello waved a dismissive hand.

'Can you even tell me what ingredients are in them?' Zoe demanded.

'I did not come on here to fight,' Contiello said.

'Which brings us to our challenge,' Josie interrupted a little too eagerly. 'We'll be right back!' As the show paused for a commercial break, the host turned to her guests after switching off her microphone. 'This is good. Though I'd like to see more emotion.'

Zoe turned to Jackson so her back was toward Josie and raised an eyebrow. A staff member carrying a tray with bottled water hurried across the set. Zoe grabbed a bottle and took a quick drink before putting it back on the tray. Jackson did the same, though he wasn't that thirsty. He'd stayed quiet for the first segment, only speaking when directly asked a question.

'Mr Levy,' Josie continued, 'feel free to jump into the conversation. We want to hear what you have to say about this.'

Contiello snorted, before turning his attention to the crowd. He smiled at some nearby ladies in the audience, winking audaciously at them.

'One minute,' someone yelled.

'You're doing great,' Jackson whispered to Zoe, hoping to reassure her. She gave him a little smile and he hated seeing the stress lining her eyes. All he could do was help her through this. He knew the goal she wanted and he'd help her get there. As for the two of them, he'd just have to wait and see where that led. She'd said she loved him, and showed it was true with small smiles and quick glances, but she never spoke of the future. Maybe, like him, she didn't know what the future would bring.

'And we're back!' Josie said. 'Mr Levy, what do you think of this whole situation?'

'I believe Chef Matthews,' Jackson answered, without pausing.

'Really? I'm not surprised. Isn't it true you're seeing Chef Matthews?' Josie looked pointedly at her audience with a knowing smile, as if conveying some secret message. 'Privately?'

'Yes,' he admitted, not caring that the world knew. 'But truth is truth.'

A wave of frustration washed across the host's features. He knew she wanted some big battle, some explosion of wills, declarations of love and wild jumping excitement. Instead she got adult calm. Well, from Zoe and Jackson at least. From Contiello she got childish snorts and flamboyant gestures.

'Before the break, we were discussing the true ownership of certain culinary masterpieces. In a few weeks, on this station, Chef Contiello and Chef Matthews will battle it out for the recipes on *Battle Chefs*!' Applause met Josie's announcement. Time seemed to crawl as the show continued. Josie asked more questions, doing her best to promote lively debate. A few times she came close, but Zoe restrained herself well.

'I'd like to welcome our next guests, who might be able to shed some light on this debate.' Josie stood, holding her hand out. 'Please welcome Chef Matthews' sisters, New York City Detective Megan Brady, photographer Kat Richmond and their mother, psychic Beatrice Matthews.'

Zoe gasped, standing to see her sisters and mother. Beatrice's ageless face made it impossible to guess her age, and only the fact she had five grown daughters suggested she must be in her fifties. Her blue eyes glowed and it was easy to see the strong resemblance between the sisters and their mother, even if Kat's long blonde hair were streaked with blue, matching the trendy empire-waist dress and heels. A polar opposite, the more serious Megan's dark-brown locks were pulled into a large bun, a perfect utilitarian match to her black slacks and fitted white linen shirt. All that was missing from her image was the police badge secured to her waistband.

'Welcome,' Josie announced, as if inviting people into her home. Zoe hugged her sisters and mother, exchanging questioning looks that couldn't be expressed in words. As they sat on chairs that must have been brought out during the break, Jasie said, 'So, Beatrice – a psychic, how interesting. What exactly do you do?'

Zoe looked across the table at her mother. The show had gone as well as could be expected, neither wonderful nor completely horrible. Beatrice had been only too happy to give her television debut talking about the art of tasseography, going so far as to do a tea-leaf reading of Josie's future. Fortunately, it looked bright, as far as Hollywood careers went, and the host had been thrilled. The second half of the hour-long show had mostly involved talking about reading tea leaves and how Beatrice had got into the career.

Megan and Kat had defended Zoe's recipes in no uncertain terms. Contiello had flinched under Megan's stare and left making comments about being sabotaged by Josie and her producers, as there had been no one on the show to defend his position but his agent. Kat had called him several names that would undoubtedly be beeped out by whatever regulating censors the control booth used to keep profanity off public television.

At the end of the show, before the host wrapped up, Kat had gone on to say to Josie and the audience, 'Zoe has proven herself time and time again every bit as talented as Conti over there. It's only a matter of time before she opens her own restaurant.'

Even now, the comment made Zoe smile. Kat's unwavering faith in her never failed to brighten her day. At least the show had ended on a good note.

Jackson had ordered a limo as a surprise for Zoe, but their cosy party of two had turned into five. Instead of the intimate evening she'd envisaged driving around town and making love, they'd ended up at dinner with Zoe's mother and sisters. Beatrice had insisted on an Asian steakhouse and they'd ended up at a place that resembled a Japanese palace. The center and one side of the table were taken up by a grill where the chefs cooked the food in front of the customers. Zoe and Jackson sat at the end. Megan was at her other side, then Kat and her mother.

'So, Jack, what are your intentions towards our Zoe?' Kat asked bluntly, eying Jackson.

'Ah.' He glanced at Zoe. 'I really like your sister, I mean, I love her and –'

'Wait.' Kat held up her hand. 'I was talking about her career. What do you mean you –?'

'Oh, Zoe! I knew this would happen. I told you, remember, when you called and –' Beatrice began, her chin-length hair barely moving under the weight of hairspray.

Megan stopped her. 'Mom, enough, please. You promised no more future-reading tonight. Don't make me call Dad.'

Beatrice made an exasperated noise and waved her hand. Megan winked at Zoe.

'I've offered Zoe a job in New York at a new restaurant. She has yet to say yes, but I've given her a contract for the next eighteen months,' Jackson said. The chef appeared at their table, beginning his performance of cooking. Zoe glanced at him, watching with interest as he flipped his utensils in the air, catching them before tapping the metal edges along the grill.

'Oh, she says yes,' Kat answered for her. 'We want her back in the city. I *need* her back in the city. She says yes.'

Zoe thought of protesting, but the truth was she had no

reason to other than that she didn't want to leave Jackson. This thing they had just started and moving back to New York meant a long-distance relationship. Those rarely seemed to work.

'Yes,' she said to Jackson. 'I'll take it. It's a dream come true. Kat's right. How can I say no?'

Kat cheered. Megan grinned. Beatrice said, 'I knew it!'

The chef made a joke and flipped an egg into the air, then cracked it on his spatula. Each of his fluid movements had both grace and purpose. Next, he placed rice, onions, shrimp, steak, calamari and vegetables on the grill. The sizzle of food wafted around them, carrying with it the overpoweringly fishy smell of the squid her mother had ordered.

'I've been thinking about writing a cookbook when this *Battle Chefs* is all over,' Zoe said, her stomach tight as she wondered what the future held. Contiello might be an ass, but the truth was he was a good cook: not very original, but he knew what he was doing. A show like *Battle Chefs* didn't demand originality so much as perfection. The more she thought about what could go wrong, the more she worried. What if the judges happened to hate whatever she did for some unknown reason? What if Contiello's presentation was better? Or a judge was single and he flirted with them? The man could be charming.

Jackson's hand slid onto her knee, squeezing her gently in reassurance. She gave him a small smile.

'I think that's a fine idea,' Beatrice said. 'I always thought I'd have a writer for a daughter.'

'I don't know if it's really writing so much as creating,' Zoe protested.

'Let her count it,' Megan interrupted. 'I don't want her

trying to get me to write some book. I barely have time to read my case files.'

'You took time off for this show, though,' Zoe said. 'I don't think I've said thank you enough for coming. I know you're busy.'

'Ah, a few Upper East Side break-ins.' Megan waved her hand in dismissal. Once a complete workaholic, she'd been much better about taking time for family since meeting her husband. 'No one was hurt and the paperwork can wait.'

'Excuse me, what's this about being in love?' Kat broke in. 'I don't remember getting a phone call about this new development.'

Zoe looked at Jackson and blushed. She slipped her hand over his under the table, holding it to her leg.

'Ah!' Kat bounced in her chair. 'You love him back! This is so great. So, what's the plan? You both move to New York?'

'Ah, we haven't really talked about that stuff,' Zoe answered, staring at Kat and hoping her sister would get the secret message to shut up.

'It's not an unreasonable question, honey,' Beatrice said.

Zoe frowned. Not her mother, too.

'I have family in South Carolina,' Jackson said. 'And a home.'

'That is a problem.' Beatrice nodded. 'Family is impor-tant.'

'Hey, can we not talk about this?' Zoe asked. 'Jackson and I will discuss it when the time is right.'

'Fine,' Beatrice said. 'But, for the record, I think a winter wedding would be beautiful.'

*

'I am so sorry about my mother,' Zoe said, the second she was alone with Jackson in their hotel room. 'She seems preoccupied with us getting married. It's gotten worse since Kat and Megan took the plunge. Now she's on me because Sasha's still in school and Ella's the baby of the family.'

'It's fine. I liked her.' Jackson wrapped his arms around her from behind. 'I like your sisters, too. Megan's funny.'

'Funny?' Zoe turned in his arms. 'I don't think any living person has ever called her funny before. Scary, maybe, but never funny.'

'But she makes all those jokes.' Jackson placed a kiss on her neck, breathing deeply next to her.

Zoe giggled as his long sigh tickled her ear. 'Jokes?'

'About having people arrested, the story about chasing bad guys in her underwear.' Jackson licked along the ridge of her ear, sending a shiver over her entire frame.

'Ah, those weren't jokes. She really did chase a bad guy down in her underwear. She caught him harassing a neighbor – some escort girl she's been trying to get out of the business.'

'Mm, can we play that?' Jackson chuckled. 'I want to see you chase me around in your underwear.'

'And I want a massage,' Zoe said, kicking off her shoes. 'No running tonight.'

'Promise a raincheck?'

He looked so hopeful, she couldn't help but nod.

'Lie on the bed. I have some lotion in my bag.' He tilted his jaw toward the mattress. Zoe slid out of her clothes before stretching out naked on the bed. She lay on her back, watching him move. Just looking at him made her wet. He stripped down and her breath caught. The lights dimmed. 'You're beautiful.'

'And you're incredible. How do you stay so fit and not work out?' Zoe ran a hand along his arm.

'I haven't since I met you, but I normally run five miles every morning and lift weights six days a week.' He gave her a playful wink. 'Besides, I wouldn't say I haven't been getting my workouts in.'

He rubbed lotion on his hands, then brought them to her feet. Zoe laughed, jerking the foot he'd touched away. 'Ah, that tickles!'

'Keep still,' Jackson ordered, grabbing it again. This time, he deepened his touch. 'You wanted a massage, you're getting a massage.'

His expression became serious as he set to work. He rubbed the other foot, his fingers like magic against her skin. Heat warmed her body, centering in her sex. Knowing she'd have to wait for him to finish, wait for his hands to make the trip over her body, made the anticipation both delicious and unbearable.

She closed her eyes, taking in every touch. He worked one calf and then the other, keeping a leisured pace. Zoe made small wiggling movements against the bed. Tender hands ran over her knees, moving up her thighs.

Jackson breathed hard, moaning loudly. When she looked at him, she saw his stiff erection towering from his thighs. His gaze stayed on her pussy and he licked his lips. Zoe shivered with the knowledge that he wanted her. To her surprise, he didn't run his hands along the needy folds. Instead, he moved up her body, over her shoulders, arms and hands. Touching her hips and sides, he caressed his way to her hard nipples, tweaking them before grabbing both breasts fully into his palms. The lotion made their flesh glide. He leant over and sucked a nipple between his lips.

'Turn over. I'll do your back,' he ordered, his eyes hot with pleasure.

Her nerves already tingled and she felt relaxed. Somehow, she managed to turn around. The backs of her legs and her back received the same treatment. He pushed his thighs between hers, spreading her legs.

Zoe's body jolted as she felt lips brush along her ass. Jackson cupped her ass, eliciting a moan. His thumbs dipped along the edge of her slit. Insistent hands pulled her to her hands and knees, even as she wobbled in her aroused, relaxed state.

Jackson guided his body to hers, his arousal pressing along her pussy. She thrust back the instant she felt him, taking his cock deep inside. The tight stretch felt too good and she rocked back and forth. It didn't take long before they were both crying out, meeting their release in perfect unison.

Chapter Thirteen

Two Weeks Later

'Welcome to *Battle Chefs*!' The big voice boomed over the metallic set. Jeremy Wayne, the announcer, might have been a small man in stature, but his voice made up for what he lacked in height. A small crowd sat in the seats, lured in with promises of prizes and free food.

Zoe nervously looked around, not hearing everything the man was saying as he introduced her and then Contiello and spoke of their individual qualifications. The feud was mentioned several times during his spiel. Contiello smiled, pristine in his white uniform. Her uniform matched his, except for the colored sashes hugging their waists – a blue one for Contiello and a crimson one for her. In the corner of her vision, she saw Jackson standing next to a cameraman. She drew strength from his presence.

Zoe had brushed her hair back, spraying it with hairspray to ensure that not a strand fell out while she worked. The last thing she wanted was a judge finding hair in their food. Apparently Contiello felt the same way. His bulbous chef hat covered his ears while the bottom blur band wrapped around his head. All but the back ponytail of his hair was covered.

From her perspective, the studio looked like a warehouse. To the television viewers at home it would look like she was standing inside a giant oven. Even the red lights that glowed around them made her feel like a turkey about to be cooked. Two kitchen sets were positioned facing each other so the competitors could each watch the other cook. Along the back, a row of shelves held baskets filled with different vegetables, fruits, nuts, spices and oils. A rack of cooking utensils and every kind of pan known to man sat waiting. She forced her attention back to the announcer, concentrating on keeping her smile intact.

'. . . special treat for you. Not only will this be a battle to create the best culinary dish out of the ingredients provided, but the contestants will also get points for originality, presentation and ingenuity.' A loud, short blast of low music sounded, adding to the tension. 'There will be no assistants. For this task, each chef will have to make every cut, every decision. Judges, can we have an hour and thirty minutes on the clock please? Delivery boys, bring in the main ingredients! As you know, the chefs must use all of the main ingredients provided. The shelves along the back are extras. Every dish must contain one of the main ingredients. That does not include any garnish or sauces. Chefs, please remember you're cooking for two.'

Two young men dressed all in white pushed two carts into the kitchens. Long white sheets covered them. Zoe waited, staring at the cart nearest to her, anxious to see what was under the sheet. The anticipation was worse than that of a five-year-old waiting to open a giant stack of birthday presents.

'Let's see what we have,' Jeremy said. The delivery boys pulled the sheets off with a swoosh of movement and backed away, going off stage. Small sounds of approval and interest came from the crowd, followed by a uniform clapping that made her suspect a small sign had lit up to prompt the onlookers' response. A cameraman came close to the table, focusing in on the items. Zoe held her breath, her eyes scanning over them. The announcer continued, 'Each chef has two Cornish game hens, two green tomatoes, cloves of garlic and a bag of *haricots verts,* which is a thin French green bean. That pile may look like rice, but is really orzo, a rice-shaped pasta.'

Nervous, Zoe could barely move. The ingredients provided were basic, though she feared the green tomatoes would be hard to utilize. Clearly the challenge was to make the ordinary extraordinary. Almost in a panic, she looked at Jackson. He nodded in encouragement, giving her that charming smile she loved. Suddenly, she knew what she was going to do.

A low rumble sounded in the announcer's voice. 'Let the battle begin!'

Contiello whistled and Zoe glanced at him. He winked at her, appearing completely at ease. A large drop cloth fell between them, preventing each from seeing what the other was doing. In some ways, not seeing was worse than seeing. On the one hand, she wouldn't be able to stare at him while he cooked and on the other, her mind would run wild wondering what he was going to do.

Zoe took a deep breath, clearing her mind of everything but the food. She ignored the camera as she preheated the oven to four hundred degrees. The game hens would take the longest to cook, needing to roast for about an hour. Next, she started a lime-and-orange reduction on the stove in one pan and poured olive oil into another, then grabbed the garlic cloves and smashed them with a mallet.

'You can do this, Zoe,' she whispered, only realizing too late she'd said it aloud in front of the camera. She managed a small smile into the lens before turning her attention to her work once more.

Jackson wasn't completely sure where Zoe was going with her creation, but she'd been moving nonstop for over an hour. He saw the tight set of her lips, the sweat on her brow, and they worried him. Did she even know where she was going? His entire body tightened as he watched her, stressed on her behalf as she moved around her kitchen. A few times she fumbled her hands, but she quickly recovered, managing not to spill anything. From his vantage point, Jackson could see Contiello as well. The man's lips moved, as if he were talking to himself while he worked.

Zoe wiped her brow before pouring liquor into a pan. She lit it and flames blazed, seemingly out of control. She jumped back. The audience gasped. Firelight shone over the floor and the faces of those in the front row.

'It would seem things are getting a little hot over there,' Contiello yelled arrogantly. 'You know what they say; if you can't take the flames, stay out of the kitchen.'

The crowd laughed at the joke. Zoe glanced up, looking nervous. Jackson urged her to think of a snappy comeback, to give him a sign that she was all right, but she just kept working. Maybe it was for the best. His momma always said, *if you don't have anything nice to say don't say anything at all.*

While Zoe was roasting the hens whole, Conteillo had cut them into sections as he would have cut a chicken. The tiny, delicate pieces were rolled in eggs then breadcrumbs and fried in a skillet. Frowning, he noticed Contiello scratch his ear before talking to himself again.

He glanced around the crowd, scanning the enraptured faces watching the two chefs work. On seeing Contiello's agent, he followed the man's gaze to the side. There, on Zoe's side of the stage, stood a man talking on a cell phone. The agent glanced between the man on the phone and Contiello. Pretending to go to the restroom, Jackson arced around to the side of the seating area to come up behind the man on the phone.

'She's taking the roasted hens out of the oven and placing them aside. She seems to have recovered from the blazing fire, but I'm still not sure what she's going to do with the sautéed black mushrooms,' the man whispered, cupping his hand over the mouthpiece. 'I'm telling you, Contiello, it looks like she knows what she's doing.'

Jackson frowned, tapping the man on his thin shoulder. He jolted in surprise, dropping his phone. Jackson leant over and caught it.

'Ah, thanks,' the man stammered, reaching to take the phone.

Jackson lifted his finger, gesturing for the man to hold on a moment before lifting the phone to his ear. Contiello's distinct voice hissed through the earpiece. 'Get me someone who knows what they're talking about. So help me, this sniveling bitch isn't going to out-cook me!'

Contiello was cheating. Jackson glared at the thin man, flipping the phone shut. At the click, Contiello looked up.

'I, ah . . .' The man backed away slowly.

Jackson ignored the man and stared instead at Contiello, forcing a smile he didn't feel as he lifted the phone. He wiggled it back and forth to taunt the chef. Even from a distance, Jackson could see the man's enraged expression.

Jackson turned, throwing the phone at the man. 'Get out of here.'

*

'Ten minutes,' Jeremy said, his voice booming overhead.

Zoe trembled. She'd been going at a fast pace since the timer had started, wishing for it all to be over. Now, as the end loomed, she wished for just twenty more minutes of time to make sure everything came out perfectly. She quickly shook the skillet and dropped it back down on the burner, then hurried to the rack with all the utensils and pots. Along one edge square plates, rounded plates, serving trays, trenchers, trio plates and bowls were laid out in pairs.

She chose the set of square plates for their larger size because of the hens, then grabbed the sliced green tomato she'd cut earlier. She dipped the slices in an egg-and-buttermilk bath before coating them with flour and spices. A loud sizzle sounded as she threw them in the oil. As they cooked, she took the hens from the oven, then paused to flip the tomatoes before moving the glazed hens stuffed with apricots to one corner of the square plates. They took up nearly half the space. Taking the fried green-tomato slices, she stacked three on one side and then piled on orzo mixed with the green beans, Romano cheese and vine-ripened tomatoes. She made the second plate exactly the same, as per the competition rules.

Breathing hard, she looked up and backed away. The audience clapped. Her eyes scanned them for Jackson, but he wasn't in his place.

'One minute,' Jeremy announced.

Zoe's eyes darted back to the plates. She'd forgotten the green-herb sauce drizzle. Her heartbeat had never really calmed, but now it practically leapt from her chest. Frantic, she looked for where she'd placed the bottle.

'Thirty seconds.' The clock counted down the time.

Seeing it shoved in a corner behind a stack of her dirty

pans, she rushed toward it. The white cloth separating her from Contiello caught her eye briefly. She wondered how he fared. Was he done? Was his meal brilliant? Shaking, she grabbed the bottle and hurried across to her plates. The crowd began to shout the countdown. 'Six, five, four, three ...'

Zoe squeezed the bottle, dripping several dots and lines on the white porcelain plates around the orzo.

'... two, one!'

A buzzer sounded. Zoe put down the bottle and stepped away. A strange mixture of relief and fear washed through her. She again looked up, needing to see Jackson. Her eyes scanned the crowd, finally finding him along the edge. He smiled at her and her heart nearly melted. A calmness came over her. When she looked at her sexy boyfriend, the stress faded. Though nerves still fluttered in her stomach, she had a sense of reality. No matter what happened, Jackson would still be there for her.

Getting the plates in front of the judges took what seemed like an eternity. When it was aired, the show would be scaled down to an hour, but now they had to wait while the judges' table was set up and the cameras moved into place. The first judge, Margot Littman, was a culinary reporter for a major California newspaper and the second, Jonah Mirran, worked as an instructor at a culinary school in New York. Since the school had a sister institute in Paris, Zoe felt her stomach drop. Before they'd started, they hadn't been told who the judges would be. She'd known that Jackson had pushed for a couple that would be fair, but he hadn't cheated and told her who he'd asked for. Jackson had said that if he'd told her, she'd always wonder if she could've won without the advantage. He'd refused to rob her moment from her in such a way. Though curiosity had nearly killed her, she'd had to admit he was right. He'd also assured her that they would be fair and not give her special treatment because of who she was dating.

Contiello went first. The round white plate displayed the hens fried up like a mini-chicken and placed on a bed of orzo and a sauce. Since she couldn't see the green tomatoes or the beans, she could only guess he'd puréed them and mixed they with the orzo.

The judges took a small bite, studying the taste as they dined. Contiello said, 'I am naming it Peppercorn Hen with Pepper Orzo. I wanted to showcase the delicate nature of the bird.'

'Interesting use of the green tomatoes,' Margot said. 'I noticed you made a big batch of the sauce when you were cooking. It watered down the flavor of the tomato itself and is overpowered by the peppers.'

'I think the sauce is good,' Jonah said. 'An interesting idea. I'll definitely give you points for creating it, but I agree the green tomatoes were too washed out of the flavor.'

'The hen is adorable when cut in such a way, but frying the bird takes much of the flavor of the meat from it,' Margot added.

Zoe swallowed, waiting on every word as they picked apart Contiello's meal. When they'd finished, there were just enough compliments and critiques to make her worry. Contiello nodded and smiled, thanking them.

When it was her turn, Zoe stepped up to the tables as her plates were served.

'This is a hearty meal,' Margot said, giving a small laugh. It was hard to tell if the words were a joke or a criticism.

'I was inspired by my recent time in the South. I wanted to draw from that experience, as I believe cooking to be an extension of who we are and what we do. I call it

Apricot Hen Dabery with Romano Orzo and Fried Green Tomatoes.' She glanced at Jackson, letting a small smile curl the side of her lips briefly. Zoe tensed as the judges took several small bites, tasting it much as they had Contiello's.

'I love how the sweetness of the apricots flavors the meat. They were cooked just enough before insertion not be over-powering, leaving the Cornish hen tasting like hen,' Jonah said.

Margot didn't smile, her eyes steady as she looked at her plate. She chose her words carefully. 'The tomatoes are a fun, Southern accent to the meal. Their texture comple-ments the orzo.'

'Thank you.' Zoe nodded once, encouraged.

'The glaze is a little sweet,' she continued. 'But when I push it aside and get to the meat, I have to agree with Jonah. The flavor of the hen is quite good.'

Jeremy ushered the two chefs to the kitchen area so the judges could confer and make their ruling. Zoe waited, her feet tapping in apprehension. Finding Jackson, she stared at him.

'I love you,' he mouthed slowly so she could read his lips.

'The judges have made their decision,' Jeremy said, joining them in front. 'Chef Contiello.'

Zoe felt her heart drop. Contiello bowed his head.

'I'm sorry, but you are not our winner.' Jeremy turned his beaming face toward her. 'Chef Matthews, you have reigned supreme today on *Battle Chefs*!'

The crowd cheered, but she didn't hear it. Her mouth open wide, she turned to Jackson, lifting her hand. He hurried to her, hugging her tight as he spun her around in circles.

'I knew you could do it,' he whispered. 'I'm so proud of you.'

'This is rigged!' Contiello fumed. Not even trying to be a graceful loser, he marched off stage.

Zoe barely paid him any attention. She felt vindicated. She'd won, proven herself the best chef. Gazing up at Jackson, she ignored the camera zooming close to her face. 'Thank you, Jackson. Thank you for everything.'

Jackson held her in his arms, studying her in the strong studio light. 'I like the idea of a winter wedding.'

Zoe, unsure she'd heard right, pulled back. 'I don't understand.'

'I've wanted to say this for a long time, but I wanted to wait until after today. I've never felt like this, Zoe. I want to be with you.' He kissed her mouth before pulling back. 'Always. I know it hasn't been very long, but when you know, you know. I want to be with you.'

A loud cheer went up over the stage. That's when she noticed Jeremy's microphone next to them and the announcer standing to the side.

'Jackson?' Zoe asked, trying to take it all in. This was the perfect moment. Her emotions soared and she was afraid of them coming down. 'I don't think I understand. Did you just say ... ? Did you ask me to ... ?' She gasped, unable to breathe.

'Say you'll marry me in the winter,' Jackson whispered into her ear. 'I want the world to know I love you.'

Her heart beat fast in her chest and a tear slipped over her cheek. A single word piped from her throat. 'OK.'

'Really?' A wide, happy grin spread over his features.

Zoe nodded enthusiastically, still unable to say everything she wanted to tell him. Her emotions overflowed, too many and too powerful to be expressed in words, so instead she kissed him, pouring her heart into the embrace.

'And there you have it!' Jeremy pulled the microphone in front of him to address the crowd and cameras at the same time. 'Anything really can happen when you're in the kitchen! Be sure to join us next time on . . .' He held the microphone toward the crowd as they yelled, '*Battle Chefs*!'

'I love you, Zoe. I don't care what happens, so long as I have you. Things like houses and where we live don't matter, so long as you're mine. Everything else will work out.' Jackson lifted her off the ground, laughing as he twirled her in the air.

Zoe finally managed to speak, saying, 'I am yours, Jackson. I love you. Forever.'

Epilogue

After his poor display of sportsmanship on national television, Chef Contiello had a hard time finding a new position after *Sedurre* closed its doors for good. He is now the head chef at a sports bar and grill. His agent won't return his calls.

Jefferson and Madelyn adopted a young girl from China. They plan on going overseas several more times until every corner of their house is filled with children. Jefferson is applying to his brother for a loan. He wants to open his own winery.

Callie is happy to have Bob back at work. Over half the things he fixed around the house while on vacation from work broke. Bob has revamped *Renée*'s menu. Gaz-pay-cho Salsa is a big hit with the customers.

Jackson and Zoe were married in winter following Zoe's win on *Battle Chefs*. The ceremony took place at their South Carolina home, just as Beatrice knew it would all along. They lived in New York for eighteen months while Zoe made a name for herself in the culinary world. It wasn't always easy with Jackson's work taking him all over the country, but she went with him whenever she could. After her contract was up she moved to South Carolina, where she is currently working on her first cookbook. The Silverback investors were sorry to see her go. Zoe had guest spots on *Battle Chefs* a few times and these days there is talk of her own culinary show. No contacts have been signed.

Kat takes the Richmond family jet to visit them often, using the new private airstrip on the edge of Jackson's land. Beatrice is now content to bother her two youngest daughters for sons-in-law. As for Megan, Zoe and Kat, she's begging them for more grandchildren. Zoe and Jackson haven't told her yet, but they're expecting in fall.

If you enjoyed *Recipe for Disaster* check out the following for extracts from other books featuring the Matthew Sisters.

BIT BY THE BUG
ISBN 978 0 352 34084 3

Kate Matthews is in love . . . with her art. As a photographer, her greatest desire is to one day create a photo so potent that it will stand the test of time, the kind of picture that is looked at for centuries. If she can accomplish that, she will be content. Not all dreams have to end in romantic love, marriage and children. As for intimacy, she has Jack – a man who understands her needs. What hip New York woman needs more? And when an eccentric couple offer her a chance to have her own art show in the coveted gallery, Faux Pas, she's willing to do whatever it takes. Their terms should be simple – teaching their reclusive son, Dr Vincent Richmond, how to date without him finding out. A young preoccupied man who unwittingly holds the key to her dreams in his hands . . . if only he'd notice she existed.

Why did he think she was Margaret?

'Well, come on then,' he said

'I'm Kat,' Kat said. 'Not Margaret.'

'What? Oh, right, Kat,' the man answered, straightening slightly. 'I'm always forgetting that, aren't I? So sorry. Kat.' He nodded his head and repeated her name softly as if doing so would help him remember it, 'Kat. Kat. Kat.'

She just watched, her hand absently straying to the latch on her camera bag. The man was absolutely distracted. He was looking right at her, but she had a feeling he wasn't seeing her at all. She could envision his mind racing with thoughts.

'You think I'd remember your name as you've been working so long for me.'

Kat didn't move. He still thought she was his employee? Having seen the fashion nightmare that just walked out of the office, she wasn't sure whether to laugh or cry.

'I will try to remember, Kat,' he promised. She decided he had a nice voice, deep and low. The kind of soothing tone a girl could fall asleep listening to. 'Sorry, I guess my other assistant must have been Margaret.'

'That's perfectly all right,' said Kat, not moving.

'Come on, you're not paid to stand there.' He motioned, as if to insinuate she was to follow him down the hall.

'But, I'm not paid,' Kat said, slowly moving to go after him. How could she not? The man was so strange, she found herself utterly fascinated. True, mildly attractive nerds weren't usually her type, but there was something all too appealing to his lost looks and his wild hair. Besides, there was a kindness in his voice, in the tone of it that she detected right away. Maybe it wasn't a tone so much as it was a feeling she got when she heard it.

The man stopped again. He shook his head before fumbling to pull up his lab coat. She leaned to the side, getting a better view of his trim waist. The man was in shape, either he worked out or he was so busy he forgot to eat. Hmm, maybe science guy had a little more to offer than she first gave him credit for. Perhaps with a clean shave and a lab coat-free wardrobe, he'd be passable.

OK, why was she suddenly having very sexual thoughts about Mr Distracted? Maybe it was the lab coat and glasses, but her mind turned on a very wicked fantasy involving the man before her, a science lab and being fucked from behind.

Get a hold of yourself, Kat, she told herself.

Even so, her body stirred, becoming moist between her thighs. Maybe playing patient and mad scientist would be a better scenario. He could do naughty little science experiments on her with his tongue.

Whoa, Kat, reign it in.

'Sorry, I must have forgotten again.'

His words jerked her out of her fantasy and she blinked several times, trying to follow what he was saying.

'Don't hesitate to remind me in the future.' Shoving his hand into his pocket, he pulled out a wallet. He began walking, digging through the wallet for cash. 'How much do I owe you?'

'Ah, nothing,' Kat said.

'That's ridiculous. You can't work for free. I know the college calls this an internship, but still, I prefer it if you made something as my assistant. I remember what it is like to carry a full class load and an internship.'

He stopped at a door. The glass window in the door was frosted over and a gold plate read, 'Laboratory 1A Dr Vincent Richmond, PhD Entomology'.

This poor adorably lost man was Dr Richmond? Her Dr Richmond? This was the guy she was supposed to date? Kat took a deep breath. This was going to be harder than she'd first thought.

Step one. Get him to actually look at her.

Vincent grabbed the doorknob, opened the door and turned seemingly all at the same time. In his hand was a hundred dollar bill.

'Take this,' he said, thrusting it back at her. 'I'll figure out the difference later. Right now we have work to do.'

Kat looked at the money, very tempted to put it in her pocket. He shook it expectantly. She wasn't a saint, but she also wasn't so mean as to rob this preoccupied man.

'But, I'm not –' she tried to say, but he sighed heavily, stopping her.

Vincent grabbed her hand and put the money in her palm. His fingers were warm, but he didn't let his touch linger. She frowned as he turned away, ending any discussion over the money. She watched him closely, but he didn't even look at her. His hands were on his hips as he looked up and down the laboratory studying the floor and ceiling in turn as he walked beside the long line of tables.

Row upon row of narrow drawers filled one of the walls. They were each marked with a white sticker written on in small precise script. The stickers were labelled with a letter and several numbers. Opened books were piled high on one of the tables. Some had highlighted passages in them, others were marked with paperclips. A notepad, filled with the same script that was on the drawers, was by the books. They were compiled of long lists of Latin words and strange notations.

The door had said this was a laboratory, but Kat found the room odd for a lab, though the old brown tables and the library atmosphere were probably suited to a guy who studied word history. Cluttered along the edge of the long counter, there were beakers, microscopes, an array of instruments from tweezers to little slides and some sort of machine that looked like it belonged in a science laboratory, but Kat had no idea what it did. She'd failed science in high school and never went to college. There'd been no point. Ever since she was little, she'd wanted to be a photographer. She deduced easily that the drawers had to be filled with old texts and maybe the equipment was used for carbon dating or whatever it was these types of men did.

'I don't work for you.' Kat set her camera bag on the table. Thinking she'd seen movement on the floor, she glanced down. It was nothing.

'Sorry, what was that?'

'I don't work for you,' Kat repeated.

Vincent stopped, standing very still as if it took him a moment to process what she said. Slowly, he turned. 'You can't quit on me. I've had too many quit on me this year.'

'But –'

He held up his hands and came back to where she waited by the door. As if seeing her for the first time, he blinked, his eyes roaming over her face and clothes. 'Ah, wow, you're . . .'

Kat waited. Beautiful? Pretty? Sexy? Dateable? This was more like the reaction she was used to from men.

'. . . ah, different.'

ALONG FOR THE RIDE
ISBN 978 0 352 34145 9

Detective Megan Matthews is cursed with always being right. Her instincts are good, her deductive reasoning even better. She's found her hard-headed ways to be too much for most men, so she's given up on trying to find Mr Right and has settled for arresting Mr Wrong. Crime Scene photographer, Ryan Andrews, has had a crush on the sexy detective since he first took her photograph by accident at a crime scene. That picture became headline news and she hasn't talked to him since. He's tried everything to get her attention, but when nothing works he's left with only one option. But is blackmailing a cop into marriage really a good idea?

Ryan stepped through the beam and for a brief moment she got a good look at his face – not that she needed to see him to remember what he looked like. His hair was longer, falling to his chin in soft brown waves. The man had an endless supply of T-shirts and blue jeans, which always bulged at the pockets with the canisters that held rolls of film. She wondered why he carried print film when all she'd seen him use at crime scenes was a digital camera.

Megan didn't know why she noticed the small detail. Perhaps it was her training or maybe it was because Ryan kept popping up around her – at work and even a few tiimes when she went to see her sister. Kat worked with her entomologist husband at the American Museum of Natural History. Dr Vincent Richmond had helped them solve the serial-killer case and Ryan had gone to take his picture for an article. Kat and Ryan hit it off, making it even harder for Megan to avoid the man. He was like a cockroach she couldn't get rid of.

OK, so maybe cockroach was a bit harsh. But he was a pain in the ass and she was too tired to deal with him tonight. Truth be told, Megan understood the friendship between Ryan and Kat. They were both photographers with laidback artistic mentalities. Megan has always been too edgy for such an easygoing lifestyle. She needed to be up and moving, needed the mental and physical stimulation, needed to be constantly challenged. Work did that for her.

Dazed from lack of sleep, she merely stared as he put the marker down by the diamond. When he turned to her, his dark-blue eyes struck her like a shock of cold water over the head. She blinked, coming out of her daze. Ryan would have been a handsome man, if she didn't resent him so much. He was athletic, but not too muscled. When he smiled, two dimples lit up his face and, when he spoke, his words were infused with hints of a lazy New York accent. It was enough to give a girl chills.

'Are you going to be at Sunday dinner?' Ryan asked, clearly trying to make small talk.

He always did that. Didn't he realise he'd nearly ruined her life? Well, her career, which *was* her life.

'Is there a department banquet?' Megan frowned. She didn't remember there being any city functions on her schedule.

'Sunday dinner with your parents,' Ryan explained.

What in the world did *he* know about Sunday dinner with her parents? Megan automatically knew the answer. Kat. Her sister had told him.

'Um, yeah, probably, if I can get away,' Megan said. It was Monday night and she really hadn't thought that far ahead in her schedule. Who knew what the weekend would hold. She did miss her family and hadn't been able to attend dinner the day before because of paperwork. At least now that her parents lived on Ninety-Sixth Street and Columbus, she did get to see them and her sisters more often.

Altogether, Megan had four sisters. She was the oldest of the bunch. Then there was Kat the photographer, Zoe the chef, Sasha the undecided college student and Ella the baby who was off serving in the Navy.

'You must be pretty excited,' Ryan said.

'Excited?' Megan repeated, confused. Maybe she needed sleep more than she'd realised because she couldn't, for the life of her, figure out why they were talking about Sunday dinner with her parents while in the middle of working a crime scene.

'Because Ella's coming home.' Ryan gave her a small smile.

'Oh, yeah.' Megan pretended to know what he was talking about. The news perked her up some. It had been a while since she checked her personal messages. Was Ella making it home Sunday? It would be the first time any of them saw Ella since she left for basic training.

'I'll be excited to meet her.' Ryan took the lens cap off his camera and made a few adjustments before aiming it at the jewel she'd found. His flash went off and Megan blinked hard, suddenly seeing bright spots in her vision. 'Actually, it'll be nice meeting the rest of your family. I've met Kat, obviously, and Zoe at her restaurant about a month ago when Kat and I were having lunch. I haven't met Sasha or Ella or your parents yet, but –'

'What are you talking about?' Megan broke in. Didn't this guy have a family of his own to go to? Why was he so worried about meeting all of hers? It's not like she wanted him in her life any more than he already was. And it wasn't as if Kat was going to date him. Kat was happily married and madly in love with her husband.

'Sunday dinner. Kat invited me to come,' he said, studying her. 'Hey, are you all right? You look . . .' He shrugged.

'Yeah, I'm fine.' Even to her own ears, her voice was flat and unenthusiastic.

'Anyway,' Ryan continued, again fiddling with his camera before moving to another marker to take the picture, 'Kat's got a meeting before dinner and she gave me the address to meet her there, but I was thinking –' he paused, clearing his throat '– that maybe we could go together.'

Megan blinked slowly, not answering. Did she hear him right? Did he just ask her out on a date – to her parents' house? Unable to answer, she actually felt sorry for the poor man. What kind of sorry loser asked a woman to go on a date with her mom, dad and sisters? It would have been mildly disturbing, if she didn't find it somewhat pathetic.

'You know . . . since we're both heading there anyway,' he said, as he took another picture.

Megan suppressed the urge to laugh in his face. He *was* asking her out on a date to her parents' house. The fact that she'd not had a real date since her picture hit newsstands almost made her say yes. But remembering that he was the reason for it made her answer, 'Um, no.'

DEGREES OF PASSION

To be published in December 2008